Winds
OF CHANGE

Jo Adams McAuley

Black Rose Writing | Texas

ISBN: 978-1-68433-134-5
PUBLISHED BY BLACK ROSE WRITING
www.blackrosewriting.com

Printed in the United States of America
Suggested Retail Price (SRP) $19.95

Winds of Change is printed in Palatino Linotype

In loving memory of my mother,

Helen Sayers Adams

and to the Sayers family, especially my cousin

Pauline (Polly) Sayers Diskey.

I hope you enjoy reading it as much as I enjoyed writing it.

ACKNOWLEDGEMENT

I give my sincerest appreciation and gratitude to Erik Larson for his magnificent work-- *Isaac's Storm: A Man, a Time, and the Deadliest Hurricane in History*. This riveting account of the Galveston hurricane of 1900 is a non-fiction book that reads like a suspense novel. His exhaustive research saved me untold hours in the library and on-line. I highly recommend it to everyone who is interested in learning more about this awful calamity. Likewise, *Gilded Lives, Fatal Voyage* by Hugh Brewster provided me with insight into the lives of first-class passengers aboard the *RMS Titanic* and personal details surrounding the tragedy they endured. My versions of both events (other than the inclusion of my fictional characters) are very accurate, but the exact location or times of some incidents may be slightly altered to fit the story.

I also thank my cousin, Polly Sayers Diskey, for her assistance in researching Joseph D. Sayers, my great-great uncle. Her late mother, Irene Sayers, did extensive genealogical and historical research and Polly helped me sort through these documents to find specific information. His story is as accurate as I could make it given the limited information available. Ralph and Charlena Sayers were my grandparents and Helen and Mayo Adams are my parents.

On the cover: "Place of Remembrance" by David Moore was dedicated on the storm's 100th anniversary to those who perished at sea during the Great Galveston Hurricane.

Winds

OF CHANGE

CHAPTER 1

"Come along Lucy, dear, let's hurry into town and get home as quickly as possible, and it's already ten o'clock," Sister Elizabeth Ryan admonished the young woman. "The sky looks like it might turn bad." She peered into the distance at the four-story Levy Building where the U.S. Weather Bureau occupied the third level and saw the single red flag flapping in the steady wind. "Mr. Cline, the meteorologist, shows it won't be too bad. He hasn't hoisted the hurricane signal. Sister Camillus asked us to stay home. She thinks it's going to worsen soon. The morning newspaper sounded no particular alarm. The report said it will go east of us. I must buy supplies or we won't have supper tonight, so we'll go regardless. Sister Gabriel called the Bureau and Mr. Blagden said we shouldn't worry. Mr. Ellison sent word the cloth for our habits arrived two weeks ago. He insists on being paid by five or he'll send it back. Thank the Lord Mr. and Mrs. Beaumont are so generous. Without their patronage, we'd never be able to pay him. Why don't you go for the material and I'll get the groceries? It'll be faster if we split up. Here," she said handing Lucy cash, "this is for the cloth and extra. You'll take a wagon home. It's too far away for you to carry such a load. Sister said water's already in the road so be careful." At last she stopped to take a breath.

As usual, Sister Ryan talked so erratically and switched from topic to topic so abruptly, Lucy had difficulty following her train of thought. She decided Sister wanted her to fetch the cloth at the dry goods store on Post Office Street, while she picked up groceries at the market. Ellison's was farther away, at the center of the island to the northwest, and it'd take her an hour to get there on foot in the bluster. Not very far, really, but given how brutally hot it'd been for the past two weeks, it wasn't good news. Galveston, like much of the Northwestern Hemisphere, was experiencing an historic heat wave. Lucy dreaded the walk to Ellison's Mercantile and knew better than to ask for a round trip ride. Thankfully, Sister gave her enough for the return. She couldn't possibly carry the heavy bolts of black and white fabric, especially if it poured.

Today she turned twenty years old and Sister Ryan's supplies included ingredients for her cake. She looked forward to the celebration but wouldn't mind waiting until the weather cleared. Still, the children need to eat, and the Sisters deserve the habits. Hundreds of washings left the current ones faded and threadbare in places.

As the women parted company, Lucy found herself pleasantly surprised. After the lovely ginger-tinged clouds of dawn, she expected it to turn viciously hot again. Although warm, it felt cooler than the previous day. Dark, menacing clouds filled most of the heavens, yet here and there a bit of blue shone through. A strong breeze cooled the grossly humid air making it even more pleasant, regardless of the ominous clouds spanning the sea to the horizon. She smiled and recited the verse to herself, "Red sky at night, sailors' delight. Red sky at morning, sailors take warning." Orange is close to red, she mused, and if true, we should be in for a big one.

Across the way, ocean waves, the peeks a dirty umber from the churning sand, loomed bigger than normal and crashed noisily onto the shore dangerously encroaching on the bath houses, restaurants, and shops nearest the tidal line. The breakers left streams of water in the avenue. Spider webs of white foam crisscrossed the flat waters between the swells. The island, nine feet above sea level at its highest point and most of it half that or less, routinely experienced flooding and Galvestonians took it in stride. Curbs, as much as three feet in height, kept the overflow in the streets and out of the buildings. The majority of the structures rested on pillars raising them more. Some were a few feet tall and others tendered as much as twelve feet of added protection. It was unimaginable the water could climb to such a level.

For days, she saw articles saying the waves and tides swelled higher than usual or commenting on the noticeable increase in the mosquito population due to recent heavy rains that saturated the ground and left innumerable puddles. This was unwelcome news for a community trying to recover from yet another bout of Yellow Fever. The weather reminded Lucy of the stories the Sisters told about when she was left on their doorstep. As she hurried along, she remembered every word of the tale she heard dozens of times....

•   •   •   •   •

As the sun peeked above the overcast horizon, Sister Theresa Clair hurried to the door thinking she heard Mr. Wilkes, in a wagon pulled by a dappled mare named Hayseed, delivering milk and eggs at the front door. He always showed up at dawn. The wind whipped sharply around the edge of the building and she feared the fragile provisions might be smashed during a heavy gust. Instead of bottles and cartons, she discovered a baby girl lying in an old, tattered basket. The note pinned to her well-worn blanket said "please take care of my sweet, innocent Lucy". No one knew why her mom left her at the Saint Mary's Orphan Asylum run by the Sisters of Charity, but children regularly came there. The nuns made it their purpose to take care of those with no place else to go.

A lot of these unfortunates were orphaned due to recurring Yellow Fever epidemics, both parents passing away at the infirmary established by the Sisters fourteen years ago. Youngsters whose parents succumbed to different diseases or accidents lived here if no relatives could, or would, take them in. A lot were loved and cherished, but the family already had too many mouths to feed. A few landed there as foundlings, the product of indiscretions on the part of unwed parents. Whatever the reason, Lucy reached the doorstep on the day of her birth, September 8, 1880. The Sisters honored the mom's wishes and christened her Lucy Marie Dubuis, also paying tribute to Claude Marie Dubuis, bishop of Galveston. Lucy chuckled softly, thankful they didn't name her Claude.

She struggled to keep the wind from pushing her tiny frame off the walk and continued her reflection on the past two decades. Besides the orphanage and infirmary, the nun's ran a school. Here the Sisters educated her and she excelled in reading, composition, and mathematics. In the first six years of her life, several couples offered to adopt her. Once the excited pair carried her home, Lucy refused to eat or speak. Even as an infant, she became sullen, withdrawn, and depressed. In weeks, she was returned to the orphanage. They deeply regretted the decision, but it just didn't work out. The terrified couples were frightened she'd die of starvation and worried there might be something terribly wrong. In reality, Lucy missed St. Mary's and the Sisters. She'd accept no substitute. The fourth placement fell through and the nuns never again forced her to leave. The women raised her to adulthood with devotion, tenderness, and affection.

At the age of sixteen, Lucy told Mother Superior she wanted to join the order. The wise woman counselled her frequently and gently guided her to understand she felt love and gratitude for the Sisters, her surrogate parents, not God's calling. Knowing she adored her home, Mother hired her at the orphanage. She cleaned, helped cook, assisted at the infirmary, and tended the children. At seventeen, Mr. and Mrs. Beaumont provided financial aid and Lucy attended Miss Mildred Cooper's Business Academy for Young Ladies and earned a certificate in secretarial arts and bookkeeping. Following graduation, she served as Mother Superior's secretary and managed the order's financial affairs. It took a lot of creativity to keep them afloat, particularly since Bishop Nicholas Gallagher forbid the Sisters to beg on street corners to raise additional funds. She received a minuscule salary and room and board at the orphanage. Lucy deemed it a perfect life of security and tranquility.

•   •   •   •   •

She turned north, the wind hit her full in the face, and progress slowed. Her large, green eyes stung from the dust coursing through the air. Her light brown hair, usually tidy and neat on her head, blew wildly, the hat hopelessly lost. Lucy always considered it a blessing to have a petite stature and small frame, but a little bulk would be useful right now. The rain started well before she made it to her destination. Day turned to night as low, thick, black, saturated clouds completely blotted the sun. Bands of rain pelted her painfully and turned the boulevards to torrents of mud. Lucy hugged the edges of buildings, hoping for protection, as she trudged forward. The faster she accomplished her mission and returned to the dry, safe orphanage the better.

Conditions continued to deteriorate. At noon, water in the roads rose to a depth high enough teens floated by on improvised rafts or in canoes. Lucy caught her breath under the awning of the Tremont Hotel and a fellow soggy traveler offered advice. "Miss, you need to get to high ground right away. I came from the south and buildings by the shore, bath houses, the boardwalk, and such, are falling apart. The waves are beating them down." He trudged on toward his destination, head bent low against the lashing gale.

Weather that a few minutes ago presented merely discomfort, now created heart wrenching panic. The orphanage sat a short distance from the ocean. Surely its sturdy brick walls could withstand this tempest. The weather turned fearsome, the rain and wind horrible, but no worse than innumerable storms battering the small island over the years. Right? By now, Lucy hit a point closer to Ellison's Mercantile than St. Mary's. Going back wasn't a good option so she decided to continue on. She'd ride out the monsoon at the store. The water in the avenue licked the knees of those foolish enough to try and cross the debris-littered flood. She saw no street cars running up and down the lane and the few wagons braving the flow were half buried by murky liquid.

About one o'clock, she reached her goal. The trip took three times longer than she expected. On numerous occasions, Lucy waited for the deluge to abate and wind to slacken before she continued her journey. So much debris-filled water rushed through the boulevards, she detoured many, many blocks looking for a place to cross. The refuse created a hazard and more than once she witnessed some fool hardy soul injured by a charging plank or tree branch. Water gushed past the tall curbs and now flowed through yards and lapped the bottom of buildings with the same determination as it did through the streets. It edged ever closer to the sidewalk where she stood. Lucy paused on the porch for a moment to remove her dripping coat and survey the spectacle around her. Here a new sensation assaulted her senses. She could smell the water, but not the stench of overflowing sewers often accompanying a torrential cloudburst. The distinctive sharp smell of salt filled the air. The flooding wasn't merely an excess of rain. The ocean itself inundated the city.

On the way, she saw refugees toting packs of clothing on their shoulders struggling to get as far from the sea as possible. Rabbi Henry Cohen, leaving the synagogue for the Sabbath, noticed them, too. He distributed food, blankets, and umbrellas to children and the elderly, trying to make the evacuation easier. As Lucy turned to open the door, she stared in horror at a small, pale object in a floating tangle of debris. As it rushed from sight, she decided it'd been her imagination. Surely, she hadn't seen the body of a baby amongst the floating rubbish. It must be a pig, or other animal, or a sack of corn, she reasoned in an attempt to comfort herself. Anything except what she thought at first glance.

Mr. Ellison saw her grappling with the door. The wind hit so forcefully, it didn't budge under her efforts. He and two large men wrestled to open it for her. It instantly slammed shut with a ferocious bang that rattled the windows and shook glass bottles standing on a shelf. "Girl, what on Earth you doin' there?" He yelled to be heard over the roar. "Ain't you heard?"

Inside was even darker than outside. Lucy asked, "Heard what, Mr. Ellison? Can we turn on the lights? I can't see. May I use your phone to let the Sisters know I'm here?"

He howled in laughter, but not the funny kind. It resonated disdain—and anxiety.

"Power went black 'bout half hour 'go. Phone, too. I reckon I can light candles. This guy, there, says the last telegraph blew 'bout thirty minutes 'go, too. The big news is Ritter's Café just fell apart. He," indicating a tall man to the left, "says it caved in. Those huge printing presses on the second floor crashed down. Folks got killed, he swears. It was crowded due to it being lunch and all." The eatery and bar occupied a corner lot two blocks to the north and eight blocks east on Mechanic Street. "Lots ain't been takin' the hurr-cane too serious like 'til now. A couple gents come by since and said a general panic broke 'round town, 'bout time, too."

Lucy turned ashen gray as she heard the story. If this happened north of her, toward the bay and away from the ocean, what might be happening at the orphanage? She didn't know the northerly blast she fought pushed the normally calm bay waters into the lanes with as much force as the storm brewing to the southeast. She had no idea the wind served as a buffer for the Gulf water being rammed toward shore. It caused a virtual tidal wave to build up at sea. The girl wouldn't be ignorant of the oceanographic condition for long, because the winds were changing.

She abandoned all plans of returning to the orphanage as more and more refugees entered the shop seeking shelter from nature's onslaught. New arrivals related stories of rising water, strengthening winds, and houses and buildings ripped from pilings and smashing to bits or floating out to sea. A tearful woman told of chopping holes in the floor of her parlor in a vain hope of keeping her home from floating off its ten-foot-high legs. Several talked of watching heroic actions of parents valiantly trying to protect offspring, strangers struggling to rescue each other, and individuals laboring to save themselves. Mr. Kellogg, who also sought shelter in the store, braved waist deep water to trudge from the Santa Fe Depot half a mile away. He hitched a ride partway on the Tremont Hotel wagon, there to pick up passengers with reservations, even though the water lapped at the seats.

Kellogg arrived about noon on the train from Houston, one of the last two to make it into town. When it crossed the three-mile trestle spanning Galveston Bay, the water surged to the tracks. Before getting to the depot, however, rising water washed it out. Passengers transferred to a relief train and nearly made it to the station prior to the fire box flooding. Kellogg, like all the men, formed a human chain allowing women and children to reach the platform.

At 2 pm, three dozen people crowded into the small store. They listened in enthralled terror as person after person related stories of destruction and harrowing escapes. Suddenly, a devastating eruption of wind battered the door, shattered all the front windows, and sprayed asylum seekers with daggers of glass. Water gushed in toppling women, toddlers, and the elderly. The winds shifted causing a rise in the water level and increase in wind speed. As the stronger helped the weaker upstairs to the Ellison's living quarters, two teens, a woman, and a man beheaded by a spinning slate tile wrenched from a roof across the street, lay dead from the wind-bomb that exploded in front of them.

CHAPTER 2

Most huddled in the bedroom. Some of the men managed to retrieve hammers and nails from downstairs and fastened the dining table on the lower portion of the small window. Above it Mr. Ellison nailed a door in an effort to render the refuge as secure as possible from flying glass and projectiles. A few bunched in the windowless storage cupboard, but the majority chose to cluster in a group. Mrs. Ellison gathered all the blankets, sheets, bandages, candles, and lanterns she owned. Fortunately, a doctor was stranded with them. He and Lucy, who'd learned a lot from assisting the Sisters at the infirmary, tended to the injured. She removed shards of glass, large and small, and wrapped the wounds. As she and the doctor worked, volunteers ripped sheets for dressings. Two additional people died and the doctor doubted three more could survive until dawn.

Not a single individual escaped injury. Some were fatal and others relatively minor. Lucy proved to be among the luckier ones. She'd been at the rear of the store, behind the sturdy counter. It, and those at the front, shielded her from the worst of the lethal glass. She suffered cuts on her scalp and face, lacerations on her neck and shoulders, and sustained two badly bruised ribs from being thrown against the shelves behind her. Falling cans hit her on the head and shoulders, adding bruises and scrapes to her inventory of injuries.

Families clung together and parents tried to comfort their terrified children. From time to time, a brave soul ventured to the front of the house to check the depth of the water on the staircase and look out the shattered windows in a futile hope the storm might abate. Twice, the observers came back with additions to the band. Victims clung to planks of wood, tree branches, and anything else to stay afloat. A makeshift raft drifted close to the mercantile and the occupants scrambled onto the porch roof and were pulled in by those assessing the progress of the rampaging deluge.

At about 7:30 the wind shifted to the south. It no longer shielded the island from the ever-growing liquid mountain building at sea. A deadly wall of water hit the shore packing the power of a speeding locomotive and demolished any remaining structures within blocks of the coast. Buildings crumbled, trees uprooted, and most living creatures perished. The wind linked forces with the cyclone now barreling inexorably for Galveston. It seemed impossible, but the situation grew exponentially worse. Waters from the Gulf and bay joined, submerging the entire island under a blanket of raging brine fifteen feet high in some places. Wind speed increased and became an accomplice to the water's destructive rampage. No one doubted this was a hurricane of monstrous strength and size.

At ten o'clock, Mr. Ellison and his clerk inspected the water's progress. It passed the three-quarters mark on the staircase and the men saw it slowly rising. A man caught in the trellis tried to climb in the kitchen window. The pair helped him and all three retreated to the relative safety of the bedroom. The stranger, after coughing up copious amounts of water and catching his breath, related what information he had.

Much of the town ceased to exist. Bodies of the dead floated eerily among the debris, lifeless limbs undulating in the current. At two-thirty, he went to the weather station to monitor the storm's progress, when it'd subside, and ask if he should evacuate the area. Mr. Cline urged him to shelter in place. He couldn't say for sure when it'd end, but felt the worst already passed. Shortly afterwards, Mr. Cline left the station, the assistant stayed, and so did this man. As the two watched, wind speeds increased and the barometric pressure fell. At 5:15 the anemometer shattered registering 100 mph, the maximin wind speed the instrument measured, and the intensity continued to rise. By now, the water reached his waist and, regardless of what Mr. Cline said, he decided to seek higher ground. Ultimately, he grabbed hold of a passing grand piano and floated into their midst.

Sometime in the wee hours of Sunday morning, the winds stopped shrieking and the rain ceased hammering the roof above the refugees in Ellison's Mercantile. The young ones dropped off to sleep and the adults followed the lead, too, exhausted from struggling to survive and the terror of the calamity. As dawn crept over beleaguered and assaulted Galveston, the curious cautiously emerged from sanctuaries to see what devastation the storm wrought.

Lucy was the first to wake in the crowded, stuffy chamber. She opened her eyes and, as they adjusted to the dim light, she surveyed the unimaginable sight around her. A girl of about fifteen, whom she'd never seen before, had her head in Lucy's lap and a little boy snuggled close to her. Stranger lay next to stranger haphazardly on the floor without regard to gender or age. Families clustered in whatever tiny space they found. Most were curled up on the floor while some slept propped on the wall or crammed in the closet. Half a dozen small children had crawled underneath the bed. The three severely injured by flying glass occupied the blood-soaked bed but all succumbed to their wounds.

She tried to gently reposition the teenager's head without disturbing her, but as Lucy struggled to stand, the movement cascaded and began a general awakening. People woke, looked up, checked on loved ones, and listened. An eerie quiet replaced the howling, thunder, and roar of the tumultuous night. The stiff sleepers gingerly rose, stretched sore, cramped muscles, and ventured warily out the bedroom door. Tentatively, a few walked across the hall toward the front of the building. Debris accumulated on the second step from the top and blocked the way downstairs. A gentle breeze and clear skies reassured them the hurricane spent its fury. The humidity and temperature, even at that early hour, told them the unrelenting heat returned.

In all directions, open spaces replaced homes or stores. Mounds of wreckage as high as roofs dominated the scene. Parts of dwellings, railroad ties, utility poles, desks, chairs, mattresses, cribs, clothing, toys, wire, fencing, ship fittings, and other remnants of lives clogged the streets. But worst of all, bodies lurked everywhere. Bloody, battered, dismembered corpses of humans and animals lay caught in the mangled mess now part of Galveston's landscape. Many were unrecognizable. Many were naked, their clothes being torn to shreds by the force of wind and water. Here and there survivors walked zombie-like among the dead, dazed and bewildered and horrified at the holocaust that befell their beloved island. Some already searched for those who were buried in the infinite destruction or beneath the water standing in the roads. Sporadically, someone was rescued. More often than not the poor soul was unreachable. The shrieks, calls for help, and moans continued for days. Gradually they ceased as victims died of trauma, heat stroke, or dehydration.

Fortunately for the occupants of Ellison's Mercantile, the refuse blocking the staircase wasn't tightly packed or heavy. Men and women passed pieces of rubble from hand to hand and labored to clear the steps. Five more bodies were added to the three on the bed and reverently draped with a blanket. Once on the bottom floor, they gingerly picked through the remnants of the mercantile's inventory and wreckage to create a narrow corridor to the door. Twice, they all froze when deadly snakes slithered past and disappeared into the debris. Everywhere, frogs and toads jumped and scurried for cover as the survivors worked their way to the outside. The first thought was joy at being spared, then reality hit. Had cherished husbands, wives, children, parents, cousins, friends survived? No one escaped heartbreak that vile day. A lucky few suffered just material loss but were in the minority. Nearly every person lost loved ones, entire families ceased to exist, and only the very youngest avoided the emotional scars of such a cataclysmic event.

Lucy's dread increased as she tried vainly to hurry to the orphanage and help in whatever way possible. She climbed heaps taller than her head, detoured blocks to find easier, safer, drier passage, and saw horrors nobody should ever experience. Yelps of pain, wails of grief, and cries of anguish replaced the roar of wind and water as people, still in a state of shock, slowly realized the depth of the havoc left behind.

It took her longer to get back than to battle her way through the storm. As she neared the ocean, Lucy lost her bearings. Trees, buildings, signs, and landmarks were obliterated. The familiar boardwalk, bath houses, trolley tracks, and restaurants she'd seen all her life disappeared into the sea. The shoreline itself bore an unfamiliar profile. Eventually she reached the area she believed to be the location of the orphanage, but nothing remained save small piles of scattered rubble. The water and wind scraped the ground clean, pushing everything in its path inland. Where before stood charming homes, a house-high mass of ruble stretched across the neighborhood.

At the horrendous sight, Lucy's knees buckled and she fell to the ground in uncontrollable tears. On other days, the spectacle would bring good Samaritans running. Today it went largely unnoticed in the aftermath of the disaster. All around, men and women collapsed in grief and wept openly, wailing uncontrollably. She got up, dried her face, and instead of a tortured look of horror, Lucy donned the mask of daze, hopelessnes, and disbelief worn by most of those in town.

As she wandered away aimlessly, she heard an amazing sound. Bells. The chimes from Ursuline Convent sounded clear and strong as usual on Sunday calling the faithful to mass, even in the wake of calamity. There. She'd go there. Surely if nuns or children survived the destruction of the orphanage this is where she'd find them. Trying to avoid seeing the loss of humanity around her, she walked as in a trance toward the familiar tolling. Although badly damaged, the sturdy walls offered protection and solace. A crowd of hundreds gathered at the sanctuary. Some came to worship, the preponderance searched for family, others to give thanks for being spared, or to seek comfort in tragedy. The Sisters passed out what food and water remained in the pantry. No living soul got turned away. Survivors arrived in clothing so tattered it barely swathed their traumatized bodies or they were totally naked. Here, too, the nuns provided relief. Lucy saw women in trousers, men in skirts, and a man wearing a habit.

She combed the convent thoroughly, met many she knew, but none from St. Mary's. Nobody had any idea what happened. She sat wearily on a bench in the courtyard next to a woman in a chair with a tiny baby in her arms and a toddler clinging to her ragged skirt. The mother and toddler were bruised and cut, but well enough considering the circumstances. For a time, nobody uttered a word. The little boy started to cry so Lucy introduced herself and comforted him.

Indicative of the shock and denial shrouding the city's residents, Mrs. Heiderman spoke dispassionately, almost as if it happened to someone else. When the bad weather commenced, she, eight months pregnant, and her husband decided to ride it out at home with their son. As the house fell apart, she clung to debris and floated away, becoming separated from the rest. She hugged the toddler tightly as she continued her story. A swell washed her right through a second-floor window of the Convent. An hour later her second son arrived, she stroked the tiny head, but she feared the others were lost. In the rage her bother-in-law, stranded in a tree near the Convent, plucked a screaming toddler from the torrent. It was his nephew, her son. Mother and child were unexpectedly reunited a few hours ago when the waters receded and her brother-in-law brought the boy in to find shelter. Her husband wasn't so fortunate and he perished beneath the raging brine.

Lucy moved on, being told by the nuns the Tremont Hotel harbored about a thousand. Maybe she'd find them there. The journey turned out to be both dangerous and miserable. Besides dodging streets clogged with debris and corpses, the heat soared to one hundred degrees adding to the inconceivable grief. Bodies, and dismembered body parts, blocked doorways and lay on porches. Human remains hung from the railroad trestle remnants and in trees. Those in tress often showed the bite marks of venomous snakes seeking safety in the same branches. She trudged north to the luxury hotel now resembling a third-class tavern. Nonetheless, it was structurally sound, something that couldn't be said of many of the buildings standing around the decimated city.

She didn't find those she sought but heard heart-wrenching stories of death or survival. George Burnett, his wife, child, and mother, and dozens more sought refuge at Judson Palmer's abode.

When it failed, Burnett convinced his family to escape out a window and climb onto a passing section of roof. Seconds later, the house collapsed and most of those inside died. Mr. Burnett survived, but late in the night the rage took his wife and child. Likewise, Mr. Palmer made it through alone.

A man sitting in the hall listened to the story and related an account he heard earlier. Dr. Young, a prominent citizen and amateur meteorologist, lived at the corner of 25th and P½ Streets just blocks from the sea. He watched the storm's progress with great concern. He had noted the rising swells and falling barometric pressure and deduced a cyclone loomed in the Gulf of Mexico. The narrator stopped the story for a moment and asked the question often repeated over and over during the weeks ahead. Why hadn't Isaac Cline, or someone at the Weather Bureau, come to the same conclusion and issued a hurricane warning? Acting on his insight, the doctor cabled the San Antonio station master and instructed his wife, traveling back to Galveston with the babes, to wait there. Then he returned to weather the blast.

Upon going upstairs to escape rising water, Dr. Young heard banging and thudding from below. He peered between the spindles and saw furniture sloshing from side to side, bumping against walls and causing a racket. As he turned to go, an onslaught of wind stampeded up the staircase and penned him firmly to the wall, preventing him from moving until it lessened. At 5:40 a sudden four-foot tidal surge ripped apart his refuge. He unhinged a door, used it as a raft, and sailed out as his house tumbled into the sea. For eight hours, he floated on the door amid the roof-tops of the few homes still standing. It'd been harrowing, terrifying, but he survived. His wife received the message and stayed in San Antonio, safe and sound. The physician counted himself among the fortunate.

Dark engulfed the quiet, brutalized city. As the hotel's guests, registered and unregistered, settled in, a woman shared her corner. Lucy gratefully accepted and soon fell into an exhausted, restless sleep punctuated by dreams of floating corpses and screaming wind. She, like all of those in town that fateful morn, would rerun these nightmares for decades.

As the citizens struggled in the hurricane's wake, people in the rest of the world wondered what happened to them. No word of the city's fate got out after four o'clock on Saturday when all the telephone and telegraph lines on the island fell. The wires between the Weather Bureaus in Houston, Dallas, New Orleans, and Washington, D.C. buzzed with activity as colleagues tried to discover why Galveston went silent.

On the 9th, at about eleven in the morning, a contingent of six citizens set sail on the *Pherabe*, one of the few remaining seaworthy ships, for the mainland since no railroad trestles or bridges stood intact. The going was rough as the crew carefully navigated a bay congested with all manner of debris plus thousands of bodies. Once ashore, the emissaries used a handcar to pump north toward Houston. A southbound train passed by, the envoys flagged it down, and tried to get it to turn around. The engineer refused, but the group climbed aboard anyway, knowing he'd be forced to go back when the tracks became impassable. The men reached Houston's Western Union office at 3 a.m. Monday and sent an urgent message to President William McKinley and Texas Governor Joseph D. Sayers: "I have been deputized by the mayor and Citizen's Committee of Galveston to inform you that the city of Galveston is in ruins." It estimated thousands died in the melee, but every person hearing the figure passed it off as a fantasy brought on by the trauma of the event.

CHAPTER 3

Governor Sayers slept soundly until the clerk knocked on the door and handed him the telegram. It shook him to the core. He received a few notices concerning a storm lashing the island on Saturday and, in case the worst happened, ordered supplies stockpiled and prepared for quick shipment if it proved to be a disaster. He'd heard nothing since and momentarily breathed a sigh of relief. Wouldn't they call for help if it got that bad? He realized the message originated in Houston and the official understood. There was no way to contact the outside. Surely it was a gross exaggeration or mistake. The next few days, precious little information trickled in from the city and each report sounded worse than the last. Very slowly, the state, the country, and ultimately the world realized Galveston experienced an apocalyptic calamity.

Lucy thanked the woman who made room for her on the floor and ate one of the rolls the hotel staff passed out. The traumatized girl continued her quest for the Sisters from St. Mary's and the orphans in their charge. She heard from those she met the western section of the city suffered terribly. The Episcopal cemetery was devastated and some of the coffins unearthed. St Patrick's Church and the First Baptist Church lay in ruins. She knew the highest part of town ran across the center of the island, where she found shelter, and it probably fared the best. This is where she went.

She headed north toward the island's crest. It relieved Lucy to see the German Catholic Church sustained relatively minor damage. She asked those inside about the welfare of St. Mary's residents and again no one heard anything but it'd been completely obliterated.

Several blocks north and slightly to the east, her heart leapt with joy to see the Cathedral stood in all its glory and appeared in good condition. Like every institution and most inhabitable private dwellings, refuges crowded in. Lucy shared the meager soup and bread the fathers served for dinner. The men weren't stingy, but supplies were limited and a lot of people needed to eat. She listened intently to story after story in hopes of gleaning a tidbit of information to lead her to any who survived the orphanage's destruction but heard nothing to aid her hunt.

Here she heard the story of Isaac Cline's journey through the night. The Weather Bureau manager decided he, his pregnant wife, and their three daughters would ride out the blast at home. He assumed his strong house could withstand nature's worst. Fifty neighbors also viewed it as a safe haven and a crowd gathered within its protective walls. As the wind and water levels rose, the refuges moved to the second floor. While Isaac proclaimed it safe, his brother Joseph, who worked with him at the Bureau, warned of its collapse. Joseph was right and the structure began crumbling.

Isaac latched onto a heap of boards, but lost sight of his family. Before long, he spotted his 6-year-old daughter clinging to a pile of wreckage and pulled her in. He saw a man and two girls drifting toward him. It turned out to be his brother and two youngest daughters. All five boarded a larger piece of wreckage and felt reasonably safe. Hours later the raft bumped into one of the few upright residences in the area and they climbed in. These five survived but Isaac unearthed the body of his wife under a heap of timbers. A mere eighteen of the fifty who sought shelter with him made it through the hurricane's vengeance.

Survivors in the Cathedral drifted to sleep and again Lucy slept on a church floor. In the morning, she'd search for her adopted clan from the orphanage. Right now, she craved rest, both her mind and body needed to heal. The physical wounds soon faded, the emotional ones took significantly longer.

On Tuesday, as a tiny bit of the shock wore off, dread of disease from decomposing corpses sparked action from Mayor Walter C. Jones, who headed the relief committee. If a loved one recovered the body, it was laid to rest in a cemetery. Recovery crews buried some in place. However, most were unidentified and the numbers astronomical, so burying everyone proved impractical. Disposal of the deceased became a priority. Dead gangs, as the bands were called, performed the gruesome task. These consisted of black men who received whiskey as payment in order to make the odious chore bearable. When city leaders decided to bury the dead at sea, these crews, running in thirty-minute shifts, stacked bodies in wagons and carried them to the docks. Here the deceased were loaded on barges, sailed 18 miles into the Gulf of Mexico, weighted, and had their souls committed to the sea. Within hours, bodies returned to the shore in droves and washed up on the beaches. The weights slipped off a lot and others simply lacked enough ballast to submerge them.

By then, corpses were becoming hard to handle due to decomposition. Burial at sea failed, so leaders made the difficult decision to burn them. It seemed the most feasible method of disposing of overwhelming numbers of dead quickly enough to prevent the onset of typhoid fever and cholera many believed to be imminent. Cremation, a new idea in America, upset people as much as the loss itself. Regardless, funeral pyres appeared all around the island and the dead gangs stacked bodies five deep awaiting their turn to enter the flames. The fires lit the sky and the smell of burning flesh and hair overpowered the stench of decaying bodies, rubbish, and sewage that permeated the air. Stories of bands of men roaming the city robbing and desecrating corpses and looting spread throughout town. Some were true, most were not, but it created an atmosphere of fear and disgust nonetheless. The searing heat accelerated decomposition and added to the misery of those already suffering unimaginably.

Lucy, at a loss where else to hunt, tried all the churches still standing or partially standing. She visited the few open medical facilities and found no one she sought. City hall, the gas company, and water works were either destroyed or severely damaged and not functioning. Suddenly she remembered the synagogue. It sat near the German Catholic Church and it survived well. She hurried as fast as possible through the rubble and wreckage to the last place she knew to try.

She couldn't believe it. Sitting huddled just beyond the doorway of the synagogue were William Murney, Frank Madera, and Albert Campbell, three thirteen-year-old boys from the orphanage. Lucy rushed over and hugged them tightly. "I'm so happy to see you. Where are the others?"

Frank answered through tears of joy at seeing a familiar face. "Don't know, Miss Dubuis. We hid in the chapel at first, singin' hymns. Mother Superior cut clothesline and the Sisters tied the littlest to 'um in a row. She said it'd keep 'um safe. We done gone upstairs, but the waves come all the way to the second floor. 'Bout now the chapel and boy's dorm was goin', so we got to the girl's dorm, crosswise from the Gulf."

Albert took up the story then. "The Sisters tried everything, but they washed away, though, and I ain't got no notion where. Everybody—tried—so—hard—." He stopped for a moment. "Don't recollect how it all happened, but we been stuck in a tree, all three of us together."

"I remember. A big tree floated by and we grabbed a hold. We held on a whole day, ain't sleepin' a bit 'cause we might fall out. A man come in a boat and fetched us out o' it and brung us here. He said we was in the sea, not even on dry land." William finished the tale.

What slim hope she held vanished at the description of the orphanage's demise. It was possible a few survived and were out there, but she doubted it. Lucy and the boys spent the night at the synagogue and then went back to the Convent. She spotted the Beaumont's helping the nuns care for the injured and destitute. "These are such special people," Lucy thought. The couple donated generously to the orphanage and to her when she attended business school. Maybe, just maybe, they'd take in the boys.

Mr. and Mrs. Beaumont greeted her and the youngsters exuberantly. Both assumed all at St. Mary's were lost in the buildings disintegration. What about the nuns and children, Mr. Beaumont asked? Did she know? Lucy said no and tears of sadness rolled down Mrs. Beaumont's cheeks as she, too, realized in all likelihood none survived. She asked, "Lucy, where are you and the boys going?"

"I think I'll settle here if the nuns let me, but can you take the boys for a while, please? The Convent is overcrowded enough as it is."

The woman smiled and took her hand. "Yes, dear, and you, too. We have a few others with us, but can find a spot for you all, if you like. We're fortunate. Ours is raised high and we didn't sustain a tremendous amount of damage, besides the fact all the windows are broken and part of the veranda roof blew away. Say yes." Lucy and the boys gratefully accepted and returned to the center of town where the Beaumont's place stood amid the ruins of so many structures.

Mrs. Beaumont's declaration that a few were at the house was a huge understatement. Thirty people occupied the large residence. All over, refugees sat on the floor, stood in the hallways, lounged on furniture, dangled legs between the spindles on the second-floor gallery, or congregated on the porch trying in vain to catch a breeze. The Beaumont's found space for the newcomers in the attic. At one end a small group of boys who arrived without parents clustered together. They were watched by a Baptist minister whose church was demolished. A clothesline supported blankets hanging across it and separated them from the girls who occupied the far side of the garret. Lucy supervised them and helped in the kitchen. Like the reverend at the opposite end, she slept in a small partitioned area offering her a bit of privacy. These humble, crowded, uncomfortable quarters were substantially better than countless in the city claimed.

The day leading to the storm, the Beaumont's made their quarterly trip to stock up on supplies. Dried beans, bread, canned goods, preserved meat, and other staples overflowed the pantry and storeroom. A huge rain barrel tied to the porch miraculously survived and provided water. Nonetheless, the daily rations for everyone, including the Beaumont's, were short. With so many there, it wouldn't hold out very long and help could be days or weeks off.

Unbeknownst to them, it was on the way. At dawn on Tuesday, a relief train left Houston and chugged its way southeast transporting food, water, and vital provisions to their ravaged neighbor. Among the passengers were officers and men of the Texas Voluntary Guard and the Texas Department of the U.S. Army sent to maintain order, distribute provisions, and provide aide. William Sterett, a reporter for the *Dallas News*, boarded as the train left the station. Mr. Sterett happened to be at the paper when telegraph communications from Galveston ceased Saturday afternoon. He heard the wild speculation about a monstrous hurricane completely submerging the island, killing hundreds. He didn't believe it for a moment, but agreed it'd probably been badly hit. He intended to get the story as soon as possible.

The train headed to Virginia Point, the last depot on the mainland. From here, depending on what they found, it would cross the trestle bridge or transfer supplies to a ferry. As it progressed, those onboard questioned the belief the storm couldn't possibly be as bad as the outlandish rumors suggested. Tall grasses lay flat against the ground instead of standing erect in the sun. Trees stood naked, stripped of leaves and bark by the violent wind. From his seat, Mr. Sterett saw swollen, drowned cows and wrecked barns. Debris littered the landscape and cluttered the roads. Here and there fierce rages tossed boats far ashore.

In the distance, a large steamship was pushed two miles inland and rested lopsided on the prairie. Long before Virginia Point, water and large piles of debris halted progress and made the tracks impassable.

The train stopped, instead, at the coastal town of Texas City roughly ten miles north of Virginia Point. Here the rescuers set out on foot, wading through water and mud, in hopes of finding a means to make it the rest of the way to the island. The travelers faced even more terrifying sights than they had from the train. Personal items such as clothing, photographs, toys, and treasured cats and dogs lay all around. To their horror, dozens of battered, broken, swollen bodies came into view. Men moving parallel to the shore buried fifty victims in shallow, unmarked graves that day. The Army officers seized a lifeboat from a British ship blown from its pier in Galveston. Soldiers loaded it full of supplies and rowed across the now placid bay.

As he walked by the sea, Mr. Sterett and his companions noted mountains of wreckage and an ever-increasing number of bloated bodies. In the distance, a yacht moved lazily toward the group. When the large craft reached him, he and a hundred others, primarily residents trying to check on family, caught a ride. It took four hours to cross the narrow stretch of water due in part to the calm air. The second reason was debris and corpses littered the way and the craft constantly bumped into it impeding progress.

Darkness fell by the time the craft neared the shore, yet all was black but a solitary flickering light shining from what just days ago had been a vibrant downtown. As the schooner got closer, the stench was overwhelming, causing some to gag and retch in horror. A few, desperate to find the fate of their family, went ashore. Sterett stayed put as the captain backed into the bay, beyond the putrefying smell, and anchored for the evening. The next morning, the captain sailed in to see what remained of the city and the reporter realized the rumors were, in deed, fact.

CHAPTER 4

In the days following the storm, the *Galveston News* published abbreviated editions, smaller in both size and content, mainly filled with lists of the dead. Some, who didn't find a body but assumed the worst, submitted names. Infrequently, corrections needed to be made as those presumed lost struggled back alive if not entirely well. Miss Anna Delz, age sixteen, washed ashore on the mainland, miraculously survived, and spent a week trying to return. Whenever a name disappeared from the registry of fatalities, it raised false hopes others could ultimately come home, but it didn't happen. Only a precious few turned up safe. The *News* also printed the contents of hundreds of telegrams, undeliverable as so many of the addresses no longer existed.

On Thursday, the periodical reverted to its original size and carried information above and beyond lists of the departed. In its pages, Galveston got a birds-eye view of what happened overnight. These articles gave the world its first glimpse of the devastation that rained on the town. As it documented the damage, residents realized a third of the city lay in ruins at the hands of the gargantuan hurricane. At least one thousand buildings and twenty-six hundred homes were either entirely destroyed or so severely damaged they had to be razed. Ultimately, every structure within fifteen blocks of the beach was demolished. The island itself lost three hundred feet of shoreline due to the force of water and wind. Estimates of the death toll varied from source to source. Most placed it at 8,000, with figures ranging as low as 6,000 to as high as 12,000. An exact count would not be possible since no one knew exactly who was on the island as the storm raced ashore. The paper also recounted the harrowing experiences of survivors.

Lucy already heard of A.V. Kellogg's perilous train trip from Houston as the storm barreled toward shore. She read about an even more terrifying encounter on Thursday. John Poe arrived in the area at approximately the same time as Mr. Kellogg, but he came from New Orleans. He expected to go to Bolivar Point where the entire train would transfer to a ferry, sail across the channel, and resume its journey. When he and the ninety-five others arrived at the Point, the wind raged furiously. Although the captain tried repeatedly, it proved too dangerous to dock in the fearsome wind and he aborted the effort.

By then, water covered the tracks and threatened to swamp the cars where the riders nervously debated what to do. Poe and ten fellow travelers decided to try and make it to a lighthouse standing on a slight rise a quarter mile away. They abandoned the train, fought wind and water, and finally reached the tower, the last ones to do so that fateful day. Eighty-five remained onboard, sure the heavy beast could survive the tempest. Poe entered, glanced over his shoulder, saw the train moving once more, and questioned his decision to leave. Further down the way, water overwhelmed the train and all drowned.

Two hundred crowded into the turret seeking safety from the blast. Wet, terrified people sat on the steps of the staircase coiling its way a hundred feet up to where the beacon warned sailors of navigational hazards. As the water rose, so did the refugees. They climbed farther and farther upwards. Those at the top moved to the highest platform and crowded into the small space allowing those below to be dry. In the distance, canon fire from Fort San Jacinto sounded out the soldiers' call for help. The group in the lighthouse spent a nerve wracking night of terror but all lived to tell the story to reporters who flocked to the island in the weeks ahead.

The *News* confirmed Lucy's worst nightmare. Crews unearthed the bodies of several nuns from St. Mary's, youngsters still tethered on. The clothesline, meant to keep them safe, actually facilitated their demise. It tangled in the debris coursing through town and dragged everyone under. Nobody can say for sure, but if not tied together, some might have made it through like the three boys.

Another story about people she knew well caught Lucy's attention. Anthony Credo walked for a short distance beside Isaac Cline as both men trudged through the deluge. Mr. Cline said he possibly miscalculated the storm's intensity and worried it'd be much worse than he originally thought.

Taking his fears to heart, Mr. Credo instructed his family to prepare to leave immediately. He had eleven children, with eight currently at home. Two of his daughters, Irene and Minnie, lived elsewhere in town. His son William went to visit his fiancée. The rest obeyed his instructions and stayed inside. In an effort to keep the house from floating, Mr. Credo chopped holes in the living room floor.

As they were preparing to leave, Mrs. Goldman and her son arrived. She feared her cottage was too flimsy to bear up to the blast and wanted to stay here. Mrs. Credo provided dry clothes and food. Meanwhile, Mr. Credo decided against leaving since the water was now much higher. One by one he swam the kids to a storm shelter he'd built in the yard. As the water continued to rise and buildings to the right and left disintegrated, he concluded this wasn't safe either, and brought them back.

Water threated to overtake the second floor as it did the lower level. All scrambled to the attic. Nightfall took away what little light filtered through the heavy clouds and it went completely dark. Suddenly, a streetcar rail dove through the roof, narrowly missing Mrs. Credo and Mrs. Goldman. The sanctuary shook. Wind lifted the roof and slammed it down. Pieces fell on Mrs. Credo and left her bleeding and bruised. The house left its pillars and floated away.

It was time to leave. Mr. Credo pulled his family out a window and each grabbed onto whatever floated by. Mrs. Goldman refused to leave, however. Time and again driving wind scattered them and Credo struggled to gather everyone together. A bobbing telephone pole struck his son Raymond in the head and the boy lost consciousness. It took all his strength to keep his son's head above water. Though he believed him dead, or dying, the desperate man continued to carry the boy with him.

An upturned portion of roof came close. The beleaguered group relocated to it and felt relatively safe on the larger raft. And, they didn't have to fear being separated. Some of the younger passengers drifted to sleep, lulled by the swaying of the eaves. After a while, this refuge started to fall apart. A section of porch passed by and the clan transferred to it, taking the unconscious Raymond along. Suddenly a particularly heavy gust of wind exploded across the raft. Vivian got hit with flying debris, thrown into the water, and disappeared below the surface. At the same instant, a sharp dagger of wood shot through Pearl's arm and her parents extracted it. About an hour later, the survivors scaled a twelve-foot-high pile of rubble and made it into a home standing firm in the face of the hurricane's onslaught.

To his horror, Mr. Credo lost nine of his sixteen loved ones that day. He found the body of Vivian under ruble where the others climbed into the house and buried her. His daughter Irene, her newborn baby and two-year-old son, were not identified. Minnie, her husband, and their two children disappeared forever. William failed to return from his fiancée's home. Amazingly, Raymond survived the head trauma. Mrs. Credo recovered and Pearl's arm healed. The Goldman's were never seen again.

Help reached the besieged island at last. Food, water, medical equipment, clothing, and various necessities were transported in by boat and barge. Cash donations, large and small, poured in from individuals, institutions, corporations, cities, states, and foreign governments. The smallest donation, eleven cents, came from a girl in Chicago. The Sabbath School in Illinois contributed $4.10. The city of Liverpool, England, and the Cotton Association of Liverpool sent a combined gift of $28,000. The state of New York sent the largest single amount, $93,696, while New Hampshire and Moose Jaw, Canada, chipped in a dollar a piece. The hands at the Cambria Steel Company, of Johnstown, Pennsylvania, donated $61. In 1889, Johnstown lost 2200 citizens in a flood caused by a collapsed dam.

One of the first reporters on the scene was Winifred Bonfils, a woman who worked for William Randolph Hearst's publication. Her riveting reports of the massive cyclone prompted Hearst to send a train load of supplies, as did publisher Joseph Pulitzer.

The bulk of the money and donations flowed through the Red Cross. Volunteers, including its creator Clara Barton, aged 78, arrived on scene with food and provisions. The group oversaw its distribution and provided aid. Not all donations went to this organization. The State of Texas received direct contributions, too.

Many urged him to call a special session of the Texas Legislature and form a committee; Governor Sayers declined. It'd take too long to make it happen and he wanted relief to flow as soon as possible. Instead, he disbursed the cash himself to speed the process and save the expense of hiring contractors to do it. Every cent must be used for those devastated by the disaster. Throughout his public service, Joseph Sayers earned a reputation as an honest, fair, and talented administrator and insisted on making sure the money quickly and equitably benefitted those desperately awaiting aid. Unfortunately, he had experience in the area. A year ago, the Brazos River flooded and he received high praise for the way he managed the recovery effort. Now he sat at a small desk in the foyer of the executive mansion and distributed money to those seeking support. He shifted his bed into the hallway, near the telephone, and directed rescue programs via phone and telegraph. Joseph made himself available twenty-four hours a day, seven days a week, during the crisis. Simultaneously, he spear-headed the fundraising campaign by contacting governors, mayors, politicians, and wealthy individuals to solicit donations. His wife Lena headed the Austin Relief Society's drive to help, making it a double effort.

In addition to funds or supplies, telegrams and letters arrived daily offering aid to those displaced in the calamity. Ordinary individuals, business leaders, politicians, and heads of state sent words of concern and sympathy. President McKinley personally dispatched a telegram to Governor Sayers extending condolences and pledging financial assistance, provisions, and tents.

Most of those who took shelter at the Beaumont's moved into tents once enough arrived and the soldiers set them up. They'd be eternally grateful for the succor and didn't want to impose any more. Lucy, the boys, and a few others stayed on. Lucy transferred from the attic into a bedroom and the boys shared what'd been the library. The books were ruined when the windows shattered and rain and wind poured inside. The girls she supervised also remained and now shared a bedroom instead of the attic.

The adults and older children trekked daily to the center of town to collect the household's daily ration of food. The following week the boys and girls managed to secure additional clothes, too, so one set could be washed and the other worn. Lucy was a bit smaller and shorter than Mrs. Beaumont. The generous woman gave her two dresses, and the requisite undergarments, to replace those tattered in the storm. Lucy altered the outfits to fit her. In her prayers, she thanked the Lord for sparing her and the boys and for the Beaumont's philanthropy.

For weeks, fires for the dead burned around the island. To no one's surprise, more were unearthed as crews cleared the wreckage, as many as a hundred a day. Salvaged siding, timber, fixtures, and fittings lay stacked next to curbs for use in rebuilding. For now, however, disposing of victims and clean-up had to be job one.

The marauding fiend of 1900 left death and destruction all along its path. It drenched Cuba in twenty-four inches of rain and skirted southern Florida causing gale force winds but little damage. It hooked an unusual turn to the northwest causing warning flags to pop up the length of the coast between Florida and Texas. In the Gulf, it tossed ships like matchsticks and they went careening wildly across the waves. A number of the vessels sank or sustained irreparably damaged. Here the deadly brute claimed its first victims.

It slammed into Galveston causing the demise of thousands of souls. The eye passed forty miles west of the city. The barometer dropped to an unbelievable 28.48 inches of mercury, the lowest ever recorded by the US Weather Bureau to that point. It would have been lower still in the eye of the beast. Three-quarters of a century later, when the Saffir-Simpson Scale was adopted to quantify the strength of hurricanes, meteorologists labeled it a four on a scale of one to five. Category Four's pack sustained winds of 130-156 miles per hour. Eye witnesses placed sustained winds even higher, possibly pushing it to a Category Five. Experts estimated gusts probably exceeded 200 mph.

It swung west a bit and turned sharply north. Houston got a taste of its high winds resulting in property damage then it hammered the central part of the state. The tempest traveled through Oklahoma where it joined a low-pressure system and regained some lost power. It took an easterly route, roared through Ohio, and battered Chicago and Buffalo with cyclone force winds causing severe damage and some loss of life. Manhattan experienced winds in excess of sixty miles per hour. The monster wreaked havoc on Price Edward Island, Canada, before rushing into the Atlantic Ocean and finally ending its rampage.

Characteristic of the indominable American spirit and Texas determination, rebuilding commenced immediately. Water service returned in forty-eight hours and the trestle was repaired in less than a week. By Christmas, the island was reborn. Fresh construction replaced the carnage. New or repaired homes, stores, shops, municipal facilities, and churches rose, like a Phoenix, from the ruins of the Great Hurricane. St. Mary's Orphan Asylum relocated and reopened in 1901. In 1911 the huge, luxurious Hotel Galvez opened on the site of the destroyed orphanage. Nicknamed "Queen of the Gulf", the lavish hotel had the audacity to charge an exorbitant rate of $2.

For years, a group of civil leaders touted the benefits of building a seawall to protect the city from just such a catastrophe. It never gained wide-spread support until the storm. In January of 1902, a committee of three engineers proposed building a barrier seventeen feet tall and sixteen feet wide at the base to guard the island. Construction began in September and the initial three-mile section was completed in July of 1904. Ultimately, it'd be extended to ten miles.

Simultaneously, Galveston launched the unimageable task of raising five hundred city blocks to a higher elevation behind the wall, including water pipes, fire hydrants, sewer lines, trolley tracks, 2000 buildings, and the Cathedral. Engineers divided the city into quarter mile sections, surrounded one at a time with dikes, pumped out the water, and used jackscrews to lift the structures within. Sand dredged from the channel filled in the space below. Section by section, the city increased in altitude. Some parts rose inches, others in excess of sixteen feet. A gentle slope from the seawall toward the bay allowed water to run off away from town. The Herculean task ended and instead of being less than nine feet at its highest point, Galveston's crest exceeded twenty-four feet. Two unexpected benefits resulted from the improved grade. The island's inefficient sewer system worked much better and bodies still hidden or hastily buried in shallow graves where they lay would forever rest in peace beneath the new landscape.

CHAPTER 5

In the days and weeks following the calamity, Joseph Sayers slept very little. The phone rang constantly and he answered each himself. As he contemplated the future of the battered city, he also reflected on the past.

•   •   •   •   •

He was born in Grenada, Mississippi in 1841. When he was ten, his mother died and the family moved to Texas. His father, a frontier doctor, set up practice in Bastrop not far from Austin. Joseph earned a bachelor of arts degree from Bastrop Military Institute and received a commission in the United States Army. At graduation, Sam Houston handed him a diploma; his classmate Sam Houston, Jr. got one, too.

Although opposed to secession, when the Civil War became a reality Joseph, age twenty, enlisted as a private in the Fifth Texas Mounted Volunteers on the side of the Confederacy. Because of his exceptional valor and leadership, he received numerous promotions, eventually becoming a major. He cherished this title above all the others he attained. He sustained several injuries in the war, the most serious a bullet wound to his left leg slightly above the ankle. It took him out of action for a short period, but he quickly returned. His presence prompted Governor Lubbock to remark in his memoirs that Sayers was the only man he ever saw in active military service on crutches.

The war ended and he went back to Bastrop where he taught school and studied law in the evenings. He passed the bar exam and

Joseph declared himself ready to settle down. He met, courted, and married Miss Ada Walton in 1868 and formed a close relationship with her kin, also originally from Mississippi. Joseph and his sister-in-law Orline, Lena for short, became good friends. Three years later, the couple felt blessed when Ada discovered she was expecting a child. Tragically, the dream turned into a nightmare when both she and the baby died from complications at the birth.

To assuage his grief, Joseph threw himself into politics. In 1873, the people of Bastrop elected him to the state Senate. The voters of Texas again sent him to Austin in 1878, this time as lieutenant governor. A month after the inauguration, to her family's delight, Joseph married his late wife's sister Lena. Instead of taking a trip, the couple spent their honeymoon in Austin so he could attend to the business of his office.

Soon he and Governor Oran Roberts clashed over the best use of public lands and funding for public schools. Sayers championed free education. He decided he'd better serve the citizens of Texas in Washington, D.C., won a seat in the U.S. House of Representatives in 1884, and served for seven terms. During his tenure, he secured federal pensions for Texas Rangers who fought in the Indian Wars. Joseph earned the reputation of being a diligent public servant, a frugal trustee of tax-payer money, and for conducting the affairs of government with the utmost integrity.

In 1898, Texans brought him once more to Austin where he served two terms as the state's highest elected official. Governor Sayers faced three disasters that tested his considerable administrative abilities. In 1899, a fire destroyed a number of buildings at the Huntsville Penitentiary and a devastating flood of the Brazos River caused enormous property damage and 289 died. Unimaginable until September 8, 1900. The thought of a third tragic event ended his reverie and planted him firmly in the present.

•   •   •   •   •

He'd done a tremendous amount to help the victims of the hurricane financially, but as January approached, he wanted to honor those who perished and acknowledge the perseverance of survivors in a personal way. His wife Lena formulated the perfect idea. Admirers dubbed her the Dolly Madison of the Mansion in recognition of her superb skills as a hostess and impeccable social acumen. She suggested he invite a contingent for a memorial service to commemorate the dead and a New Years' Day banquet in honor of the living. He loved it and recruited her to plan the menu and prepare a guest list.

She put the three orphans from St. Mary's and a chaperone on the list. Lena sent these invitations in the envelope with the one to Mayor Jones. Mrs. Sayers tucked in a note requesting he try and locate the boys. The children, he discovered, lived at the Beaumont house. Mr. and Mrs. Beaumont gladly offered to pay all expenses and insisted Lucy escort them.

"Oh, Mrs. Beaumont," she urged, "why don't you go?" Lucy grew up in an orphanage and knew she'd be out of her element at the governor's soiree.

"I need to stay here and supervise construction. The repairs are at a critical stage and I can't get away. Neither can my husband. You simply have to go, there's nobody else. Ellison's received a large shipment yesterday and we should be able to find you something suitable to wear."

Excitedly, Lucy agreed. She'd never been off the island much less to the capital city. The next day she, Mrs. Beaumont, and the boys went to the dry goods store where Lucy spent a harrowing night four months ago. It conjured up horrible memories and she shuddered when she entered. This time instead of high water, fierce winds, and terrified people she found warmth and smiling faces. It smelled of raw wood and fresh paint. Shelves held canned goods, hats, hardware, rope, pickles, and flour from trains arriving at regular and predictable intervals. At the east end of the store, racks displayed an abundance of ready-made clothing for every size, age, and taste.

Lucy tried three dresses and decided on one with a blue and white starburst print skirt that brushed the floor and flowed to a short train behind. The ruffled blouse had a high lace collar and a bow at the waist. The ensemble came with a bolero jacket in the same blue print as the skirt and trimmed in a wide lace band. It was the fanciest and most mature she'd ever owned. Mrs. Beaumont insisted she select an elaborate hat and stylish black boots. For four months she'd worn a pair of Mrs. Beaumont's that were slightly too big.

The boys, too, got appropriate clothes. The generous woman bought each a dark blue sailor-style suit with wide white collars tied in a bow in the front. Black stockings covered their legs beneath the knee length britches. The outfits were fashionable, attractive, and itchy. All three scratched vigorously while thanking Mrs. Beaumont for her gift.

The train ride was amazing. The travelers watched excitedly as the powerful locomotive slowly puffed away from the station and gradually picked up speed. None ever rode one before. In town, they saw new buildings and repaired boulevards. As it progressed farther, however, the scenery cruelly reminded them not long ago the whole island lay in ruins. Here houses sat in heaps, the owners' dead in an unknown resting place. Trees, wreckage, and land-locked boats still littered the prairie. Fortunately, no bodies were in sight although Lucy knew some likely lurked in the piles by the way.

Passing through Houston awed them all. Established by the Allen brothers in 1836, just three years prior to the founding of Galveston, it'd grown much larger than the island town. The city, population 45,000, was twenty-five percent larger than Lucy's home and vibrated with movement and excitement. It developed into the transportation capital of the state. The hub hummed and rail lines from all corners of the country jammed the tracks. Trains transported cattle, lumber, cotton, and produce to ports on the island and New Orleans, to all forty-five states, and beyond. Ox drawn wagons clogged the streets and bulged under loads of sugar cultivated and processed in Sugarland, Texas or boards from local mills. From the railroad car flour mills, blacksmith shops, saddle and tack stores, hotels, restaurants, and a few boulevards paved with bricks and gravel came into view. Most roads were dirt. They saw the town's two papers, the *Post* and *Chronicle*. At the far southern outskirts of the city, Lucy noted new construction. A gentleman told her George Hermann donated the land for a charity hospital. Years later it'd become Memorial Hermann Hospital, part of the world-famous Texas Medical Center.

After transferring at the downtown station, the small group headed west to San Antonio, the state's largest city. The boys, once enthralled by the train and fascinating sights of Houston, got restless and bored when the ride passed onto the flat lands of south central Texas. The youngsters alternately slept, wandered from car to car, visited other Galvestonians, or inundated her with endless questions for which she rarely had an answer. Their interest peaked again a bit near San Antonio. The terrain rolled into gentle swells and for people used to the plains, it presented an amazing sight under a full moon. One last change and the engineer pointed his locomotive north toward Austin. The swells grew into hills and all four enjoyed the unfamiliar sight. As the train slowed and she looked around, Lucy mentally dubbed the capital a tiny berg compared to Houston and San Antonio. Even in the dark she knew it wasn't large. Claiming 22,200 citizens, it's population made it less than half the size of Houston.

Mrs. Sayers sent a carriage to the station and it whisked them toward 1010 Colorado Street. Lucy spotted the governor's mansion and admitted to herself it disappointed her. Somehow, she envisioned a palace. It was lovely, to be sure. The edifice stood among beautiful trees, picturesque gardens, and a fountain sparkling in the bright moonlight. The gleaming white Greek Revival structure sported six thick columns across the front supporting wide porches on both levels. But it paled in comparison to Gresham's Castle, as Galvestonians called it. Built by the Gresham family of native Texas granite, white limestone, and red sandstone, the ornate Victorian style residence was three-fold the size of this splendid estate. Thankfully, the hurricane inflicted relatively minor damage. The Catholic Diocese eventually bought the property and the bishop lived there. It then became referred to as the Bishop's Palace.

Inside the governor's home the recently installed electric lights beckoned the tired group to an elegant foyer with a curving, carved staircase at the back. Governor and Mrs. Sayers welcomed Lucy and the boys warmly and ushered the travelers into the front parlor while a footman took charge of the trio's meager luggage. The maid served tea and cookies and the boys inhaled every bite. They left at dawn and now the clock in the hall chimed ten o'clock. All three ate a quick meal at a café during one of the stops between Houston and San Antonio, but that'd been hours ago. An extremely nervous Lucy managed to sip a few drops of tea.

"Now my dears," said Mrs. Sayers, "I know you must be exhausted. I've taken the same journey myself and it's slow and tiring, especially the wait. I'll show you to your rooms."

Her graciousness stunned Lucy. She expected to go to an inn not sleep in the mansion. The girl very politely explained Mrs. Beaumont provided money for a hotel and ended by saying, "we don't wish to be a burden".

"Nonsense, we have enough space to accommodate you and more to spare. The boys can share and you'll be in a private one across the hall. I insist." She could hardly argue with the governor's wife. The trip drained her and the boys struggled to keep their eyes open. The exhausted girl thanked her hostess profusely and gladly trailed her upstairs.

The next morning, Lucy woke as the sun peaked above the horizon and she dressed in the same brown suit she wore on the train. Tip-toeing through the cold house, she curled cat-like into a large chair beside a fire in what she thought might be the library. She was wrong. The room where she warmed herself turned out to be the governor's private office. He walked in a few minutes after she sat down.

"Well hello Miss Dubuis, aren't you the early riser."

His voice startled her and she jumped to her feet. When she saw the governor standing by the doorway her knees shook. "I'm so sorry, sir, I didn't mean to—. I wanted to warm up a bit...so I'll.... leave...". Her voice faltered.

Joseph Sayers chuckled heartily and indicated she sit. He tried to reassure her by saying, "Relax young lady, I don't bite." A footman announced breakfast and Joseph requested she join him. By now she was, indeed, famished and happily let him lead her to the dining table. Once served, the governor asked her about her life in Galveston.

She told him what it was like growing up at St. Mary's, going to business school, and working for Mother Superior. She smiled as she related these good memories. Then she frowned and trembled when she got to the storm. Joseph listened intently to the story. He found it an enthralling account, Lucy spoke well and articulately, and this made it all the more interesting. He sensed her keen mind and eye for detail. He conveyed his sorrow for what she'd been through and asked a totally unforeseen question.

"Do you know how to use a typewriting machine and take shorthand?"

Dumbstruck at his query, she hesitated a moment and replied. "Why, yes sir. I learned both at Miss Cooper's Academy and we used a typewriter at the orphanage. Why do you ask?"

Since its introduction in 1864, more and more women acquired jobs as secretaries, a profession formerly dominated by men. Smaller hands and nimbler fingers allowed the ladies to type faster and more accurately than most of their male counterparts. He'd always hired men, but his current assistant gave four weeks' notice and would leave for a position in Dallas. He took a shine to this intelligent woman and decided to offer it to her.

"Miss Dubuis, I find myself in need of a secretary. Are you interested? There's a small suite with a private entrance at the rear of the kitchen if you'd care to use it. Mr. Woodson lived in it until he married last year."

"Sir, what about the boys?"

"You can escort them back if you prefer and retrieve your things or I'll get a police officer to do it. Your choice. It is essential you start soon, though. This is Woodson's final week and he'd like to leave sooner if possible."

Lucy hoped her mouth hadn't dropped open. When she boarded

the train, never in her wildest imagination did she foresee this. She thanked him profusely and requested a day to consider it. Later in the morning she'd attend the memorial and in the evening the banquet. She and the boys planned to see the sights the next day and return to Galveston the following afternoon. She promised to give him an answer after the tour.

The service was dignified and mournful; the banquet sumptuous and thrilling. Lucy knew several of those in attendance, the food was delectable, the music delightful, and the room glowed in the light of dozens of candles. Local ladies and gentlemen dressed grandly, while those from Galveston wore garments closely resembling her own or even humbler. Not all had a generous benefactor. Everyone treated the survivors kindly and took great pains to make them feel welcome and at ease. Lucy's attention wasn't focused on her surroundings that night, whereas on other occasions her eyes would be big as saucers. Reflection on the governor's proposal occupied her thoughts and swirled through her mind where the music should have been. She envisioned a quiet life working at St. Mary's and, perhaps, marrying and living on the island with her husband and family. Now, there were no jobs, no nuns, and a lot fewer men. The Beaumont's were amazingly kind, but she couldn't intrude on them forever. Striking out on her own in a strange city frightened her, but less so than the hurricane. She'd survive this, too. Slowly and surely, she began talking herself into taking the position.

CHAPTER 6

Lucy accepted the governor's offer and his suggestion someone else take the boys home. She carried her entire wardrobe on the trip, owned nothing else, and thought of no good reason to go to Galveston. She'd like to personally thank the Beaumont's and say good-bye, but it'd be a waste of money. Governor Sayers telegraphed them with the change and, at Lucy's request, said she was sending back the unused funds for the hotel. The policeman assigned to escort the children would give it to her when he arrived. Mrs. Beaumont quickly answered and sent congratulations and best wishes for her success. She wanted Lucy to keep the money and use it to get a foothold in Austin.

Lucy wrote her sponsors a lengthy letter expressing her eternal gratitude for their love and generosity toward her and the boys. She deemed the advance to be a loan and vowed to reimburse the whole amount. She appreciated the wonderful gesture, particularly since they already did more for her than she'd ever be able to repay. The magnanimous duo may have saved her by taking her in. She said how sad she felt at the thought of leaving her friends, especially them. However, getting a job wasn't optional and it might be a while before any became available in Galveston. Mrs. Beaumont sent a warm and loving reply. They'd miss her very much, too, and truly intended the funds a gift. If she insisted on repaying it, please make it easy on herself. It took fifteen months, but Lucy refunded every cent. In her letter, Mrs. Beaumont assured her Frank, William, and Albert could stay until the orphanage reopened in its new location.

It broke her heart to see her charges off at the station. She helped care for the boys at St. Mary's and had a soft spot in her heart for the trio as she did for all those now lost forever. It still brought tears to her eyes when she contemplated the Sisters' fate and the orphans who perished so cruelly. Since the storm, Lucy developed a unique bond with these three and it hurt her to think she wouldn't see the youngsters again. Maybe she'd go to Galveston for a visit. Lucy hugged each boy tightly, handed Frank a huge basket packed to the brim with food for the trip, and waved until the train disappeared from sight. Then she returned to the mansion to begin anew.

The housekeeper, Mrs. Elvira Laney, showed her to the suite at the back of the manse. It was small, clean, and cozy. The parlor held two comfortable chairs, a table, a potbelly stove, and two doors. One led to the hall by the kitchen and the second to the exterior. A single bed stood against the south wall and a chest on the north side of the tiny sleeping alcove. The arrangement permitted her access to the stove and ice box if she fixed her own meals. The cook, Carrie Plunk, told her Mr. Woodson generally ate in the kitchen with the staff and invited her to do so, too. As a state-paid secretary she earned a very small salary and having room and meals provided gave her a livable, if modest, income.

Lucy decided to enhance her wardrobe as she owned only three outfits. The one she wore to the banquet was far too elaborate for business. The brown and gray hand me downs from Mrs. Beaumont sufficed, but she wanted a little more. She worked for Governor Sayers and must dress appropriately. Mrs. Laney recommended a reasonably priced shop in town and Lucy went there after her charges left. She bought a black skirt and two blouses to match it, one solid white and the other white and black striped. Lucy got additional undergarments, stockings, a hat, a nightgown, and warm wool shawl. Just as she was about to walk out, she noticed a green dress with subtle pink stripes. It was too tempting to resist and she added it to her pile. The leftover travelling money paid for some of it and Governor Sayers granted her a week's advance, too. She never before owned so many clothes.

On a cold Monday in January of 1901, she excitedly walked the short distance to the capitol. Lucy sat beside Governor Sayers' door and answered the phone, greeted visitors, took letters or notes in shorthand, and typed them. She filed memos, placed calls, and scheduled appointments for her boss. She regularly accompanied him to outside meetings to take the minutes. While employed by the governor, Lucy had the honor of meeting a variety of famous people. The most exciting of all was William McKinley, President of the United States.

At the beginning of his second term, President and Mrs. McKinley embarked on a seven-week, cross country, ocean to ocean trip through the south and southwest part of the U.S. He left on April 29th and arrived in Houston May 3rd, the first sitting president to set foot in Texas. Here Governor Sayers and political dignitaries greeted the Chief Executive and accompanied him on to Austin. Citizens of the capital city surpassed the imagination by elaborately decorating the streets and buildings in honor of the visit. A procession down Congress Avenue for the First Couple included a military band, fifteen companies of the state militia, and Confederate veterans. The city lit the route with glowing, shimmering lights. As he and Mrs. McKinley rode in an elegant carriage, the *Austin Statesman* estimated a crowd of 20,000 spectators waved and cheered him on his way. A reporter wrote "Never before in the history of this city has there ever been anything to equal the reception of yesterday". A lot of the onlookers traveled long distances to catch a glimpse of McKinley. The throng completely overwhelmed city facilities, restaurants, and hotels.

The procession culminated at the capitol building where McKinley made a public speech on the steps and then addressed the Texas Legislature. At the end of the speeches, a fragile elderly woman shuffled forward bearing a gift. Mrs. Anson Jones, widow of the last president of the Republic of Texas, presented McKinley a tiny silk Lone Star flag. Later, the society ladies of Austin held a reception for the honored guests at the Sachem. They dined with the Sayers' at the Executive Mansion and departed for San Antonio, the next stop on the journey.

For months, McKinley dominated periodicals and casual

conversation. People rehashed the story over and over often embellishing their interaction with the dignitary. Instead of seeing him from afar, they'd been standing very near. Others boasted about shaking his hand. Few actually came so close, but as time passed thousands claimed to have done so. Lucy was one of the few who really shook his hand and exchanged a few words as well.

Mr. Sayers introduced her and mentioned she survived the Great Hurricane. The President expressed sympathy for what she went through and asked a few questions regarding her experiences. She relayed a short version, he had a busy schedule, nonetheless spoke well and poignantly. Her rendition enthralled him and he said she should write a book chronicling her ordeal. There'd been an abundance of articles, but her eye witness testimony created a deeply powerful and compelling story.

The furor over the Chief Executive's sojourn eventually settled down and other happenings filled the Austin paper. The Texas oil boom was in full swing. Spindletop, that gushed forth in January, ignited an ever-increasing frenzy to find the black gold. As more and more petroleum-driven engines came into use, the demand for crude oil soared and Texas grew into a major player in the industry. Also during the year, J.P. Morgan incorporated US Steel and in May the stock market crashed for the first time ever. In June, Cuba became a U.S. territory and on September 2nd, while at the Minnesota State Fair, Vice President Theodore Roosevelt proclaimed America should "Speak softly and carry a big stick."

For Lucy, the burgeoning fall meant an end to the brutal summer. Trees would soon don glorious golds and oranges and reds. She eagerly anticipated the day cool breezes wafted through the window across from her desk instead of hot, oppressive blasts. Even better, it was Friday, September 6th. On Saturday the governor usually locked up at three o'clock and she'd have the rest of the day off. Mandy O'Brien, secretary to Lt. Governor James Browning, was a good friend. If the office closed early, the pair planned to see *Love by the Light of the Moon*. The movie mixed live actors with animation and everyone marveled at the special effects. Mrs. Ledbetter, the pianist at the theater, played well and the score added to the enjoyment of the silent film. For now, she wanted this day to end. Fridays were always busy. The Governor held staff meetings then and she took notes. He dictated a lot of letters for delivery the following week. In ten minutes it'd be five o'clock and he showed no sign of slowing. Sayers and the Attorney General were meeting privately in the chamber behind her.

Just then, the boy who worked for Western Union walked in with a telegram. Tears brimmed in his eyes as he handed the envelope to Lucy and shuffled out sadly, not even waiting for a tip. She opened the message per the Governor's instructions. As part of her job, she culled the urgent from the merely important and decided if it warranted an interruption of his schedule. Given the expression on the boy's face, it promised to be urgent. On reading it, she too broke down in tears.

"Come in," he said gruffly, "it better be important."

Lucy opened the door softly and entered. She tried to assure him of the wire's significance but couldn't trust her voice.

As he read the telegram, Governor Sayers turned pale:

To Gov. Sayers
Austin, Texas
McKinley shot at Pan-American Exposition in Buffalo, New York at 4 p.m. Culprit apprehended. President expected to survive.

The country and the world reacted with shock and disgust at the senseless act of violence. Twice an assassin's bullet ended a president's life and now a third tried to do it. Thank heavens the attempt was foiled. The evening paper gave details about the tragic event. Leon Czolgosz, an anarchist from Michigan, shot as he stepped up to greet McKinley at the Temple of Music, a pavilion at the Exhibition. The fiend fired a revolver hidden beneath a handkerchief. The first bullet hit a button and stuck there. A second projectile tore through the president's abdomen and lodged precariously near his stomach. The perpetrator tried to fire again and that's when bodyguards wrestled him to the ground and prevented another assault. The Cabinet notified Vice President Teddy Roosevelt but urged him to continue his camping trip to the Adirondacks since McKinley seemed well. So well, in fact, McKinley instructed police to take it easy on Czolgosz.

Unfortunately, the optimistic prognosis rapidly turned to one of despair. Surgeons missed gangrenous tissue and the poison invaded his blood stream. The president's condition steadily declined and no hope remained. He died on the morning of September 14th and Roosevelt rushed back to Washington to assume the office. The entire nation mourned the loss. After a hundred twenty-five years, the United States grieved for its third slain leader.

Czolgosz confessed to the murder saying he deemed it necessary because McKinley posed a threat to the good people but failed to explain what he meant. He pled guilty, the judge rejected it, and entered a plea of not guilty instead. The assailant refused to talk to his lawyers, refused to testify, and refused to help in any way with his defense. The attorney's only choice was to use an innocent by reason of insanity defense. The jury didn't buy it and convicted the assassin of murder. On October 29, 1901, the state of New York executed Leon Czolgosz, age 28, in the electric chair.

Throughout his tenure, Governor Sayers worked hard to promote Texas' interests and improve her status in the country. He used his influence to convince Teddy Roosevelt to authorize funds to enlarge Buffalo Bayou making it deep and wide enough to accommodate large sea going cargo vessels. Houston, located fifty miles from the coast, turned into a major port. It expanded time and again, eventually becoming one of the busiest in the U.S. Due to its inland location, Houston was less vulnerable to the ravages of Atlantic hurricanes than Galveston and quickly outpaced her in size and importance.

As January of 1903 approached and the end to his term neared, Governor Sayers pondered what to do. He decided to resume practicing law and chose to move to San Antonio, Texas' largest city. He invited Lucy to go with him and she gladly accepted. He paid her more than the state since she no longer had access to the apartment and needed to find her own place to live.

Lucy rented a room at a small boarding house catering to women located three blocks from the office. It provided the perfect, respectable accommodations for a single female. Mrs. Ethel Daffodil, a widow, allowed no male occupants. She enforced an eight o'clock curfew during the week and a ten o'clock deadline on Saturday. The woman allowed no drinking or smoking and she restricted gentlemen callers to the parlor. Mrs. Daffodil earned a reputation as a diligent chaperone and surrogate mother to the three ladies who stayed with her. The rent included meals so Lucy didn't have to bother cooking. Since she worked blocks away, she walked home for lunch most days. Ethel loved to cook and all the girls enjoyed her efforts. Now and then one of the lodgers complained about the rent, or a draft, or the chores, but the food got A+ ratings. The landlady insisted her tenants keep the establishment spotlessly clean; Thursday evening all the women pitched in to scrub the domicile from attic to cellar. Following dinner, they took turns washing the dishes, sweeping, and cleaning the bath. Each made the bed and tidied her room before leaving the house.

On the rare times Lucy didn't eat in Mrs. Daffodil's kitchen, she dined at the Sayers' or went to a cafe, but with a date or companion. Unescorted ladies were not always welcome in reputable eateries. Lucy and Dorothy St. Martin became best pals. Dorothy worked across the street from Lucy at a bank and the two went out together when finances permitted. The girls decided to splurge and paint the town red by eating at a fine restaurant and taking in a movie. Neither could afford the cost of two activities very often and it took months to save enough. Dorothy picked the spot, the Elite, and Lucy the movie, *Mary Jane's Mishap*. The spooky comedy told the tale of a maid who accidentally started a fire, died, and came back as a ghost to haunt her employers.

The friends wanted to make it an event and dressed in their best. Lucy chose the outfit she bought for Easter. It's pale pink color, three-tiered skirt, wide bell sleeves, and short train exemplified spring. Dorothy picked a frock of light blue with a slim skirt and matching jacket trimmed in a darker hue. Both looked pretty, young, and happy as they walked from Dorothy's to dine. It promised to be a delightful interlude until a mishap nearly ended the adventure before it began. Just as she grabbed the knob to push open the door, a man yanked it forcefully inward from the opposite side. Lucy was suddenly thrown off balance and she tumbled—into the arms of a stranger.

CHAPTER 7

Harry Fawcett grew up in San Antonio and figured he'd die there as well. His great, great grandparents, Ambrose and Chastity, immigrated separately to the United States from England in the 1700's as babes in arms. Ambrose's father, Reginald Fawcett, boasted an extended line of blacksmiths and brought tools of the trade to the New World. His employer died and he scrounged enough money to purchase the inventory and book passage in steerage on a packet ship, the *Renowned*. An anvil, bellows, heavy hammers, and tongs were loaded into the hold of the ship. A violent storm at sea threatened to shatter his dream of owning a business, but he, his family, and the equipment survived to thrive when they landed.

The ship docked at the Port of New Orleans in 1798, just prior to the expiration of the treaty between the U. S. and Spain allowing Americans to freely use it and navigate the Mississippi River. Within months, King Charles IV closed the harbor to U.S. vessels and none landed there for several years. In 1800, even though Napoleon secretly acquired the region, Spain administered it. The Louisiana Purchase Treaty was signed in 1803, the area reverted to U.S. control, and her ships again put in at New Orleans.

From Louisiana, the Fawcett's headed west to Spanish Texas, hammering and shoeing horses to pay the way. Reginald set up shop under a tree in San Antonio. The city, the first chartered settlement in Texas, started in 1731 as a colonial trading post and Catholic mission. Here, the native generation of Fawcett's began when Ambrose's three siblings joined the group.

It was a hard, grueling existence but the wide-open territory offered plenty of opportunity. Mexico won independence from Spain in 1821 and trade prospered until Santa Anna repealed the Constitution. The document exempted pioneers from the oppressive taxes and laws endured by Mexicans. Texans, in effect, governed themselves and liked the arrangement. In 1830, revised laws stripped this autonomy, ended the ability of Americans to settle the area, authorized troops to enforce the laws, and Mexican soldiers tried to seize a cannon at Goliad. The invasion prompted the creation of a flag bearing the picture of a cannon and the slogan "come and take it" and ignited the revolution. Two Fawcett cousins and an uncle died in February of 1836 at the Battle of the Alamo. A short time later, the Republic of Texas sprang forth. It remained an independent country before becoming the twenty-eighth state in 1845. Although not slave owners, the Fawcett's fought for the Confederacy in the Civil War believing states should control their destiny.

Many of the kinfolk continued plying the smithy trade, while others such as Harry's grandpa, switched to farming. Cotton was king and he bought a tract of land and planted as much of it as he could manage. It'd never make them rich, but it provided a comfortable, if backbreaking, livelihood. His father Oscar spent his youth sowing, hoeing, picking, and selling the white wonder.

His great, great grandmother Chastity arrived earlier. The Cornell's entered through New York in time to fight in the Revolutionary War. Mr. Cornell, a lawyer, served in George Washington's administration as an advisor to Secretary of State Edmund Randolph. Her distant uncle, Josiah, assisted Nathanael Greene who commanded the Continental Army's Quartermaster Corp. Josiah demonstrated superior organizational and logistical skills as he navigated the treacherous task of procuring and distributing supplies to the troops, what little of it there was. Later, President John Adams assigned him to help negotiate a treaty to end the Quasi-War.

The Cornell clan wandered its way to Virginia where several established large tobacco plantations. A different branch continued the journey south and west, moving into farming or ranching. In 1861 Harry's maternal grandpa, Kinder Cornell, lived in Oklahoma and owned a small cattle ranch. The band migrated farther and settled in San Antonio where Maude Louisa was born and raised.

The Fawcett's and Cornell's ran into one another occasionally at church or the general store and the kids played together at recess. Oscar dropped out in the eighth grade. He learned enough reading, 'riting, and 'rithmetic to calculate how much seed to buy, read the weather report and almanac, determine profit margins, and record sales transactions. That's all he needed. History, science, grammar, and such fulfilled no useful purpose.

Maude stayed in school to the end. She loved learning and wanted to be a teacher when she graduated. Anybody who finished qualified as an instructor, although some places required a test to demonstrate proficiency. She passed the exam easily and walked tentatively into her classroom at eighteen. The pupils adored her and so did their folks. Her parent's place sat beyond the city and she had no way of getting to work. Consequently, she boarded round, moving house to house every month of the term. She taught for two years and then Oscar crossed her path again in a dramatic way.

It was a hot, sultry summer Sunday. After church, the adults congregated to share gossip and catch up. Maude, her two sisters, and three companions walked to the river to cool off in the clear stream. The raucous group splashed and waded happily. Suddenly, Maude tripped on a submerged branch and fell into the swiftly moving water. Oscar and his cousin Ben, who'd joined those onshore, rushed in and pulled her to safety. The men carried her to Doc Beemer who pronounced her in fine shape. He ordered her to rest in bed and said she'd suffer no ill effects due to the accident.

Mr. and Mrs. Cornell thanked the rescuers repeatedly and insisted he and Ben come to dinner the next night. They'd known each other their entire life, but Oscar and Maude rarely met during the last several years. Once he left school, he stayed too busy to go to town often. At eighteen, he bought a small spread, accepted his dad's gift of two pregnant cows, and plowed his own field. In the spring, the cows gave birth, to a heifer and a bull. He had a fledgling herd and his fields were sprouting cotton and corn and a variety of vegetables to put on his table and sell at the market.

The near tragedy thrust the couple together, rekindled the crush of eighth grade, and Oscar now regularly visited town. He made it to church most weeks and frequently managed to be in the proximity of the school at two o'clock. He invited her to the Texas Independence Day dance and the Fourth of July picnic and the Harvest Ball. As he walked her to the Kayliff's, where she currently boarded, Oscar proposed and she accepted.

They set the date in January, following the end of the semester and giving the mayor time to hire a replacement. Maude wore a simple white frock with ruffles around the neck and at the hem and carried a bouquet of white honeysuckle and winter jasmine. Ladies decorated the hall in flowers and brightly colored paper and contributed dishes of luscious beans, bread, smoked meats, cakes, and pies. With lots of hugs and wishes for happiness, the elated couple left to begin life on the farm. Maude used her meager savings to add chickens to the menagerie and invested egg and poultry money in a milk cow.

By the time Harry appeared in 1875, the Fawcett's scattered somewhat, with a lot still living in the area. His parents claimed a good-sized farm, modest herd of cattle, and a large flock of chickens. When he was ten months old, an unidentified epidemic hit San Antonio. It mirrored symptoms linked to cholera and yellow fever but was neither. Fortunately, the death toll stayed low. Unfortunately, his mom succumbed to the mysterious disease. His aunt came and raised him until he turned seven at which point she married a traveling preacher. Oscar never wed again so Harry grew independent and self-sufficient at a young age.

Before and after class, he tended the animals and took care of the crops. He did it because it was necessary but knew in his heart farming wouldn't be his career. He thought of many different occupations, medicine, shop keeping, train engineer, soldier, and lumberjack. None of the notions lasted and he had no idea what he'd do, except he'd rather use brain not brawn.

His goals changed often, loyalties remained the same. He met Heath Mattery, Willie Hightower, Oliver Segar, and Charles Morgan in first grade and they bonded instantly. They suffered through bouts of chicken pox and measles together, swam in the pond on Willie's property, and hunted rabbits in the woods. Heath's dad let them build a fort at the edge of his field to fight the Coahuiltecan Tribes who formerly inhabited the region.

At twelve, the fivesome almost ruined their futures forever and landed in jail. Heath, the most mischievous of the bunch, devised a scheme to pilfer candy at the store and the rest reluctantly agreed to participate. Charles pretended to look at nails, "accidentally" knocked over the keg, and ran out. The owner chased him while the conspirators grabbed big fistfuls of gum drops and licorice and dashed to the door. The sheriff happened to walk up, saw the crime, and nabbed the shoplifters on the porch. Mr. Draper threatened to press charges and ultimately settled on four week's labor instead. The youngsters paid penance in the evenings and the entire day on Saturday.

Harry's father prospered enough to hire a hand and at fifteen freed his son to get a job off the farm. He started doing chores at the mercantile where he swept floors, stocked shelves, and packed groceries. Next, Harry worked at his cousin's blacksmith shop. This definitely wouldn't be his fate. Definitely. He hated the filthy, hot, dangerous, back breaking tasks. Harry wanted something offering potential not an early grave. The third effort took him to the stables. It was better than being a smithy, although barely. He adored riding and detested mucking stalls. He also had the opportunity to try teaching. Older students routinely acted as instructors to the others. This was more to his liking, yet still wrong.

Harry completed his education unlike the majority of boys. He graduated alongside his four best buddies. All sat tall as Millicent Moore gave the valedictorian address and then walked proudly across the stage to accept a diploma. Heath signed on as a porter on the railroad and Willie sorted mail at the post office. Charles, whose uncle served on the town council, cleared brush at the site of new roads and Oliver went to college. Harry really needed to find a job.

Walking through town and scanning the paper did little to aid his quest. He'd resolved himself to farming until he saw Mr. McKenna put a placard in the Wells Fargo depot window: HELP WANTED: MESSENGER. The manager conducted a brief interview, offered him the position, and he started immediately.

At twenty, Harry met Flora when Mr. Pincher became the bartender at the Gray Gulch Saloon. The two kept company over six months and he fancied himself in love. The romance ended due to Mr. Pincher's move to Abilene. Elsie Zantoe entered his life in May and exited in June. She had dark, curly hair, shiny brown eyes, and a lyrical laugh. As a Methodist, her father refused to allow the relationship with a Catholic to continue.

Harry received numerous promotions and now managed the mailroom. Further advancement seemed sure so he felt ready to marry and begin a family, but none of the romances worked thus far. He believed the perfect person existed and he'd wait. Finding the right mate topped his priority list. His parents enjoyed a wonderful marriage that providence cut too short. He witnessed terrible unions and was determined to avoid the path. In the meantime, his career took precedence above all else except his dad and pals.

•   •   •   •   •

Claudia's beginnings glowed with promise and hope. She had parents who loved her dearly, siblings who doted, and unlimited opportunities to enjoy a fulfilling future. She attended a private school, wore the latest fashions, and was presented to society at an elaborate ball. This, however, proved to be her downfall.

One of the guests, Bennett X. Viceman, caught her eye and she his. Her father introduced them and the attraction was electric. His wife Bitsy Sue clung to his arm and, as always, feigned ignorance of what was coming. Claudia ignored his advances, returned his gifts, and declined invitations. For a while. He wore her down and the girl caved in to the proposed trip to France. She concocted a story believable enough to fool the family and set sail for the continent. That's where Lucy was conceived. Her father disowned her upon discovering the girl had an affair with a married man. Her lover lost interest, she had nowhere to go, no way to earn an honorably living, and she fell into prostitution.

Claudia walked the streets squeezing out a subsistence living entertaining sailors on leave and men who couldn't afford better. She'd been very pretty, once, until her profession exacted its toll and she donned a rough, unkempt, and depressed demeanor. The desperate woman tried to terminate the pregnancy but the botched procedure nearly killed her, leaving the child unharmed. Ultimately, Claudia decided she loved the baby and knew keeping it impossible.

She delivered the infant herself as she'd made no friends and a midwife cost too much. The precious girl resembled an aunt so she named her Lucy. The distraught woman wrapped the newborn in a blanket, put her in a tattered basket, and deposited her at the doorstep of St. Mary's. Of course,nobody ever knew, but Claudia kept an eye on her daughter from afar hoping to contrive a means of meeting her. It never happened because she drowned on September 8, 1900.

CHAPTER 8

Harry looked forward to this weekly dinner. The four grew up together, attended the same school, and had similar professions. Harry managed the local Wells Fargo station. He advanced from messenger to mailroom manager to supervisor, and now top man in the city. Heath Mattery scheduled routes and timetables for the Galveston, Harrisburg & San Antonio Railroad, the first line to service the city in 1877. Willie Hightower, the assistant postmaster, mapped deliveries in town and for the surrounding rural areas. Charles Morgan, a city employee, plotted new avenues, sewer lines, and utility easements. The comrades shared a history and traded thoughts on improving service to customers in an effort to aid each other's career. Oliver, the fifth member of the band, went to college and earned a Ph.D. in mathematics. He stayed in Austin and was now a professor.

It'd been a particularly lively exchange and Harry intended to modify some of the ideas to fit Wells Fargo. He'd like to keep talking, but all four made plans and needed to leave. While walking toward the exit, Willie related a story about one of his postmen who was stuck in a tree for two hours because of a vicious dog. Harry, laughing so hard his eyes teared, jerked open the door. Suddenly, a beautiful young woman landed hard against his chest. Instinctively he wrapped his arms around her so she wouldn't bounce and land on the floor.

"Are you alright, Miss? I'm terribly sorry. I should pay more attention. Here, please sit." He held her arm and led her to a chair. Then he took a better look at the lady he practically threw to the ground. This is a gorgeous girl, he noticed. She stood a scant five feet tall and had a slim, petite build. Her large eyes were the greenest he'd ever seen and her light brown, almost blonde, hair curled cutely beneath the edges of her flirty pink feathered hat.

The clash didn't hurt Lucy, however the public spectacle mortified her. Her face burned from ear to ear in embarrassment. She scowled at the man, fully intending to lambast him for his carelessness, but the words caught in her throat. While not extraordinarily handsome, he possessed extremely pleasing features, sparkling blue eyes, and neatly trimmed hair several shades lighter than her own. It all came together nicely to form a very tempting package. His dapper gray tweed suit, vest, and straw hat flattered his muscular physique. He sported a fashionable mustache that curled slightly upwards at the tips and a blue bow tie. And, at the moment, he wore a worried, concerned face. His appearance, and the anxious expression, kept her from telling him off, but not from developing an instant aversion.

Lucy tried to stand and he steadied her with his strong, firm hand. Dorothy clutched her arm and gently herded her toward the door. It embarrassed her, too, and she meant to leave as quickly as possible. Lucy mumbled a nearly inaudible "I'm fine" and the women hurried away. Harry followed, to escort them to their destination, and both refused. He was a perfect stranger, albeit an attractive one, and neither wanted any interaction with him. It'd be scandalous to be seen on the street with a male neither knew. After making sure she really hadn't been hurt, Dorothy suggested eating at Leon's. The restaurant served great food and none of the customers witnessed the accident.

Over dinner, the girls discussed the mishap. Dorothy forced her to relive the humiliating incidence even though Lucy would rather let it go. She thought the men crude and ungentlemanly. Her friend voiced disdain for the quartet, but Lucy wasn't sure. The fellow who yanked her in seemed contrite and apologetic. He asked her time and again if she hurt herself, required help, and requested the honor of ensuring she arrived home safely. Maybe he meant to be kind rather than improper. The others, too, expressed regret for not being careful. It was probably rude to leave so abruptly, without giving the four an opportunity to make amends.

Dorothy conceded the point. Perhaps they should've spoken briefly, but all the customers stared when Lucy fell into the arms of the man. Begrudgingly the woman admitted she found him appealing, and the tall one next to him, too. In an effort to change the conversation, Lucy told her something she'd been keeping a secret.

"Do you remember me telling you about President McKinley's visit? Good. I told him of my experiences in Galveston and he suggested I write my memories. Well, I took his advice. I jotted notes on all I remembered, sort of like a diary. He died, I put it away, and pretty much forgot the whole idea. Last week I saw the journal in a cabinet. I think I'll give it a try."

Dorothy waited, expecting her to continue. Lucy didn't so she asked, "Try what?"

"Oh, writing a book, of course."

"Lucy, how exciting. I bet you'd be good at it. Who can say, you might become rich and famous. Will you let me read it?"

Lucy laughed at the request. She hadn't even begun writing yet, and may never do it, but Dorothy already envisioned her as a famous published author. "Sure, if I ever really get underway you'll be my guinea pig." She appreciated the fact Dorothy shared her excitement and wanted to help. If the situation were reversed, she'd beg to encourage her friend by reading the draft.

The rest of the night went splendidly. The food was excellent, they ordered dessert, and the movie turned out to be hilarious. When she got to the house, barely ten minutes shy of curfew, Lucy still bubbled with excitement from their adventure. Instead of going to bed, she opened the Galveston diary and reread it. She scribbled notes in the margins, wrote on separate sheets of paper and slipped them between pages, and generally tried to recall the tiniest details. The more she wrote, the more she remembered, and the more motivated she became. Why not? She worked until dawn, slept a few hours, and took up where she left off.

On Monday, Mr. Sayers asked if she felt ill. She looked awfully tired and red-eyed. She smiled, thanked him for the concern, and said she tossed and turned. In truth, she stayed up writing. She'd put a stop to it, at least past eleven o'clock, but over the weekend she became a woman possessed. Lucy secluded herself in her room and wrote, except for eating and doing chores. She declined joining the other boarders when Mrs. Daffodil played the piano and everyone sang nor did she participate in a game of whist afterwards. Normally she reveled in these activities, however not now. Once she started writing, the words gushed forth geyser-like from the end of her pen. Nonetheless, she had to go to bed. Even if it sold, she must earn a living in the meantime.

"Yes, sir, Mr. Fawcett. Mr. Sayers can see you on Monday at ten o'clock. Thank you for calling."

Well, his calendar for the week is totally full now. It'll be busy, she mused. At least there'd be three whole days free before tackling it. The Sayers' were going to see relatives in Austin and the office would be closed on Friday, Saturday, and Sunday. That'd give her a lot of time to write and her boss gave her permission to come in and use the typewriter. She could polish the first two chapters for Dorothy to read. It was a little scary letting someone else read it, but Lucy hoped to get an honest review. If her pal hated the manuscript, why bother continuing? Because she loved doing it! She'd keep on no matter what. It provided a great creative outlet and, since she possessed no musical or artistic talent whatsoever, it was the sole path available.

Lucy put the finishing touches on her draft and then typed the two completed parts. On Sunday she took the pages to Dorothy, who lived with her parents, and ate lunch there as well. She always enjoyed socializing at the St. Martin's. They were gracious and warm, the three younger siblings delightful, and the home welcoming. She visited frequently and always left in a happy frame of mind.

Lucy made a point of going to sleep early and arrived on Monday rested, refreshed, and prepared to face the long week. Two clients came and went exactly as scheduled. So did the third. At five minutes to ten o'clock, Mr. Harry Fawcett walked through the door, hat in hand.

"YOU??" Lucy jumped abruptly when she saw him. In front of her stood the man who pulled her roughly into the Elite. He was as shocked as she. "What are you doing here?"

"I have an appointment to see Governor Sayers, Miss???"

"Oh, Dubuis. Miss Dubuis."

He smiled and the pleasant features turned absolutely radiant. His blue eyes sparkled like sunlight on a pond, the dimples in his cheeks grew larger, and his mouth turned up boyishly. Lucy tried to remain stern, he almost toppled her, but she couldn't help responding to his charm.

"A pleasure to make your acquaintance, Miss Dubuis. I truly am sorry about the other day. Please forgive me. It was entirely my fault."

Struggling to regain her composure, she managed to control her face. "Yes, you are correct. The Governor should be ready for you shortly. Take a seat."

Moments later the door opened and Joseph Sayers walked out.

"Harry, my boy. Good to see you. Have you met Miss Dubuis? Of course you did. How's your father? I haven't seen him in ages. Come on in."

"Thank you, Governor, my mother and father send their best and …." The door banged softly behind him.

So, she mused, he knows the Sayers. Apparently, the families are friendly. Lucy busied herself typing and filing and tallying the billable hours from the previous week. Her boss learned she also studied bookkeeping so put her in charge of that aspect of his practice, too. Lucy loved having the additional responsibility. It assured she always stayed busy and she liked it just fine. She hated sitting around with nothing to do.

At a quarter to eleven, the door opened and Mr. Sayers and Mr. Fawcett emerged, laughing loudly and shaking hands cordially. The former governor said, "be sure to give my warmest regards to your parents. I don't get out their way often but will be sure to call on them when I do."

"Thank you, sir. And please give my best to Mrs. Sayers."

Harry turned to Lucy, flashed his most endearing grin, and asked, "Miss Dubuis, since we've now been formally introduced, may I escort you to lunch?"

"Certainly not, Mr. Fawcett. I go home for lunch."

"Surely you could make an exception once in a while."

"If I wished to do so. Now, I have a lot of invoices to type, so if you'll excuse me," said Lucy with finality as she turned to her calculations again.

He struck out. For now. Harry Fawcett refused to surrender easily and he'd try again. Mr. Sayers sung her praises when he asked about her relationship status. He proclaimed her bright, congenial, efficient, respectable, honest, hardworking, and unattached. He said he never understood why such a delightful young woman was still single.

A month later they bumped into each other, figuratively speaking this time, at the mercantile and at the movies the next week. He and his three comrades were seeing the same show as Lucy, Dorothy, and the two other women who lived in the boarding house. Charles suggested sitting together, but Lucy refused. Willy proposed going for a soda at the Sweet & Fine, and Lucy begged off. If the rest went, so be it, she'd doggedly avoided any association with Mr. Harry Fawcett. As the embarrassment of the incident at the restaurant dimmed, she found it harder and harder to remember why she took the vow.

As fall waned and winter settled in, Lucy and Harry found themselves running into one another all over town. She saw him at the bakery and the bank. Both ended up at the drug store counter searching for aspirin and on the same aisle at the library hunting for a book. Occasionally she'd see him at a diner or coffee house. When Dorothy and Willy started dating, it became harder to avoid him. Her chum totally changed her view of the man and encouraged her to forgive him, too.

Shortly before Christmas, the country went into a frenzy at the startling bulletin out of North Carolina. On December 17, 1903, Wilber and Orville Wright, brothers who owned a bicycle shop, made the first prolonged flight in a powered, controlled, heavier-than-air-craft at Kill Devil Hills, south of Kitty Hawk. Soaring ten feet above the ground, their four excursions covered distances of 120 feet to in excess of 200 feet. Visionaries conducted experiments in flight for centuries, but none succeeded until now. It excited the imagination and ignited a wildfire of speculation on what type of future the marvel might create.

As she read article upon article extolling the wondrous new invention, her mind wandered to the events of the last two years. On January 1st, 1902, the first Tournament East–West football game took place in Pasadena California two decades after the modern sport began. It pitted the Michigan Wolverine's against Stanford University, with Michigan crushing its opponent 49-0. In the future, it'd be renamed the Rose Bowl. In 1903 the premier World Series game was played between the Boston Americans and the Pittsburg Pirates, Boston won five games to three. Henry Ford established the Ford Motor Company and Lucy saw an automobile in November. The noisy contraption frightened horses and humans alike as it rattled raucously down the road.

Christmas holiday was on Friday and Mr. Sayers shut down at noon on Thursday and all day on Saturday as well. She'd have an unheard of three-and-a-half-day holiday. Dorothy had only Christmas off, so Lucy took her to lunch Thursday as consolation. She locked the door, walked across the street to the bank, and went in to meet her friend.

Lucy chose a seat in the small reception area and observed fellow patrons. A woman grasping the hand of a girl stood at the teller cage where Dorothy worked and an elderly gent making a deposit occupied the other station. The bank manager, Mr. Brookings, talked quietly to a short, fat man at his desk, and two men sat in chairs lining the front wall. One was a boy who nervously waited for a job interview and the second a middle-aged cowboy who didn't remove his hat and wore a buckskin coat with the collar snugly to his chin, even though the stove in the corner kept the room warm. The patrons at the tellers' stalls left, the customer in Mr. Brookings office departed, and the cowboy sprang into action. He grabbed Lucy roughly by the arm, jerked her out of her seat, drew his gun, and backed toward the front door in preparation for a speedy escape.

"Pull the shades and hang the closed sign," he ordered the boy. "This is a hold up. Put money in that there bag or I'll kill her," he threatened as he tossed the sack at Dorothy.

CHAPTER 9

Winter arrived in full force on Wednesday. A strong north wind pushed an Arctic blast all the way to Texas and at noon the mercury barely reached freezing. As Harry hurried onward, clutching his flapping coat in his right hand and his hat with the left, he pondered the elusive Miss Dubuis. She seemed to invade his mind constantly these days. If he ran into her in town and tried to initiate a conversation, she always made an excuse and left quickly. When Willie started dating Dorothy, he hoped she'd relent, but so far she remained unmoved. I wonder how long she can hold a grudge, he asked himself.

He learned a little about this intriguing woman from her friend. Dorothy told him Lucy survived the Great Hurricane and gave him a dossier on the men she dated. One practiced law and the other owned a boot and hat store in town. She went out with a minister a few times until he joined to a new congregation in San Marcos in July. Could he really call them the competition when he'd spoken only a few words to the lady? He asked if any of the relationships were serious and Dorothy said no. Lucy liked the gentlemen, nothing else. She simply never yet met the right person. He didn't know if he'd be the right man or not but sure wanted the opportunity to find out.

Harry rounded the corner and, just ahead, spotted the object of his revere at the far end of the lane. Lucy walked from her building and crossed the road. She entered the bank where Dorothy worked and he decided to try again. If the girls planned to have lunch together, maybe he'd be able to wrangle an invitation. With her pal coming, too, Lucy might agree.

Battling wind and biting cold, he trudged his way toward the bank. Through the plate glass window, he saw several customers inside. He lingered a moment to think of an excuse for coming in and to his horror witnessed a ruffian viciously grab Lucy, draw a revolver, and brandish it around. Instantly he devised a plan when she glanced in his direction.

Lucy froze in terror. Her knees turned to jelly, her heart pounded, and her breathing accelerated. She felt as powerless and panicked as during the storm. What should she do? He held her tightly to his chest and jerked her from side to side as he waved the gun erratically through the air. The tellers gathered the money as fast as humanly possible. Maybe he'd leave when Dorothy handed it over. Or maybe not. As the teen walked to the far window to draw the shade, the bandit twisted to see and Lucy peered out the window hoping to find help.

She caught a glimpse of him watching her. Mr. Fawcett stood close enough to see in but, so far, the robber failed to notice. Their eyes locked for a second and a message flashed between them like a telegram. The feeling defied explanation or rationality, but suddenly she knew exactly what to do. Lucy let her wobbly knees collapse as they threatened to do and her body went limp. She pretended to faint. The gun-toting cowboy now held a dead weight in his left arm. His body instinctively bent toward the increased burden and his right arm flew up to compensate. It gave Harry the opening he prayed for. He crashed through the door and rammed the man with all his strength and power. The gun flew away, his grip loosened, Lucy fell to the ground, and Harry knocked the thief out cold with two powerful jabs to the head. Mr. Brookings snatched the revolver, Dorothy summoned the police, and it ended as swiftly as it began.

"Miss Dubuis, Miss Dubuis, are you alright?" Harry asked worriedly. He made sure the culprit posed no threat and then rushed to her. "Here, take a seat. You look shaken."

Lucy rose to her feet, or tried to, but didn't quite make it. Her knees refused to hold so Harry picked her up and placed her gently on a chair. He put an arm protectively around her shoulders and held her tightly as she shook and sobbed. The customers tried to recover from the trauma and momentarily the police arrived.

A patrolman named O'Toole handcuffed the outlaw who was beginning to regain consciousness. A second officer wrote down the names of witnesses and instructed them to come to the station to give statements. After the police took the perpetrator away, Lucy, still in his arms and who spoke only her name since Harry broke in, turned to him and said, "well, Mr. Fawcett, I see you finally succeeded in throwing me to the ground."

Her quip completely stunned him and then he exploded with laughter. Her eyes flashed appreciation and gratitude as well as a playfulness he'd yet to see. The dam broke. She forgave him for embarrassing her and now they'd be friends...or more?

Through laughter, he asked, "Are you hurt?"

"No, not at all. I'm in shock, I think. How will I ever possibly thank you? Dorothy!" She frantically scanned the area, desperately searching for her.

The woman, trying to calm her co-worker Miss Truman, ran over. "I'm here, Lucy. Are you alright? I can't imagine how on Earth you two arranged that."

She tried to verbalize it but couldn't since she had no idea herself. She paused a minute to think and answered, "I don't know. I saw Mr. Fawcett at the corner of my eye and knew what to do. There's no way I can explain, I just did." Shaking noticeable, Lucy grasped Dorothy's hands and then hugged her tightly.

The victims were steady enough to go so Mr. Brookings locked the bank and the entire band headed to the police station. Harry took the arms of both Lucy and Dorothy and escorted the trembling ladies down the street. She no longer considered him a stranger and felt perfectly comfortable being with him. As they walked, passersby stared and pointed. Word of the attempted bank robbery spread as quickly as a brush fire and people were astounded at the outcome. This sort of action often ended badly. Unlike in the restaurant where she resented the notoriety, Lucy appreciated the attention. It was one of admiration, devoid of mockery.

The police chief, Roger Withers, interviewed Harry and Lucy

personally. The pair's action astounded him and he wanted to extract as much detail as possible. The two told him everything and yet had no words to describe exactly what happened at the crucial point. He inquired into their relationship and Lucy turned bright red. Harry simply said he met her by accident a few months ago and they had spoken briefly a few times since.

He concluded the interview and the chief told them about the man who tried to rob the bank. A flyer came in on him last week. He'd hit banks all over Texas for the past two years. Authorities estimate he stole $10,000, and worse, killed a deputy in October in Kerrville. "You two are due a $2,000 reward. I'm going to split it between you. I reckon you're the first woman ever got one, least ways far as I ever heard."

Once the police asked all the pertinent questions, Harry's wish came true. He accompanied Lucy and Dorothy to a very, very late lunch. Word of the robbery and the heroes who foiled it swept through town. Customers stopped at the table and congratulated them. Those on the sidewalk rushed in to do the same. A reporter from the *San Antonio Press-Times* rudely interjected himself and refused to leave unless he got an interview. It wasn't a pleasant meal until Mr. Brookings came by and told Dorothy he closed the bank. It'd reopen on Saturday.

When the three escaped the restaurant, it'd turned dark, cold, and blustery. Harry ushered Dorothy home where Willie and her parents anxiously paced in the hall. They heard about the incident, knew she was unharmed, still wouldn't rest easy until she arrived safe and sound. The three relived it yet again and answered a hundred questions. The St. Martin's served a delicious dinner none really wanted but ate to be polite.

Lucy and Harry headed toward Mrs. Daffodil's at seven-fifteen. She invited him into the parlor where the two were bombarded with questions. At ten minutes before curfew, the girls went upstairs and the landlady returned to the kitchen. Alone for the first time, Harry found himself suddenly at a loss for words. In desperation he asked, "What are you going to do with your share of the reward, Miss

Dubuis?"

"I think I'll invest in a savings account. It'd be nice to have a little put aside for a rainy day, as the saying goes. And you?"

"I'll add it to my fund. I plan to buy a house as soon as I save enough money. The room over the office is nice enough, but I want my own place." He omitted the fact he also hoped to marry at some point and start a family there, too. She thought his ambition admirable and very sensible.

"Lucy," Mrs. Daffodil stuck her head around the corner, "I'm going to lock the door in five minutes."

On the porch, Harry kissed her hand and asked if he might call on her again. She smiled broadly and said, "yes, I'd like that."

Back in her room, Lucy took off the gray dress Mrs. Beaumont donated to her. The high-quality garment looked as good as the day she got it. She and her benefactor corresponded regularly so she knew Galveston was a city renewed. The devastation would live in the hearts of survivors forever, however people now concentrated on the future rather than dwelling on the past. Three years later, thinking of the horror caused her eyes to tear and hands to tremble. However, the nightmares once plaguing her frequently, now intruded rarely. She slept peacefully most of the week.

She spent Christmas at the St. Martin's, as did Harry and Willie. He and Dorothy were quiet and secretive all morning. At dinner, everyone discovered why. The couple announced their engagement and a spring wedding. Her father blessed the union two days earlier but kept his promise and didn't tell, not even his wife, so the proclamation surprised and thrilled the others. They asked Lucy and Harry to stand with them on the special event. The four talked for hours about dates and dresses, food and flowers. In the end, both agreed to May 21, 1904.

As he walked her home, Harry invited Lucy on a date for New Year's Eve and she gladly accepted. Although they shared a meal at the St. Martin's and following the robbery, Lucy counted the party as the first real date. She decided to spend some of the reward and buy a gown when Harry said the ball was at the elegant Menger Hotel. Built prior to the Civil War, the luxurious manor hosted many notables including Presidents Ulysses S. Grant, Benjamin Harrison, and Theodore Roosevelt. It earned a well-deserved reputation for its lavish décor, incomparable service, and delectable cuisine.

Lucy begged Mrs. Daffodil to let her break curfew just once. The celebration wouldn't end until one, giving revelers the opportunity to ring in the New Year. The woman sympathized and simply refused to relent. The establishment provided her a livelihood and her reputation meant everything. How'd she possibly go if she needed to be back before it started, she asked? Dorothy provided the perfect solution later in the afternoon. Since she and Willie were attending as well, Lucy could stay at her house. It solved two problems at once. She avoided the eight o'clock deadline and Mrs. St. Martin breathed easier having her daughter stay out so late. If the women went together, it'd be fine.

Lucy usually patronized small shops that dealt in reasonably priced conventional garments. For such an auspicious event, she visited Madam Dominique's Emporium. The name sounded a bit pretentious, but it handled the finest women's wear in town. The store also advertised quick alterations. Given the fête was barely a week away, this might be crucial.

She splurged and bought a silvery white silk creation enhanced by gold embroidery covering the bodice and accenting the flowing skirt and train. It had a wide, low squared neckline edged in the same lace that formed the short sleeves. It was her first formal frock and a more elaborate costume than she ever dreamed of owning. The daring décolletage made her blush as she imagined appearing in public without her customary high neck and wrist-length sleeves. Dominique assured her all the ladies in France wore this style. Lucy hoped the trend reached San Antonio, too. Just in case, she bought a matching lace cape. It wouldn't keep her warm, she'd wear a heavy coat, but it covered her in case none of the other women were so exposed.

Harry gasped in delight when he picked her up. She looked stunning in the gown and it complimented her figure and complexion to perfection. He helped her on with the cape, and then the coat, and smiled to himself. He suspected exactly why she wore the cape and, although he appreciated the view, understood her caution and respected her modesty. Governor Sayers did not exaggerate when he sang the praises of the beautiful woman. Lucy's worry proved baseless since most of the young ladies wore bodices of similar design and fashion. Many wore tops with even more daring plunges.

"Lucy, my dear, your dress is stunning," Mrs. Sayers cooed. "And Harry, I've never seen you looking better." He cut a dashing figure in his black tail coat, trousers, waistcoat, and white winged-collar shirt and bow tie. Lucy proudly stood beside such a distinguished gentleman. Why'd she resist him for so long, she asked herself?

"And Joseph, why haven't you told me about these two? It's absolutely charming."

"Don't blame the Governor, Mrs. Sayers," Harry explained, "this is really the first date we've been on."

"You see, Lena, I'm innocent and ignorant. Shame on you Lucy for not telling me. I'm awfully fond of both of you and am pleased to see it."

The four talked a little and then the band tuned up. Harry led Lucy to the dance floor and the Sayers drifted away to speak with colleagues. The ambiance enchanted her and it was a better date than Lucy envisioned.

CHAPTER 10

As she walked to the office on Monday, visions of elegant dresses, soft candlelight, romantic music, and the delightful Mr. Harry Fawcett whirled in her head as she recalled the glorious festivities yet again. She and Dorothy talked far into the night and all the next morning about the enthralling interlude. On returning home, Lucy related every glorious detail to members of her household. They asked dozens of questions and insisted she model her gown again. A couple of friends dropped by the next day and she relived the perfect party with each retelling. Lucy appreciated Governor Sayers giving her Saturday off to recuperate and he magnanimously paid her for the day.

As expected, she had a hard day ahead of her. Work accumulated in her absence so she prepared invoices and emptied the overflowing in box. She'd have to catch up on it as fast as possible. Still, she couldn't entirely banish the magical time from her mind, especially Mr. Fawcett. Hard as she tried to concentrate, he intruded on her thoughts. Dismissing his presence grew harder still when the roses arrived. He sent a dozen beautiful crimson blossoms and a note reading "Thank you so much for the most memorable evening of my life. Ever yours, Harry." The gorgeous bouquet on the corner of her desk served as a constant reminder. Her roommates oohed and awed over the fragrant flowers when she came in the door. No one needed to ask who sent them.

Harry telephoned twice and dropped by on Wednesday night for a short visit. He told her he'd be leaving town for a week beginning on Sunday. Three months ago he earned a promotion and all the area supervisors were meeting at Wells Fargo headquarters in New York

City for an annual conference. He asked if she would like to go to dinner and see a local rendition of George M. Cohen's *Running for Office* when the trip ended. Lucy adored Cohen's music and looked forward to seeing the play. The amateur production would be the first live performance she ever attended.

Lucy spent every moment she squeezed from her busy schedule on her book while Harry traveled. With each chapter she wrote, the story fell into place until it seemed to take on an existence all its own. She struggled to revise and edit the pages to vividly express the shock of the event and the joy and pain of survival. When he got back, the work was halfway done. She approved of the finished portion and Dorothy declared it a masterpiece. Tears welled in her eyes as Lucy described the fear and panic the victims experienced. She confessed she misjudged the magnitude of the catastrophe and often wondered if perhaps people exaggerated its significance. Although only those involved truly felt the impact, she no longer underestimated what Galvestonians suffered.

Harry got back right on schedule and the two had a wonderful time on their date. Lucy absolutely fell in love with the theater and made a point of seeing new productions put on by the troupe as soon as it premiered. As he walked her home, Harry asked her out to a movie for the following Saturday and they decided to see *The Great Train Robbery* and several variety acts being performed on stage in conjunction with the film.

The blustery winter slowly gave way to gentle spring. All around town azaleas burst forth and turned gardens into pink and white showcases. Sunny yellow daffodils, vibrant irises, and graceful tulips added to the riot of color of San Antonio in March. Lucy enjoyed helping in the lush garden gracing Mrs. Daffodil's small front yard. She liked puttering in the vegetable patch, too, she'd done it at the orphanage, but she'd never known the pleasure of watching magnificent blooms push through the soil and explode into an endless variety of color.

Through the spring, Lucy and Harry saw each other more and more. Often as not, Dorothy and Willie joined in. The four spent hours discussing the rapidly approaching wedding and in mid-May all the arrangements came together. Flowers were ordered, music selected, and the gown altered. Dorothy chose to wear her mother's wedding dress. Simple by Victorian Era standards, the heavy cream-colored satin fabric was lavish and elegant. The longer skirt skimmed the floor, with three box-pleats in front and a train behind. A shorter overskirt, edged in an elaborate fringe trim, draped across the front and gracefully met at the back in a knot below the waist. The bodice featured a modest V-neck and three-quarter length sleeves, both edged in lace imported from Belgium. Five carved ivory buttons accented it from the point of the neckline to the peplum that flowed atop the skirt in front and then gathered up to the waist behind. A band of fresh flowers would hold the double-tiered veil in place.

The week preceding the wedding, the four met to review preparations. Mrs. St. Martin invited them all to stay for dinner and they shared local gossip and recent events, glad to put wedding plans aside for a while at least. Their discussion of the efforts of Baltimore to recover from a devastating fire in February brought painful memories to mind for Lucy. The 1500 destroyed buildings represented half those lost in the Great Hurricane, but it caused her to tremble. Miraculously, unlike the storm, the catastrophe took no lives or homes. The same month, the U.S. paid $10 million to gain control of a portion of Panama where, on May 4th, construction of a canal to bisect the narrow land mass began. Harry, who went to New York regularly on business, remarked how in April Longacre Square in Manhattan was renamed Times Square for the city's largest periodical, the *New York Times*.

The girls woke at dawn on the day of the wedding. Lucy fixed the bride's hair as the sun eased above the clear, cloudless horizon. Dorothy donned her antique dress and Lucy put on her modern one. The light, gauzy robin's egg blue fabric fell softly from her shoulders, formed a slightly scooped neckline, narrowed to a thin waist, and then draped gracefully to the floor. A ring of flowers adorned her matching wide-brimmed hat. The ceremony started promptly at nine o'clock and a wedding breakfast followed. Shortly before noon, the happy couple boarded a train to Houston for the honeymoon.

Lucy and Harry walked to the park after the joyous newlyweds left, chose a bench in the shade of a huge old Bur Oak, and watched the ducks glide silently around the small pond. The duo discussed the festivities and pronounced it perfect. Harry took her hand and she allowed him to hold it beneath a fold in her skirt. It felt bold and she enjoyed the warmth of his touch. More and more Lucy found herself drawn to this brave, honest, and caring man. He earned her trust and she decided to tell him about the work she'd just wrapped up. "Harry, a year ago I decided to try my hand at writing a book." She paused, half expecting him to laugh, or stare in shock, or convey doubt. Instead, his face registered interest and curiosity.

"Marvelous, what's it about?"

It surprised him when she said it recounted her experiences in Galveston. Harry thought for a moment it'd be one of the romantic novellas that appealed to women or perhaps a story for *The Ladies Home Journal*. It impressed him she tackled a non-fiction historical account of the terror she endured. She seldom mentioned it and he assumed the wounds were too fresh for her to air it freely. He guessed right. Putting it on paper, venting her fear, healed some of those scars.

"You and Dorothy are the only ones I've told. I finished last week and want to send it in, even though I can't imagine it'd really be printed." She liked the results, and Dorothy said she loved it, but could little Lucy Dubuis really get a publisher to buy it?

"I can. You lived through an awful experience. I've heard you mention it occasionally and you have a great gift for expression and detail. No doubt others would be as enthralled. May I read it?"

Hesitantly Lucy agreed to lend him the carbon copy of her manuscript and he carried it with him when he went to Clinton to open a small depot. Once the train left the station, he opened the book entitled *The Mighty Blast* and couldn't put it down until he read the last page. He garnered a new respect and sympathy for those who persevered the ravages of the horrendous ordeal. Harry liked it so much the instant he finished he telegraphed Lucy and gave her his opinion.

"Telegram, Miss. Dubuis." The young Western Union boy often came by. The former governor frequently got telegrams from government officials, clients, or acquaintances. She signed for it, as usual, tipped the kid a dime, and slit open the envelope to screen the message in case she needed to phone Mr. Sayers while he ate lunch. To her shock, it was addressed to her instead of him. She'd never received a telegram and it excited her as much as the contents themselves.

Lucy,
Spellbinding. Send immediately.
Harry

It was abrupt and short, they cost a lot, but she reread it a dozen times. Lucy prayed he really liked it and wasn't merely being kind. She doubted he'd go to the trouble and expense of sending an insincere telegram. He could give false flattery when he came home. His few words almost convinced her to take action. A visit to Dorothy erased all doubt. Her pal adamantly seconded Harry's advice and reminded her she'd lose nothing except the cost of postage. She worked too hard not to try. The next day she researched publishers at the library and discovered the majority were in New York, as she assumed, and she selected the largest. Carefully she wrapped the original copy and mailed it. Then she waited. And waited.

Harry got back and she told him she sent her manuscript to a publisher. He was nearly as excited as she and knew it would sell quickly. Months passed, she heard nothing, and wondered if it ever arrived. In September, Lucy decided to write and ask. She took the letter to the post office on Saturday after work. She stepped to the window to buy a stamp and Willie called out.

"Lucy, how are you? Are you looking for a letter from New York?"

"Yes. Maybe. Why?" She held her breath for an answer.

"Mr. Ashburn noticed this as he sorted the mail for Monday's delivery and showed it to me. He knows we're friends. I planned to drop it by on my way home." The postmaster reached into his pocket and pulled out a thick, ornately embossed envelope addressed to her with a return address where she sent her book. Lucy turned pale, thanked Willie, and took it to her room on wobbly knees. She wanted to open it in private; if it brought bad tidings, she'd cry. I put my heart and soul into it, she thought, and rejection will be hard to take.

She needn't worry. It held a letter from Mr. Gettings, a contract for *The Mighty Blast,* and a small advance against sales. Lucy jumped, shouted for joy, and raced down the stairs. The other residents, congregated in the parlor, ran to see what happened. Too excited to even notice the concerned gapes, she sped out of the house, down the street, and to Wells Fargo. She fully intended to have Mr. Sayers examine the document before signing it, but in the meantime, she couldn't wait to share the incredible news.

"Harry, Harry, it sold. The firm bought it." She shot into his office, not bothering to knock or close the door, and blurted the news. Harry rocketed from his desk, picked her up, and spun her around. While employees and customers looked on with amazement, he kissed her on the lips. Although blushing fiercely, she smiled from ear to ear. To explain the extraordinary public display of affection, Lucy announced to those assembled she just sold a book. Everyone clapped and congratulated her, and she thanked each for their well wishes on its success. Harry walked her to Dorothy's where she shared the joyous word with her dear pal. But for her encouragement, and that of Harry, this moment might have passed her by.

At the beginning of October, Lucy had unexpected time to complete the revisions. The Sayers' went to Jacksonville, Texas to see the Governor's brother Thomas. His wife gave birth to another son, Ralph, on September 23rd and they wanted to see the newest nephew. Without the money from Mr. Gettings and the reward, the loss of a week's pay would be a hardship. It felt wonderful to have a cushion in the bank and not needing to count every penny. Maybe she'd even take a few days of vacation and go on a trip. Maybe to Galveston.

Lucy and her editor constantly traded letters for his recommendations and rewrites. He repeatedly assured her this is normal, and in fact her manuscript required fewer changes than typical for novices. In February of 1905, Lucy saw her book in the stores. The sight thrilled her, and she wondered if it'd come too late. Four and a half years passed since the disaster all but destroyed Galveston. Were people still interested? Several Galvestonians released memoirs shortly after it happened. Would hers attract readers now? There'd been no serious hurricanes since then and she feared it'd been forgotten.

She misjudged the impact the storm made on the nation's memory. Texans gobbled it up. Those on the Gulf coast soon followed and before long her story was one of the biggest sellers. Everyone remembered its impact on lives and property. The press seared images of the destruction into the country's mind. Plus, Lucy's narrative put a different perspective on the tragedy. The others focused primarily on physical damage and the author's own story. Hers portrayed a personal and intimate side to the cataclysm. It focused on the plight of a few victims, including her own, prior to, during, and after the monster, if they had an after. To bring it up to date, she sent questionnaires to these survivors and all answered back. She told her readers how lives dramatically changed forever. It's exactly what interested the public at this point.

Lucy got more attention than she ever dreamed possible. Newspapers and magazines from coast to coast sent reporters to interview her. Locally, strangers and friends stopped her to tell her they liked the book and express sympathy for what she went through. Civic leaders and club presidents invited her to speak to their organizations. She deemed it all very flattering and overwhelming, and tried to accommodate everyone. Her editor, Wilber Gettings, even convinced her to go on a two-week lecture tour to promote it. The idea of speaking in public terrified her, but he insisted it'd increase sales substantially. The company even sent a matronly widow to act as a chaperone and assistant. Mr. Sayers gave her a leave of absence, engaged a temporary replacement, and wished her the best. He hoped the stand-in was somebody he could hire permanently. He'd hate to see Lucy leave, but had two reasons for suspecting he'd need a new secretary.

First, she published a volume that sold well. He estimated she'd make a lot from it and guessed she'd try another. When she and Harry came to Thanksgiving dinner, her eyes glowed vividly as she described the challenges of writing and the joy she experienced doing it. The second reason was Harry Fawcett himself. He and Lucy grew close the previous year and even through the arduous editing process the pair managed to go out often. With no father to approach, Harry chose to talk to him and ask if he'd approve an eventual proposal. He certainly did, too. As flowers sprung forth once again, Harry's mind focused on broaching the subject of marriage instead of the Earth's reawakening.

CHAPTER 11

As the soft spring morphed into a brutal summer, sales of *The Mighty Blast* rose faster than the temperature. Each week brought a check and she fretted over what to do with the money. She considered renting, or even buying, a place of her own and quickly changed her mind. Right now she earned a lot, but that'd slow down and end. No, she'd stay put. Plus, she enjoyed the company and convenience of the boarding house. Instead, she invested it carefully and conservatively. She bought stocks such as public utilities, government bonds, and in the printing industry. It made sense to underwrite her own field. She put a little into the bank to use for fun and provide funds in case of an emergency.

In July, her editor telephoned and asked for a second book. She laughed aloud at the suggestion. She lived through no other calamity, thank heavens. He said she should try her hand at a novel. He knew Lucy possessed a keen sense of narrative and detail and asked if her imagination was as sharp. She answered yes yet hadn't contemplated writing anything else and certainly not fiction. Lucy promised to think it over.

For weeks she turned the proposal over in her mind and tried to formulate a plot. Finally, it hit her. She endured another disaster, of sorts. The bank robbery. She could certainly incorporate the crime into any story she concocted. The harder she thought the more clearly she envisioned the tale. Lucy decided to trace the life a young school teacher who moves to San Antonio when it's a frontier town, survives the Battle of the Alamo, and finds her love. Although she'd fill it primarily with fictitious characters and events instead of real ones, it'd be based in history. OK, she told Mr. Gettings, let's see what happens.

He urged her to give it a full-time effort, but she lacked the confidence to quit the security of the secretarial job. Lucy opted to do it as she did the last, in the evenings and on Sundays. What if she couldn't finish or sell it? She wanted a secure way to earn a living regardless.

Harry shared her excitement and supported the endeavor. He never complained if she declined a date or even cancelled in order to complete an especially challenging chapter. He missed seeing her but understood how much writing meant to this extraordinary woman. Proposing had to take a backseat for the moment and he wondered if marriage even interested her now, particularly while trying her hand at a novel. He also realized she'd quit her secretarial job and compose during the day, enabling them to spend evenings together. The sudden realization tipped the scales in favor of asking for her hand sooner rather than later.

The third Sunday in October, Harry invited her on a picnic by the lake. He even supplied the food. Since his cooking skills were minimal, he paid his neighbor to prepare fried chicken, baked beans, cornbread, and an apple tart. The oppressive heat of September begrudgingly relented to a pleasant autumn. Harry chose a sunny spot feet from the water and spread out the colorful quilt his aunt made him when he left home. The couple discussed Franklin Roosevelt's March marriage to his fifth cousin Eleanor and President Roosevelt giving away his niece. In July, W.E.B. DuBois and William Trotter founded the Niagara Movement, the forerunner of the National Association for the Advancement of Colored People. In September, the Treaty of Portsmouth, orchestrated by Theodore Roosevelt, ended the Russo-Japanese War. And three weeks ago, Wilber Wright piloted an airplane he kept aloft for thirty-nine minutes, the only flight lasting half an hour so far.

Harry told Lucy his boss recommended him for a promotion to regional manager for Texas, Arkansas, Louisiana, and the Oklahoma and Indian Territory. The news thrilled her and she asked if it meant extra travel. Yes, he said, he'd be gone frequently. "Does it matter?" he asked, wondering if it gave her second thoughts about the relationship.

"Harry, I'll miss you terribly," he started to say he didn't have it yet, but she quickly continued, "because I'm positive you'll get it. It's a wonderful opportunity for you and I'm delighted." She patted his hand affectionately.

Breathing a sigh of relief, he gathered the courage to broach the subject. "Lucy, you know I've been saving for a house and now can buy an older small one begging for elbow grease. I'm pretty handy and can bring it up to snuff in a flash. I spoke to Governor Sayers since you have no family. He, well, we, well, will you marry me? I love you so much and want us to build a life together," he gushed out the question in a long, buoyant breath.

Lucy threw her hands to her mouth in surprise. She ached for him to ask, knew she felt the same way, and prayed for it to happen. He proposed and she immediately exclaimed, "yes, oh yes, Harry. I love you, too, and will be honored to become your wife."

The pair spent a wonderful day making plans and contemplating the future. Lucy suggested a spring ceremony. It gave her time to design a nice wedding, create a beautiful gown, and find a place to live. He told her he'd be able to afford a small, two-room home with indoor plumbing. She'd like to help, she said, buy something a bit larger. Lucy imagined a second bedroom or perhaps a loft that, blushingly, she said they'd use when the babies arrived. Harry balked at her suggestion because he anticipated being the provider regardless of her income. He decided to authorize the bank and investment company to keep her accounts in her name. The law required a husband's consent for a married woman to manage her own monetary affairs and he meant to consent.

His magnanimous gesture pleased Lucy tremendously. It spoke volumes of his admiration, esteem, and confidence in her ability. She respected his reluctance to let her contribute and appreciated it. To alleviate his concern, she said it wouldn't be a lot and it'd allow for more space. He trusted her to make decisions regarding her own finances and this is the way she wanted to spend a little of her earnings. Harry admitted he failed to factor in space for children, although he looked forward to having them, and reluctantly consented to a $500 contribution and increased his budget to $1,900. She intended to contact an agent soon in the hopes of finding the perfect nest before the wedding.

She and Harry dropped by to see Dorothy and Willie. Her friend grabbed Lucy, hugged her tightly, and blurted out they were having a baby. In the excitement, Lucy forgot her own elation as the ecstatic mother-to-be bubbled over due dates, gender preferences, and nursery themes. She finished gushing and Harry made his own announcement.

"Lucy and I are engaged. A while ago she agreed to marry me and be my wife."

The Hightower's shouted in glee at the thrilling news and Dorothy rushed to hug her again. Lucy asked her to be the bridesmaid even though she'd be very pregnant by then. Lucy didn't mind so Dorothy agreed to stand with her dear pal. Harry chose Willie to be with him. The two women discussed preliminary details and the men went for a walk. At this stage, it seemed best to let the ladies handle the arrangements.

Monday turned bittersweet when she told the Governor of her impending departure. She liked and admired the gentleman and hated to leave. It was still half a year away and she promised to work hard until the last minute. Lucy swore to train her replacement, too. Mr. Sayers told her he couldn't be happier about the marriage or sadder to see her go. He tried to keep her from worrying. It'd be fine and if she decided to leave earlier he'd manage, but not as well.

"You know, my dear, young ladies often quit before the wedding in order to focus all their attention on the event."

"Governor, do you want me to leave now?" she asked sadly. She had the money but hated the thought he was trying to get rid of her.

"Heavens no," he boomed. "Just know I'd cope if you did."

After Thanksgiving, wonderful news caused Lucy and Harry to jump for joy and have a heart-wrenching discussion. As she predicted, Harry got his promotion. It provided a substantial raise, more responsibility, and a change of location since Wells Fargo required him to be in a centralized spot. He had to report for duty in

Dallas on January 8, 1906. A decision needed to be reached concerning the wedding. Sadly, he said he understood if she wanted to wait for the ceremony. He'd come back in April.

She rejoiced for him, but the idea of a prolonged separation broke her heart. She dreamed of her wedding for years and hated planning it alone. She pondered the dilemma for two days and told him no, they should marry before he left. Nuptial trappings took a distant second to their life together.

"Let's do it right away. I'll cancel our reservation for the chapel and talk to the priest. Surely he can find a few minutes to marry us." Tiny tears, partly from joy at marrying him now and partly for sadness at not having her perfect wedding, filled her eyes. Harry held her tightly for a moment, asked again to be sure, and kissed her tenderly when she said yes.

Dorothy helped, of course. The women contacted the caterer, organist, and florist. Fortunately, none yet began preparations. Harry and Lucy talked to Father Brown. The kind old priest suggested a revised date and place for the union. All agreed to hold it in his study on December 23rd. Dorothy and Willie would be the witnesses and sole attendees. The St. Martin's begged to give a small reception and the pair gratefully consented. It wasn't what she hoped for but being together took precedence.

The weeks flew by. Since a seamstress wouldn't be able to design an elaborate wedding gown, she'd buy a ready-made practical one she'd be able to wear every day. Lucy selected a light weight soft wool and cotton blend fabric in a pale dove gray accented in a darker shade lace of the same color. The lace formed the lower part of the gently gathered skirt, adorned the bodice, and encircled her waist. The wide matching hat sported large feathers in varying tones of gray across the crown and cascading down the edge at the rear. She also chose a double breasted, black and white hound's tooth checked traveling suit trimmed in velvet with a narrow skirt for the trip.

The week prior to the ceremony Harry surprised her with an announcement. To ease the disappointment of a wedding and because he knew how desperately she wanted to go back, he proposed a trip to Galveston as a honeymoon. Although far from the best season to go, it might be a good while until he could take off once he took over the new responsibilities. Better to go now rather than risk not going at all. The possibility of cold weather didn't bother Lucy in the least. She'd be going home again. She telegraphed Mrs. Beaumont giving her the good news and said she'd like to come by after Christmas. The woman replied inviting the bride and groom to use their cottage on the beach. It was vacant during the winter.

Before the wedding, she stayed with the St. Martins. She let go of her place at Mrs. Daffodil's and all her belongings were packed in trunks stacked neatly in the corner of the room where Dorothy's brother previously slept. As they talked about the honeymoon trip, Lucy suddenly became pensive and quiet. Hesitantly, she asked Dorothy what to expect. The nuns told her the bare basics but lacked first-hand experience, of course. Blushing fiercely, Dorothy related what she forced herself to say and gave Lucy a better picture of the experience. It'd be embarrassing, a tiny bit painful, and eventually very enjoyable.

The morning dawned cold, dull and gloomy, however a pleasant fire warmed the comfortable room where the priest blessed the union and pronounced the two husband and wife. Lucy and Dorothy cried softly, Willie smiled, and Harry beamed. The reception proved perfect. Mrs. St. Martin served a buffet, most of the guests brought gifts, and two dozen friends wished the newlyweds well. Harry arranged to have the presents and the bulk of the luggage sent to Wells Fargo in Dallas where it'd be stored. At two o'clock Lucy, with Dorothy's assistance, changed into her traveling suit and she and Willie chauffeured them to the station to catch the train. The trip took twenty-four hours due to various delays. The engine sprung a leak near Gonzales and the bride and groom spent their wedding night sitting on a hard depot bench waiting for it to be repaired.

Returning to Galveston evoked many memories both good and bad. So much improved, so many never came home. As she watched the passing scenery long since cleared of rubble, visions of her fight to survive flooded to mind. The memory hit her less cruelly than in previous years but set her trembling. The rebuilt railroad trestle over the bay stood gleaming majestically in the sun. The industrious residents of Galveston reopened it within days of the storm and built it stronger than ever. The town shown bright and clean and optimistic. Even those structures that survived were refurbished. The landscape also looked different. Not a single vista remained the same. From the train, Lucy saw a three-square block section of town surrounded by a dike. Within it, structures stood low on the sand as the entire city once had. Around it, buildings perched substantially higher. Engineers devised a brilliant scheme to raise the whole city to lessen the impact of future hurricanes.

The locomotive pulled into the station just past five and the couple hunted for a cafe to eat dinner. Lucy recognized the name of one restaurant and she suggested eating there. When finished, Harry hired a taxi for the trip to the Beaumont's cottage. Posts lifted the charming white-frame, blue-shuttered house ten feet above the ground. A bedroom, small living area, and magnificent view welcomed them. Located steps from the Gulf, it provided a perfect hideaway to spend a honeymoon. It was obvious to both the house was new and built post-hurricane. Since the weather was mild, they'd be able to walk on the shore after all.

Their first real night together was trial and error. Dorothy's explanation helped, but she was apprehensive nonetheless. Harry approached her lovingly and gently until she relaxed. The next coupling went better and by the third Lucy began to relish the intimacy of marriage. Christmas Day shone bright and sunny so they exchanged gifts while sitting on the porch delighting in the sights and sounds of the ocean. She bought him a box of the cigars he smoked from time to time. Harry got his bride an adorable gold and pearl brooch in the shape of a butterfly. She immediately pinned it to the lapel of her dress and thanked him for the beautiful present.

"Harry, how'd you guess? I saw a pin like it once and always wanted one. Did I ever mention it to you?"

"No, sweetheart, I, well you'll probably think I'm nuts for admitting this. I saw the design in a dream and then I spotted it in an ad. I figured you'd love it." He kissed her passionately and soon they went back in.

As promised, the Fawcett's called on the Beaumont's the following day. The old friends welcomed them warmly, hugged Lucy tightly, and congratulated them on the nuptials. Mrs. Beaumont said she would have come to the wedding but sympathized with the decision. Lucy asked a million questions about people she'd known. William, Frank, and Albert, the boys she cared for, turned eighteen and all left the island. Mr. Cline, the meteorologist, went to New Orleans in 1901 when the Weather Bureau moved the station. Most of the survivors she knew still lived in town and recovered with varying degrees of success. Later, Mr. Beaumont hitched up the buggy, embarked on a tour of the city, and Lucy marveled at the changes.

The four walked atop the seawall and speculated on how different things would be if the city built it earlier as engineers suggested. She smiled to see Murdock's Bath House reborn and standing white, fresh, and solid over the Gulf. More cabanas were there, too, as well as cafes, shops, and hotels. Mr. Beaumont guided the mare to the relocated orphanage that opened a year after nature's fury destroyed the original. The boulevard led past the barren lot where the old one stood and this was the saddest sight of all. The nuns at the new St. Mary's were kind and gracious. They were aware of her miraculous survival and asked many questions regarding the fateful day. The Beaumont's picked an elegant eatery for dinner, took them to the cottage, and left the newlyweds alone for the rest of the week. Both enjoyed private walks on the beach and quiet dinners in casual cafés. It'd been a perfect way to start life together and Lucy eagerly anticipated settling into a place of their own.

CHAPTER 12

Prior to the wedding, Mrs. Sayers arranged for the couple to rent a small guest suite in Dallas, owned by her nephew, while searching for the ideal home. The building, located at the edge of a winter-bare garden, held a tiny bedroom and bath. It was perfect for the short term and guaranteed more privacy than the other affordable options. Harry's increased salary and a somewhat larger contribution from Lucy enabled them to buy a slightly bigger home than originally expected and she was determined to find the right spot.

Harry worked and Lucy rode around town with an agent viewing potential properties. Mr. Bennett steered her to twelve, and none suited her. She insisted on it being in convenient proximity to Harry's office, small but not tiny, and at a reasonable cost. On the thirteenth try she saw the ideal house and forever ended the number's bad reputation, in her mind at least. The bungalow was located on Howell Street near the Greenwood Cemetery, one of the oldest in Dallas. Established in 1875 as Trinity Cemetery, it changed name and owners in 1896.

Built in the 1870's, the lower level of the home held the living, dining, and kitchen areas. Upstairs Lucy found the two bedrooms she desired. It required some renovation, and a lot of cleaning, but not to the extent she feared. It wore a new coat of crisp white paint on the clapboards and recently replaced columns, roof, and pouch railings. Unfortunately, the owners neglected the interior for years. The paint and wallpaper were dull, shabby, and faded. The floors needed restraining and it lacked electricity and indoor plumbing. The structure was sound, the price unbelievably low, and it had the potential to be a miniature showplace.

"Hi, sweetheart, I'm here. I guess the day went well. What's our address?" It no longer surprised her when she and Harry shared inspirations and thoughts. They possessed a special connection, a bond that surpassed understanding or reason.

On Friday, she took him to see it and he agreed it looked promising. A contractor gave the pair an estimate for adding electricity, enclosing part of the service porch for a bathroom, and sanding the floors. His quote fit the budget and left a little for furniture, provided they painted, papered, and stained the floor themselves. The couple finalized the deal and hired workers. Once Lucy and Harry began their part of the remodel, neighbors came to welcome the young twosome and half a dozen new friends helped with the tasks. It took two months, but in early March Harry carried his bride across the threshold.

He loved the cozy nest she created. Lucy flanked the fireplace with two comfortable chairs and tucked a small round table between. Over time, she'd buy a sofa and coffee table to go in front of the window. The stove in the kitchen gleamed brightly beside the sink and an ice box stood at the end of the counter. A sturdy dining table with six chairs rounded out the lower level decor for now. An iron bed, crisp white linens, his aunt's quilt, and second-hand bureau made the master bedroom warm and inviting. The second remained empty waiting the time it'd be filled by a baby. Excitedly Lucy explained what else she wished to do, what pieces she planned to add, and art she hoped to hang on the walls. Harry delighted in her enthusiasm and thanked heavens for his remarkable wife.

The next morning, as pledged, Mrs. Lillian Berry walked Lucy to the market for her first real grocery shopping trip. While in the guest room, they ate out or dined occasionally with the landlord. Since she always lived at the orphanage, the governor's mansion, or Mrs. Daffodil's, she had no idea what to keep on hand or how to choose the best items. She helped in the kitchen at St. Mary's and the boarding house, but never prepared a meal from beginning to end. Lillian volunteered to help, as did many wives in the close-knit community. All remembered being in her shoes and wanted to ease the transition.

The ladies visited the dry goods store where Lillian suggested she stock up on flour for 7¢ a pound and sugar at 6¢. She bought a pound each of coffee for 25¢, bread at 6¢, and salt for a penny. She paid 27¢ for a dozen eggs and selected several tins of vegetables and soup at an average of 8¢ apiece. She and Harry preferred fresh but agreed with Lillian it'd be wise to keep a few cans on the shelf. Then came the butcher and Lucy purchased two pounds of bacon for 20¢ and half a pound of steak for 13¢. She bought potatoes, vegetables, fruit, butter and other staples. It really opened her eyes seeing the cost of these items. She grasped what Harry meant. She understood why he assisted her in establishing a budget and asked her to keep an eye out for specials and sales.

Gertrude Rehm, another neighbor, coached her on making a meal for her husband. She recommended a simple meat pie stuffed with potatoes and onions encased in a crust. The patient woman taught Lucy to season boiled cabbage with a bit of bacon and make a lemon tart. Madge Brooks, a block to the east, accepted the challenge of teaching her to bake bread in the future. For now, she settled for slicing the loaf she got at the store. It was great fun and she liked the company of Gertrude immensely. Lucy knew it'd be a pleasure living near such pleasant, obliging, and congenial people.

Harry stopped at the corner stand in the evenings and gave the boy a penny for the paper. He and Lucy read it together and discussed the day's happenings, the perfect way to reconnect. On April 18th, a horrendous headline filled the front page: GIANT EARTHQUAKE LEVELS SAN FRANCISCO. At 5 a.m., a pre-quake rumble rocked the area. Half a minute later a tremendous clashing of tectonic plates across the San Andreas fault line sent violent shock waves lasting up to a minute charging mercilessly through the region. It ended the lives of 3,000 and destroyed 28,000 buildings. When Charles Richter invented a scale to measure the intensity of earthquakes in 1935, seismologists retroactively ranked it as a 7.8. No one could imagine the destruction a 10, the top rating, might bring. Nobody even dared contemplate it.

Willie Hightower redirected several letters to her from her editor,

Mr. Gettings, who desperately wanted to know what happened. Where is she? Was she alright? Did she have the new novel? Lucy felt terribly embarrassed by her thoughtlessness. In the rush and excitement of the wedding, honeymoon, moving, and buying a home, he and her project slipped her mind. She sat and wrote him a letter apologizing profusely for her negligence and vowed to get back to it. In the meantime, she mailed him a copy of the pages she completed before she moved and immediately bought a second-hand typewriter. Since she no longer had access to the machine at her office, she needed one of her own.

Lucy set a strict schedule for herself. She fixed breakfast first thing. Harry left at seven, she mixed bread dough and left it to rise, did chores, went to the market, and put dinner in the oven. Then she worked on her book for at least four hours each day except Sunday. It was set aside just for each other and both fiercely protected it. Following Mass, they'd stroll around town and choose a restaurant or pack a lunch for a picnic. Now and then Harry rented a buggy and drove into the country or across town. Both enjoyed playing Whist and a new card game called Rook. Harry taught her to play chess and she became good enough to give him a challenging match. When he left town, she often skipped errands and cooking to write instead.

Mr. Gettings heartily approved of her novel, entitled *Frontier Teacher*, and urged her repeatedly to finish it. Lucy liked doing the research necessary for an historically based book as well as the challenge to continually devise the means and manners to tell the story. She typed the last chapter in October, forwarded it to her editor, mentally prepared herself for an extended wait, but his response arrived in just a week. He telegraphed to say it'd be published right away and gave her a larger advance than previously. With Harry's blessing, she used much of the money to furnish the rest of the house and order drapes in a light green, fern-leaf print on a cream background. The ones the previous owners left behind provided privacy but were faded, worn, and ugly.

The volume sold better than the other since more people read fiction. The success of *The Mighty Blast* boosted sales for sure, but the charming, touching story of perseverance, courage, and love stood on its own becoming a top seller. By year's end it earned her no small amount of notoriety that turned into a blessing and a nuisance. She and Harry rarely had dinner in town without fans coming to the table to compliment her. She appreciated the kind words and always responded politely and cordially yet missed her privacy.

Mr. Gettings, who marveled at her husband's instructions, contacted Lucy directly in all aspects of her career. He deposited checks into her personal account, planned marketing strategies, and discussed future books. She decided to tackle a ghost story, she told him, and already investigated the Millermore Mansion in Dallas. Built in 1855, visitors and residents reported it being haunted by the spirits of children and adults who died there of small pox, diphtheria, and pneumonia in the days when the town didn't have a hospital. She considered weaving a story around it. He encouraged her to pursue the idea. This kind of novel was very popular. M.R. James' *Ghost Stories of an Antiquary* sold well as did *The Wind in the Rosebush, and Other Stories of the Supernatural* by Mary E. Wilkins Freeman. Classics by Edgar Allen Poe enthralled and frightened readers years after the author's death. Lucy realized basing her work on actual events or locations suited her and it developed into her trademark style.

As more and more people bought copies of *Frontier Teacher*, Lucy got fan mail from all around the country. Earlier, a few academicians and newspaper columnists congratulated her on *The Mighty Blast*. Beginning in early 1907 these letters were from ordinary readers, mostly women, who enjoyed her story. It further encouraged her to attempt a third. Besides fulfilling herself, entertaining and pleasing her fans was the reason she wrote. As she put increased effort into her book, maintaining the house and keeping up with chores proved increasingly burdensome. Lucy summoned her courage and broached a subject she feared may hit a sore spot for Harry.

"Sweetheart," she said as they relaxed on a bench by the lake in September, "Mr. Gettings is really pressuring me about my book and is already asking for a fourth. It's getting harder and harder to take care of marketing, cooking, and cleaning." She omitted the fact she disliked domestic activities from her reasoning. "How do you feel about hiring a lady to come in to help out a few days during the week? I'd have the freedom to write and she's bound to be better at it than I am." Lucy held her breath and waited for his response.

Hilarious laughter was a reaction that hadn't crossed her mind. Harry stopped chuckling, reached into his pocket, and handed her an envelope. Inside she found a clipping and several folded pieces of stationery. She read the advertisement he handed her: "Wanted-Daily maid for general cleaning and cooking. Send inquiries to Mr. Harry Fawcett care of Wells Fargo." Once again, their unexplainable link unified their minds and set them on the same path.

"I planned to give it to you for your birthday, but now is better, I guess. I know you hate cleaning and cooking, even if the latter has improved a lot. All the stations I supervise are doing extremely well. Mr. Cavanaugh, the vice president, authorized a bonus and raise last week. It significantly exceeds the cost of hiring a housekeeper. Here," he handed her the letters, "these are the replies to the ad. Interview them immediately if you like."

Lucy hugged her precious husband tightly and thanked him profusely. His kindness and consideration constantly amazed her, as did the fact he read her mind. The longer they lived together the more often it happened. She blessed the day she decided to marry him.

She interviewed the applicants she deemed to have the best resumes right away. Two lacked experience, one had a slovenly appearance, and two seemed excellent prospects. Miss Spencer spent the mornings at another home and couldn't come until two. This wouldn't enable her to bake bread or do the shopping. She liked the woman but hoped for someone to be in by eight. Mrs. Morales fit the bill perfectly. She was a widow with a ten-year-old daughter. Her husband, a railroad brakeman, died in a train wreck in Warrensburg, Missouri and she moved to Dallas to be with her sister following the funeral. The sister had two children of her own and kept Maria after school and in the summer. Her previous employers relocated to Tulsa but she declined to go. And, she needed to work as much as possible. Lucy hired her and she started on Monday.

Lucy loved being freed from scrubbing and errands. Occasionally she felt a bit guilty, but Harry came up with the idea so he obviously didn't mind. And, Mrs. Morales turned out to be a fabulous cook. Lillian had a lady twice a week. Madge and Gertrude managed by themselves, and Madge had two children. The thought caused her to pause and, not for the first time, wonder when she'd conceive. They'd celebrate their second anniversary in a few months and still no sign of a baby. She mentioned it to her doctor and he urged her to relax. It can take a while, he said. And it might never happen she reminded herself. Carl and Gertrude Rehm had none at all.

In mid-October, Mr. Gettings approached her about a promotional tour. He realized it'd be harder with a husband but urged her to go. The route he plotted took her on a three-week trip beginning in Dallas, through Austin and San Antonio, to Houston, as far east as New Orleans, north to Little Rock, and west through the Oklahoma Territory in time to celebrate it becoming the 46th state on November 16, 1907. He proposed a grueling trip involving lots of stops and she hated every bit of it. Lucy, who genuinely enjoyed meeting those who read her books, said she'd consider it. Having Mrs. Morales there to ensure Harry got good meals and handle the housework eased her conscience a little at leaving him alone. The caring woman volunteered to arrive early and fix breakfast in her absence.

That night she talked it over with Harry, expressing her reservations at being gone and, again, he astonished her by hooting and cackling. Instantly Lucy knew why he burst out laughing. Their telepathy shot into overdrive and she excitedly waited to find where their paths crossed in the course of the tour. He received a telegram earlier instructing him to go through Oklahoma to launch several more offices and implement necessary changes in advance of statehood. He'd be on the road the final two weeks of her itinerary. Both trips ended in the same city and the pair could return together. "Oh, Harry, how nice. Can we take a short vacation? Wouldn't it be fun? On top of it," she added, "we deserve a break."

The trip was punishing and more exhausting than Lucy anticipated. She fell into bed, either in a hotel or sleeping compartment on a train, as early as possible. It took all her strength to rise and dress for her appointments. As the days dragged on, she felt drained and yearned for home and husband. They met in Oklahoma City, but she looked pale, drawn, and weary. Her pallor alarmed Harry and he urged her to cancel the appearance.

"You're catching something, I know. I can't say what. It's serious, I'm sure." He sensed, undoubtedly, important business was happening inside her.

"I can't cancel. A lot of people signed up and I'd hate to disappoint them. It's the last one and then I'll rest. I promise, since I don't think I'd survive another day anyway." Lucy tried to make it a joke, but Harry knew differently.

He relented, insisted on going with her, and sat nearby as she spoke to a packed hall. Throughout the speech, Lucy gripped the podium tightly, sipped water often, and forced herself to stand. As she turned to walk off stage, she froze in her tracks, turned deathly white, and fainted on the floor.

CHAPTER 13

Lucy woke a minute later in the arms of Harry as he carried her to the buggy offered by a couple attending the lecture. Once he tucked her on the back seat, the driver sped toward the hospital. She protested, saying she was tired, but he continued onward. A middle-aged doctor examined her and Harry paced nervously in the waiting room. After twenty agonizing minutes, the physician walked out and said Lucy asked to see him. Harry expected to find her sad, or sick, or worried. Instead, his wife beamed from ear to ear.

"We're having a baby, a baby, sweetheart. It's due in June."

Harry whooped happily and ran to hug her.

"Are you okay?"

"We're perfectly fine. The doctor said I fainted from exhaustion, worsened by the pregnancy. No tours for me, at least not soon. The doctor's keeping me until tomorrow to be safe. Then he'll release me for our vacation."

Harry drove her to the hotel and required she spend time with her feet elevated or in bed, even though the physician cleared her for normal activities. He showed her a few sights on Wednesday, walking no more than an hour before taking a break. The duo repeated the pattern on Thursday. Lucy kept telling him he was being ridiculous, nonetheless he refused to relent. On Friday, Harry and Lucy boarded the train at last.

He gave Mrs. Morales strict instructions to keep his wife from overexerting herself. Lucy humored him for a while but rapidly rebelled against the well-meaning restrictions. The tug of war continued for four days and they reached a compromise. Harry let her resume her normal routine and she swore to avoid lifting heavy objects and to take a nap in the afternoon. If she didn't sleep she'd lie down, or sit with her feet up, for at least an hour.

The weather turned bitterly cold at Christmas, ice and snow covered the ground, and Lucy voluntarily stayed put for fear of falling. She spent her self-imposed confinement writing her ghost story and simultaneously began formulating a third novel. The next story revolved around a young girl in Ireland. When the Great Potato Famine hit in 1845, she immigrates to the U.S. to escape starvation. There the heroine meets a man and marries him. The newlyweds go west during the 1849 Gold Rush and are one of the few to strike it rich. The story follows them as California becomes the 31st state, the Pony Express is established, the railroad arrives, and the Civil War breaks out.

Mr. Gettings loved each chapter of her spooky tale and pledged to publish it before she finished the book. She had great fun writing it, too. It allowed her imagination to soar without the boundaries of reality. Lucy understood the pleasure Jules Vern derived from conjuring an electric-powered submarine and flying machines prior to the inventions becoming a reality. She hoped her imagination remained just that, however; the image of ghosts actually haunting homes wasn't pleasant.

Morning sickness hit her hard. Harry brought her a piece of toast and tea in bed and a biscuit at night as the doctor suggested. Neither helped. Both were relieved the malady ended at Christmas since he'd leave town a week later. He needed to go to New York on business and hated deserting her. She reminded him she, herself, travelled for work and assured him she'd cope. Besides, she felt better and Mrs. Morales would be there a lot of the time. He left on December 26th and stood in Times Square on New Year's Eve to watch as a ball dropped at midnight welcoming in 1908 and introducing a tradition that'd be going strong a century in the future.

Frida's Fright was ready in April, the same time Mr. and Mrs. Jacob Murdock became the first people to travel in a car across the United States and Miss P. Van Pottelsberghe de la Poterie of France the first woman to ride in an airplane. Unbeknownst to Lucy, Mr. Gettings edited and typeset each chapter as she completed the tale. On receiving the closing installment, it took only a few weeks to prepare it for printing and distribution. When it hit the stores in May, she was eight months pregnant and miserable. Her ankles doubled in size, nothing fit, she couldn't find a comfortable position, and writing proved impossible as she had trouble concentrating. Her subsequent book, *Irish Lass*, would keep until the baby arrived.

She went into labor on June 6th and Lucy opted to go to the hospital with a doctor in attendance, although most women still delivered at home. She declined anesthesia because she read of adverse effects in the paper. Fortunately, she suffered through a relatively short labor and her daughter emerged in seven hours. It seemed much, much more, but Lucy got lucky. Lillian averaged fourteen hours with her three and Madge even longer. No matter the length, Lucy was delighted and Harry in awe of the tiny bundle.

"What should we call her?" he queried as he gazed in amazement at the girl and marveled at her perfect, miniature features.

"I'd like to name her Helen Pauline for your late mother and grandmother."

"It's perfect and thank you for remembering. I wish we knew your mother's name."

"If anyone," she said, "I'd pick a Sister. I, well, have no feelings for people who abandoned me at birth." She told the truth, but her expression betrayed a sense of loss nonetheless. And, on especially pensive moments, she pondered if somewhere out there she had siblings. Harry often wondered if his wife resented the anonymous parents for deserting her. If she did, her optimism and loving nature hid the pain well. Suddenly, her face glowed. "What about making it Helen Pauline Mary. The Mary will honor those who died at St. Mary's Orphanage." He applauded the addition and wrote it in the church records and newly required civil birth registration.

"Remember when Philadelphia declared May 10th Mother's Day?" he asked. "Maybe we'll proclaim it our own holiday, too." Lucy liked the sentimentality of honoring them and wondered if it'd catch on nationwide.

She tended children in the orphanage, but never cared for infants. Mrs. Morales loved having a baby to care for as much as Lucy and patiently taught her to change diapers, bathe a newborn, and properly hold and handle Helen. It required a lot of work and lost sleep and Lucy cherished every minute of it. Harry hurried home from the office to spend time with his family and couldn't imagine a happier life.

As soon as Lucy recovered from Helen's birth, she visited her favorite shop. The two dresses Mrs. Beaumont gave her desperately needed replacing and she wanted updated, fashionable frocks. She'd worn both for years and they were utterly obsolete. Contemporary styles were simpler, casual skirts narrower, trains shorter or nonexistent, and hems very slightly higher. Instead of dragging the ground, it ended an inch or two above it. It looked odd to see the tip of her shoe peeking out underneath as she tried on the dresses. She instantly warmed to the extremely practical fashion change as it reduced the risk of tripping, lessened the wear and tear on the garment, and kept the edges cleaner. It also lowered the chances the hem would accidently catch fire from a hearth and injure or kill the woman wearing it.

Miss Campbell, the owner, declared them wonderful choices. The light lilac ensemble was perfect for the hot summer to come. Cooler, modestly scooped necklines replaced the high, scratchy collars of her old ones. The sleeves touched the elbows instead of the wrists. A wide satin ribbon trimmed the neck, sleeves, waist, and bottom of the hem. The narrow skirt required fewer petticoats, a plus in sweltering weather. The second, in a sunny yellow, had black stripes on the bodice and lace on the skirt. She'd pay Mrs. Morales extra to shorten her other outfits so they'd be stylish in one way at least.

Lucy thought the lively conversation in the boutique about the recent World Congress for Women's Rights in Amsterdam interesting. Most of the ladies in the store were happy as wives and mothers. They had no interest in voting, having a political voice, or getting a job. A few disagreed, including Lucy. She absolutely adored being married to Harry and baby Helen set her world on fire, but she had the luxury of pursuing a career and being there for her family, too. On top of that, she hired a maid to help. Few had the option of doing either of these things. Those ladies who must or wished to work should be given the right to do so and protection to keep it safe. Women now organized a trade union, competed in the Olympics, one in Boston owned a book publishing house, and countless more owned florists, stores, and restaurants. She read about female doctors and lawyers who practiced in big cities or on the frontier. Why shouldn't business owners, regardless of gender, vote on laws affecting their livelihood? A few states already gave them the right to vote in selected or all elections. She saw no reason they shouldn't have a voice in running the country.

Helen grew every day and Lucy marveled as she lifted her head and rolled over. Like all parents, the pair believed her truly gifted to accomplish such a brilliant feat. Even if Helen broke no records, in September Thérèse Peltier of France became the first woman to pilot a plane by soaring eight feet above Turin, Italy. In October, Henry Ford unveiled his Model T and Harry suggested getting one. It cost $850, a fortune, and Lucy disagreed. Roads were few, fuel expensive, and the contraptions noisy and dangerous. They discussed it and reluctantly he admitted her point was valid. Eventually he'd buy it, but for now the buggy sufficed.

Her third novel sold as successfully as the other two. *Irish Lass* enchanted readers from coast to coast and an overseas company paid for the right to distribute it in Europe. With the latest check Lucy earned the status of what people called a woman of independent means, still Harry insisted on paying all the living expenses. It didn't create a hardship because his wages continued to grow as well. His expert management and innovative procedures made him increasingly valuable to the company. His boss recommended him for an upper management position in New York just before Helen's second birthday; he declined. Texas was his home, the family put down roots here, and he chose to stay. Lucy encouraged him to take it, said it'd be a great opportunity, and secretly rejoiced when he said no. She loved Dallas, could go to Galveston and San Antonio, and despised the idea of moving. She would, though, and support his career as he did hers.

Moving notwithstanding, Wells Fargo continued to expand his responsibility and salary. Their combined income made the young Fawcett's quite wealthy. In February of 1910, on the same day W.D. Boyce founded the Boys Scouts of America, they bought a new home. Located a few blocks from the first, it held over twice the square footage, was ten years old, and completely renovated. It had four bedrooms, a bath on both floors, a separate parlor and dining area, a large eat-in kitchen, and maid's quarters by the pantry Lucy turned into an office. Harry allowed her to contribute equally so once the old house sold they'd be mortgage free.

They moved in and Lucy busied herself repainting, changing the dining room wallpaper, and buying additional furniture. She had the most fun decorating Helen's room. Her tiny space in the other place held a crib and miniscule chest. She put a "big girl" bed, crib, large dresser, rocker, toy box, and shelves in the new one. A wool rug covered the floor to make it warm and comfortable for the toddler. The walls were pale pink and the fabrics pink, white, and yellow. Helen found playing in front of the large window with a view of the big back yard to be the best part of her day.

Irish Lass generated a sensation. It took the U.S. by storm and Europeans clamored for it as well. It'd been translated into French, German, and Italian. Lucy received courtesy copies and found it unbelievable she couldn't read her own story. Regardless, it sold countless volumes and now the world knew her name and demanded prior books be translated, too, particularly *The Mighty Blast*. Her charming tales, grounded in history and featuring strong women, appealed to a wide audience from the humblest to the elite. She received dozens of invitations, a few from overseas, to speak, make personal appearances, and attend social gatherings. She and Harry accepted a precious few. Neither had a desire to go often or far. To the majority, Lucy sent her deepest regrets and gratitude for being invited.

Even with Mrs. Morales, having a toddler slowed her writing.

Lucy's next effort took longer to finish, as did the one after. Instead of completing them in a year or less, she spent eighteen months finalizing the editions. Mr. Gettings resented the delay, but Lucy loved her precious little distraction and wouldn't change it for the world. She delighted in each milestone and achievement. She and Harry celebrated when Helen crawled, walked, and began to talk. The stories she crafted now featured children as an integral part of the plot. Her latest work was a bit autobiographical. It chronicled the life of a girl who grew up in an orphanage and went on to become a writer. It sold more copies than any other and presented Lucy with a wonderful opportunity.

A new forensic tool debuted at about the same time Lucy's book hit the stands. Fingerprints found at the scene of a murder in Illinois the year before led police to Thomas Jennings. He was convicted but appealed the verdict. The Supreme Court upheld the validity of the evidence in 1911 and his death sentence was carried out in 1912. The landmark case gave authorities one more way to enforce the law and bring criminals to justice.

At three and a half, Helen eagerly anticipated Santa's visit. She helped decorate, hung a stocking, and squealed every time a package arrived. Although Helen had no aunts, uncles, or living grandparents, gifts from friends, neighbors, and Mr. Gettings crowded below the Christmas tree. The one from the Sayers' arrived a week earlier and Dorothy's two days ago. Santa brought her a brightly colored rocking horse and a doll. Lucy wrapped a red jumper and green stuffed dog in a shiny silver and gold box and tagged it from Mom and Dad. She wanted to preserve the belief in Santa and wondering why there wasn't something from her folks might help shatter the illusion.

To ring in 1912, the Fawcett's gave a big party. Friends from all around and Harry's business associates arrived in buggies and cabs. Governor and Mrs. Sayers traveled in from San Antonio ensuring the newspaper's social editor sent a reporter to cover the story. The ladies wore their best gowns and the gentlemen suits or tuxedoes. Lucy engaged a seamstress to design the perfect dress. She decided on a luscious peach colored creation topped by an elegant shirred empire-waisted bodice accented by rich chocolate brown embroidery in an art deco pattern. The narrow, soft underskirt ended at the floor with a wide lace band edged in tassels. The slightly gathered overskirt of heavy, glimmering silk did not quite come together where it attached to the waist, leaving a glimpse of the filmy lining beneath. Halfway to the floor, the sides met in a gracefully draped knot. Behind, a flat, short train complemented the look. It was modern, flattering, and a perfect choice for her coloring and petite figure.

Mrs. Morales and her sister came in to cook and serve the guests. The two prepared lavish dishes of oysters on the half shell, roasted stuffed goose, crab patties, onions in cheese sauce, coconut cake, and vanilla ice cream with chocolate sauce, as well as a variety of relishes, salads, and sweets. She invited too many for a formal dinner, so Lucy served it buffet style on her prized Blue Willow china. She thought the contrast of the bright blue oriental pattern against a field of pure white beautiful. Revelers crowded in and feasted on the delicacies, chatted quietly amid soft candlelight, and enjoyed the string quartet playing softly in the gallery. At twelve, the guests toasted the New Year with Champaign, streamers, and noise poppers. It was a glamorous goodbye and hello that held the promise of a wonderful future.

In January, Lucy got an invitation she felt obligated to accept. Her foreign publisher forwarded a request from Lady Phoebe, wife of the Duke of Westerbridge, who was a big fan. She proposed hosting a tea party in Lucy's honor in late March or early April and it'd be unconscionably rude to decline such a tribute. Harry arranged a leave of absence and Lucy sent her acceptance and appreciation to the Duchess. The occasion afforded the perfect opportunity to tour England and Ireland as well. Both wanted to go, but never took the time. The pair couldn't go anywhere until they replaced Mrs. Morales.

The housekeeper tearfully gave Lucy her resignation the middle of January. Part of the tears were for leaving her wonderful employers and the others in elation at her impending marriage. Lucy, too, cried for joy and sadness. Before the woman left she must find someone else. Instead of a daily maid, she and Harry decided on live-in help and to take her to Europe. Helen needed care while her folks attended the tea and tours planned by Mr. Owens, her European associate.

The ad generated three applicants since few in Dallas sought a live-in position. Lucy and Harry interviewed the candidates and selected a young Irish girl who recently earned her citizenship. Fiona O'Malley stood five and a half feet tall and had curly, brassy red hair, and bright blue eyes. She reminded Lucy of the heroine in *Irish Lass* and it probably tilted the scales in her favor. She worked for two years as a maid so she knew how to cook and clean. As the oldest of ten, she raised her siblings when her mother died in labor, so she gained plenty of experience there, too. Although twenty, she seemed perfect and was eager to go in service with a nice family. Besides, she relished going to Ireland and seeing her clan.

CHAPTER 14

Preparations started immediately and frantically and Fiona proved up to the task. As soon as Lucy relocated her office upstairs, the housekeeper moved into the room off the kitchen. The girl acclimated to the surroundings quickly and the women began packing for the voyage. They stayed so busy the statehood of New Mexico in January and Arizona in February passed largely unnoticed amidst the frenzied preparation. The additions completed the United States from sea to sea. It'd be 1959 before Alaska and Hawaii joined the union and extended the country's borders beyond the contiguous boundaries. Just prior to departing, Lucy noted the establishment of the Girl Scouts by Juliet Gordon Low. She anxiously anticipated Helen joining an organization emphasizing the outdoors and self-reliance.

Mr. Owens booked a first-class suite on a ship sailing from New York to Southampton, England on March 17th but it was her responsibility to purchase tickets to New York. The accommodations onboard included a bedroom for Harry and Lucy, a crib in the corner for Helen, and a cot in the parlor for Fiona. The accommodations weren't ideal, but it's what he provided and she appreciated his generosity in paying their way.

The train ride north enthralled Helen...for a short time. Her parents brought along lots of toys and these distracted her for a few minutes. She became restless and bored so Fiona carried her from car to car trying to entertain the ball of fire. Mostly, she toddled around the compartment exploring every corner, ran up and down the aisles, and playfully accosted other riders. Fortunately, there were several children her age to play with so the trip passed pleasantly enough. Word spread and fans stopped by to greet Lucy and ask her to sign books they carried for the trip.

The troupe left the train in New York and Lucy met Mr. Gettings face to face. The two corresponded for years, talked on the phone sporatically, and she looked forward to knowing him personally, too. He treated Lucy and Harry to dinner while Fiona watched Helen in their room at the Plaza Hotel in Manhattan. The next morning, he arrived bright and early to take them to the pier where the vacationers laid eyes on the White Star Line's pride, the gigantic *RMS Olympic*, the same liner they'd return on in eleven weeks. On that trip, the *Olympic* would be commanded by a different master. This excursion ended Edward Smith's tour of duty on her. Once he got to England, he'd be reassigned to a sister boat still under construction in Belfast. That newest one, the *Olympic*, and the yet to be built *Britannic* were the largest, speediest, and safest vessels in White Star's fleet.

Immediately on walking up the gangplank, the glamour and luxury of the magnificent craft took Lucy's breath away. The entry foyer had a gleaming black and white patterned floor, white paneling, and comfortable chairs. As the group rounded the corner, both she and Harry gasped at the sight of the Grand Staircase. Lustrous ornately carved curved oak railings bearing wrought iron grills soared beside tiled steps. In the center, a matching straight rail divided the twenty-foot-wide flight in half. At its base, a tall bronze cherub hoisting a glowing torch lit the way upward. On the landing, where the steps split in opposite directions, designers recessed an ornate clock into the paneling and surrounded it with intricate mahogany carvings of Honor and Glory. The entire structure was topped by a magnificent dome.

While walking through the passageways, Lucy glimpsed into the Palm Court and found the white wicker tables and chairs, pristine white paneling and columns, richly carpeted floors, arched windows, trellis-clad walls decked in lush greenery, and potted palms delightful and charming. She knew she'd enjoy spending time in the lovely spot. A peek into the decidedly masculine main lounge with is dark, wood lined walls, deep wool carpeting, plush chairs, and mahogany cupboards beckoned Henry to relax in its tranquil arms.

The stewardess who guided them, Miss Violet Jessop, pointed out the cozy fireplace in the comfortable reading room and mentioned ladies often congregated there to play cards or write letters. She indicated to Harry the direction of the barbershop and pointed to the hallway leading to the well-equipped gymnasium, Turkish bath, and heated swimming pool. Lucy wished aloud she'd brought a bathing suit and the woman assured her she'd find whatever she desired in one of the *Olympic's* many shops. Prior to reaching their cabin, Violet showed Lucy the main dining area. It contained small, intimate round wooden tables, deep upholstered chairs, ornate paneling, and sparking chandeliers. The bar in the corner boasted elaborate multi-colored marquetry, carved flourishes, and expertly painted accents. Here, for an additional cost, they could savor what Charlie Chaplin declared was the best food anywhere, either on land or at sea.

Gossip is always ripe onboard and this trip promised to be no exception. Mostly the chatter revolved around fellow travelers, only today Captain Smith was the prime target. Over the years he served on many White Star vessels and earned a reputation as a sociable, gregarious, and competent officer who won a loyal following among transatlantic crossers. Those familiar with his record spread the word far and wide. In 1911, this very ship slammed into the *HMS Hawke*, a British warship, in the strait of Solent adjacent to the Isle of Wight. The crafts survived but suffered extensive damage. The crash ripped a hole in the *Olympic's* hull and smashed the bow of the *Hawke*. An inquest blamed Captain Smith for the incident. The tattletales wondered aloud and often why he deserved a command.

They had a smooth crossing yet Lucy experienced an unsettled stomach she assumed to be sea sickness. Fortunately, the others suffered no such discomfort and enjoyed the adventure and sumptuous surroundings. 'A' deck was magnificent from the luxurious furnishing to the delectable meals. Giving in to curiosity, Fiona toured the lower levels and found the space tremendously better than what she endured before. Everyone, from the loftiest to the lowest, slept in clean, comfortable quarters and ate well. Fiona put Helen in her crib for a nap and told her employers about the trip to

America and painted a vivid contrast of life in steerage on the *Olympic* and previous vessel.

The scheduled arrival date in Southampton was March 24th and it couldn't come fast enough for Lucy. Seasickness plagued her the entire trip so setting foot on dry land sounded heavenly and she rejoiced at the prospect. When word spread the coast loomed on the horizon, Lucy and Harry hurried to the promenade deck to get a glimpse of England. They stood hand in hand peering to the distant horizon to see the tiny speck of land. After tea, the two leaned against the railing and marveled at how much larger the island now seemed. Suddenly, a terrifying jolt shook the hull and caused passengers to lose their balance, stumble or fall, and cry in alarm.

"Lucy!" Harry instinctively called to his wife, grabbed her waist with his left arm, and gripped the railing vice-like in the right hand. "Are you alright?"

"Yes, I'm fine. What happened? Let's go check on Helen and Fiona!"

He couldn't imagine the problem until stewards swarmed the decks to ensure nobody got hurt and spread the word not to worry. The craft rammed an unknown submerged object, probably debris floating from shore, and a piece of the propeller broke off. The captain slowed a bit, otherwise the trip continued as planned. And, the men repeated, it posed no danger. The gossip she heard on the initial day at sea popped to mind and Lucy considered it very odd the same captain was involved in two accidents on the same boat. "I wonder if he'll be fired for this one," she mused to herself. "I wonder if he's jinxed," a superstitious few asked.

Mr. Owens greeted them and showed porters where to put the luggage. It thrilled her to meet another associate, but the countryside enthralled Lucy more than the publisher. As the train steamed toward London, sights such as thatched roof houses, Tudor architecture, grand manors, and ruined castles dotted the landscape and captured her imagination. "Our trip will definitely find its way into a book," she thought.

The group checked into the Savoy, Britain's most luxurious hotel.

The establishment boasted electric lighting throughout, automatic lifts, private baths in the priciest rooms, and hot and cold running water. Their opulent suite provided all the amenities and dining surpassed even the *Olympic's* fare. As Fiona unpacked, Harry took Helen for a walk and Lucy lay on the sofa for a moment—that turned into a two-hour nap. She never stirred as her daughter stormed in the door. She woke, her energy renewed, and Lucy eagerly anticipated sightseeing, the party on the 6th of April, and Ireland afterwards.

The couple toured all the usual sights: the Tower of London, Westminster Abbey, a number of museums, Parliament, Trafalgar Square, and several parks. They took side trips to Stratford on Avon, Oxford, and the mysterious Stonehenge. Helen came on a few of the excursions, but her parents often went alone reliving the romance of their honeymoon. Intermittently, Lucy experienced waves of nausea so they returned to the hotel early. She assured herself, and Harry, it was the excitement and she'd be back to normal soon. At the end of the second week, Mr. Owens insisted she spend the afternoon at his office. He wanted her to meet the staff, sign some papers, and see where her novels were printed. She dreaded the ordeal, assumed it'd be boring, and eventually admitted it proved an interesting interlude. The time sped by and the tea party drew near.

Before leaving Dallas, Lucy combed through fashion magazines and patterns from Europe. She'd be meeting titled men and women and the cream of London's society. She knew she'd be a fish out of water, but at least could appear as if she belonged. She decided on a slim white frock with a light weight silk lining and an elaborate lace overdress falling in asymmetric layers. The neck scooped low on her chest and had a lacy insert at the bottom for modesty. The unlined lace sleeves stopped at her elbow and the hem ended at the ankles. She wore a large, wide white hat covered in the same fabrics and crowned by white feathers and flowers. She chose two-inch square heeled shoes with pointed toes and a thin leather tie across the bridge of her foot. To Lucy it didn't seem elaborate enough even though it's what the periodicals pictured. She prayed it'd be appropriate.

The ensemble was perfect and she and Harry spent a delightful day at the manor house. Her Grace, a charming and thoughtful hostess, put them at ease right away. The gracious woman quickly calmed the pair's fears and soothed the nervousness both experienced from being in such an unfamiliar setting. Despite an early fog, it turned unseasonably warm and bright, so the Countess served tea in the garden. Several gauzy marquees provided shelter from the sun, white wooden tables and chairs dotted the lawn, and buffets held sandwiches, cakes, scones, and tempting delicacies. Liveried footmen darted to and fro serving food and drink and maids discretely refilled empty platters behind the scenes. Guests crowded in to speak with her and say how much they liked her work. Two of the men visited Galveston in the 1890's and asked lots of questions about its destruction and recovery. One said he thoroughly enjoyed *The Mighty Blast* and then very delicately mentioned her fiction wasn't his cup of tea while lifting his beverage playfully. Lucy laughed, assured him she took no offense, and realized the novels appealed primarily to women.

Later, Harry ordered dinner sent to the suite and shortly afterwards Lucy fell ill. She threw up all night and looked drained and weak when she woke. "Surely neither the food the hotel brought or the Duchess served caused it," she lamented. "I find that hard to believe."

She wasn't better in the morning so Harry asked the concierge for the name of a doctor. The helpful man located one and made an appointment at two o'clock for Mrs. Fawcett. Dr. Buckingham escorted a beaming, pale Lucy out of the examination room and shook Harry's hand heartily.

"Congratulations, old chap, you and your wife are expecting a baby. In October, I'd say."

The announcement surprised, stunned, thrilled, and worried him simultaneously. Lucy suffered terribly when she carried Helen and this pregnancy promised to be just as hard. They were scheduled to sail for New York on the 18th, ten days from now. Would Lucy be able to endure the trip while so sick? Did she even feel well enough to try?

For her part, Lucy found it hard to believe she missed the signs yet again. With Helen, she was young and inexperienced. She failed to put two and two together when she missed a period. In this case, she guessed, the excitement and stress of the trip made her forget to notice. Oh, well, she sighed, I'll do better next time. The ominous words "what next time?" intruded uninvited into her happy ponderings like a dark, foreboding cloud.

Back at the hotel, Harry asked if she wanted to try crossing the Atlantic in her condition. "Dr. Buckingham warned me the ship's motion might make the nausea worse and also said I can go without it hurting me or the baby."

"Do you prefer to stay here until it passes? I need to sail as scheduled but you, Helen, and Fiona can wait."

"Absolutely not! I'll go. In fact, let's go now. If it follows the same course, it'll be worse before it gets better. I'd rather be home when it hits full force. I can't think of anything more depressing than being sick in a hotel. Harry," she said hesitantly, "did you sense it or know what was happening the way you did with Helen?"

"No, darling, I got nothing. How strange."

A momentary wave of sadness swept over her and then she brushed it off. "I'm acting silly," she said to herself, "I don't believe in such nonsense, not really." Nonetheless, it hurt her heart to think their mystic language, as Harry called it, was breaking up, almost as though they began losing touch or drifting apart, but otherwise were as close as ever. "Snap out of it," she chided herself, "you've too much to do to dwell on drivel."

Again, the concierge took care of all the arrangements. He called the White Star Line's reservation desk and made the requested itinerary change. The clerk happily replaced the old tickets for similar accommodations on the newest liner that'd leave Southampton on the 10th for her maiden voyage. Because it went to Cherbourg, France and Queenstown, Ireland after leaving England, it'd take longer but got them to New York a week earlier than originally planned. Lucy lamented the loss of the rest of the vacation and apologized to Fiona for canceling the greatly anticipated trip. The girl assured her it was fine and she shouldn't fret. Her kinfolk lived near Queenstown and perhaps would meet her at the dock for a brief hello.

Lucy left the packing to Fiona since she felt so queasy. The girl scurried to fill steamer trunks and suitcases and Harry tried to entertain Helen to keep her out of the women's way. He insisted Fiona wire her mother and see if a short visit was feasible during the layover in Ireland. He paid extra so the O'Malley's could reply at no cost. It'd be a short reunion, they stopped for barely two hours, but the family promised to come.

On the tenth of April, the small group climbed into a cab pulled by a pretty palomino mare and headed to the train station. The travelers retraced their route to Southampton and went immediately to the pier. It was now eleven-thirty and the ship sailed at noon. Only passengers and guests were allowed onboard today, however on the 5th the paying public was permitted to tour the vessel and view its sumptuous design. Lucy marveled at the size of the beast and noticed it closely resembled sister *Olympic*. Both had gray hulls, gleaming white decks, four smoke stacks, and two taller masts forward and aft. The one obvious difference was the name painted proudly across the bow—*RMS TITANIC*.

CHAPTER 15

The overwhelming sense of déjà vu striking Lucy the moment she walked onto the *Titanic* was quickly replaced by dismay as the Captain approached. Edward Smith, hand extended, welcomed them warmly. The reservations clerk alerted him the last-minute fares crossed with him on the *Olympic* a few weeks earlier and he pretended to remember. The man referenced her books, doubtless another PR heads up. Harry and Lucy smiled appropriately and assumed it wasn't true. The three never bumped into each other on the previous outing. Still, they appreciated the nice gesture that did nothing to alleviate the trembling in Lucy's knees when she remembered the commander caused two earlier accidents.

The interior was not merely a sister to the *Olympic* but a twin. From the magnificence of the Grand Staircase, to the airy Palm Court, and the cozy Reading Salon, the two looked virtually identical. In fact, White Star planned on triplets, the third being the *RMS Britannic*, scheduled for completion in 1914. As Lucy and Harry walked arm in arm to the 'A' deck, Lucy kept glancing at the stewardess leading the way. Suddenly it clicked and she said, "Aren't you Violet?"

"Yes, ma'am, I thought you seemed familiar, too. I apologize I don't remember your names, although I do recognize you from the *Olympic*. A month or two ago, as I recall. Nice to see you again." Her greeting sounded true and sincere.

Violet led them to the same sized stateroom as before. With Lucy ill, Harry wondered if he'd be able to upgrade to a larger space.

"I know we aren't full, sir, and will be happy to see about moving you," offered Violet. Twenty minutes later she returned and helped the Fawcett's transfer to a two-bedroom suite, with a parlor in between, that gave Lucy greater privacy. They'd use the bigger side while Helen and Fiona shared the smaller one.

The spacious compartment sported canopied beds in both sleeping chambers and several comfortable chairs. In the larger, a small table and two chairs sat in the corner as well. The center of the parlor held a large dining table and four chairs and a variety of sofa's, lounging chairs, and a writing desk balanced the decor. Lucy needed to rest and the configuration gave her a better chance of doing so without being disturbed by the rambunctious Helen.

The gangplank swung away, the anchor rose, and tugs chugged alongside to push the behemoth down the channel and into the sea at exactly twelve o'clock. Lucy dreaded the potentially sickening time afloat, but hoped the punctual departure bode well for the journey especially when Violet mentioned the coal strike. It ended on the 6th, but deliveries wouldn't arrive prior to their sortie. White Star commandeered coal from other vessels to ensure the already twice delayed *Titanic* set sail.

Lucy's optimism crumbled as the ship swerved sharply to starboard. Later, she found out the giant's massive undertow sucked in the *USMS New York*. The six tow lines tethering the *New York* snapped and the two boats missed colliding by a mere four feet. The incident rekindled the gossip regarding the captain's record and set passengers' nerves on edge. A few reported feeling uneasy being there and at least one decided to disembark in France instead of going on.

The *Titanic* got underway after an hour and sailed across the Channel for the short, eighty-four-mile jaunt to Cherbourg to take on more fares and let off those who bought passage to France. Because the port couldn't handle the beast, the tender *Nomadic* ferried the newcomers to join her. At 8:10 the *Titanic* weighed anchor and steamed north for Queenstown, Ireland where it arrived at half past eleven. Here, 120 second and third-class voyagers and 1300 bags of mail joined their numbers, and Fiona saw her family for the first time in two years. Promptly at 1:30, the captain set sail for the final leg of the trip.

Many famous people crossed on the luxurious liner, dubbed

unsinkable, including American millionaire John Jacob Astor and his pregnant wife. Mr. Astor's divorce of his first wife Ava in 1910 created a national scandal when he stood in court and admitted adultery in order to secure the disillusion. His marriage to Madeleine, thirty years his junior, in 1911 set the tongues of gossips afire once more.

Like the Astor's, Benjamin Guggenheim boarded in Cherbourg. His brother Solomon was a well-respected art collector in New York. Mrs. Margaret "Molly" Brown, part of the nouveau riche, also embarked in France. Her husband, J.J. Brown, recently struck it big in the mining industry. Artist Frank Millet, on his way to design the Lincoln Memorial, arrived too. Isidor Straus, co-owner of Macy's, and Mrs. Straus, got on earlier in England.

In Southampton, Bruce Ismay, chairman and managing director of the White Star Line, and his wife Julia, boarded as did others from the company. Thomas Andrews and nine workmen came to finish construction not fully completed in Belfast. A little interior trim required touching up as well as a few adjustments to the heating system. The craftsmen, ordered to be as invisible as possible, would take care of any problems arising during the cruise. Andrews, *Titanic's* chief architect, made a habit of going on maiden trips to monitor the ship's handling.

Lucy learned several additional well-knowns were originally scheduled to sail but, for one reason or another, changed plans. She'd loved to have meet some of them like novelist Theodore Dreiser, candy maker Milton Hershey, and telegraph pioneer Guglielmo Marconi. Word spread J. Pierpont Morgan and Alfred Vanderbilt were coming, too, but the rumor proved false.

Morning or sea sickness, she wasn't sure which, kept Lucy in most of the day. What little she ate was brought on trays by stewards for her and the family, too. Often though, Harry or Fiona, with Helen in tow, dined in the restaurant. Both tried to occupy the girl who soon rebelled against the confinement of the suite. When Lucy left the stateroom, she enjoyed taking tea in the Palm Court the best. The soothing beverage and simple biscuits suited her stomach perfectly. Helen and Harry usually chose the sweet pastries and she wished she could, too.

On Friday, since Lucy seemed to be feeling better and they already tucked in Helen, Harry took the opportunity to leave the cabin and socialize a bit. "Sweetheart, I think I'll go to the gentlemen's lounge, play poker, and smoke a cigar."

"Look, darling." She picked up the information flyer resting on the table beside her chair. "Be sure you read this first if you do play."

The cover page prominently displayed a warning to anyone who joined in card games. It stated, hard as the company tried to eliminate the threat, professional gamblers and card sharks occasionally made the crossing and cheated unsuspecting victims out of a lot of money.

"Don't worry, my dear, I'm a terrible player and won't bet much or stay long. Call Fiona if you need anything."

"Have fun. I love you." She couldn't imagine life without her precious husband.

Saturday, Lucy recovered enough to go to breakfast. The menu listed haddock and grilled ham but she selected oatmeal rather than tempting fate. Afterwards, she and Harry wandered arm in arm through the ship and checked to see if the crew posted the overnight mileage run. Everyday Harry took a guess at how far the vessel progressed and put a dollar into the betting pool organized by Purser McElroy. He never came close to winning but didn't feel bad because ten percent of the pot went to seaman's charities. The pair sat in steamer chairs on the 'A' deck promenade following that. The enclosed area provided a wonderful view of the sea and some protection from the biting cold.

The couple resumed strolling and ran into Captain Smith making his daily stem to stern inspection. This time he extended a genuine greeting. They'd encountered him regularly and the Fawcett's felt sure he really remembered.

At lunch, the family opted for the buffet instead of a formal meal. Lucy decided to be bolder and selected shrimp, boiled chicken, and cheese. Harry tried these, too, plus a small serving of herring. It was his first taste of the fish and knew the first would be the last. He indulged in a glass of beer and a tasty pudding. The heavy food and choppy sea proved too much for Lucy and she fell ill.

On Sunday, she went with Harry, Helen, and Fiona to worship in the dining salon as did a hundred fifty others. Captain Smith led the service and read from the *Titanic's* prayer book. The pianist concluded the program by having the congregation stand and sing "O God Our Help in Ages Past". Upon leaving, a question popped into Lucy's mind. She spotted Violet walking past them, stopped the girl, and said, "Hello, Violet, are you well?"

"Very well, Mrs. Fawcett. And you? Do you feel better?"

"A little, thank you for asking. Violet, a question occurred to me as we left church. Are there provisions for the Jewish passengers?"

Proudly she answered, "Yes ma'am. We have a rabbi who holds services in all sections and we serve kosher meals to all classes as well."

"How nice, and I appreciate the information."

Gossip that day revolved mainly around a small formal dinner honoring Captain Smith. Mrs. Eleanor Widener planned a fête in the A la Carte Restaurant, called the Ritz by those who recognized its similarity to the one in the famous hotel. According to the busybodies, the hostess arranged for a trio of musicians to play, elaborate decorations, and pink rose and white daisy centerpieces. Caviar, lobster, Egyptian quail, grapes, peaches, and an assortment of sweets and wines topped the elaborate menu.

At the moment, dinner was the last thought on the captain's mind. He received reports from ships ahead that icebergs littered the area. Knowing the way things worked onboard, he feared some reports hadn't yet reached him. He inspected the ship as usual and found all well. Time and again he checked for wireless messages in the Marconi Room, took note of the northerly winds pushing bergs toward his location, alerted the lookouts to watch for ice, and continued his normal routine.

At lunch, the Fawcett's shared the same table as the outspoken and vivacious Mrs. Molly Brown. The woman entertained diners with tales of her efforts to secure the vote for women, reform the juvenile justice system in Colorado, and philanthropic efforts. Lucy heartily supported feminist causes, particularly regarding suffrage. On top of that, she adored the woman's hennaed red hair, fashionable black and white striped suit, and oversized hat sprouting tall, black feathers.

Lucy came to realize many on the trip weren't on pleasure cruises. Mrs. Brown grabbed the first available transportation and rushed to get to the bedside of her ill four-month-old grandson Lawrence. The Rayerson's, of Pennsylvania, were in route to bury their son who died in a car accident. Fortunately, the rest told a happier story. The Dean family, who shared the table, was having a wonderful adventure. Bertram and Eva brought two-year-old Bertram, Jr. and 9-week-old Millvina to lunch as well. Lucy cuddled the tiny girl, the youngest on the *Titanic*, and marveled at the speed with which babies changed. She grew more excited at the prospect of having another child to love.

All day clouds dotted the sky, the wind increased, and the temperature dropped noticeably, only fifty degrees at noon. The cold weather left the decks uncharacteristically deserted. Usually people crowded them trying to walk off a big meal. Those who dared brave the frigid wind were wrapped in furs or heavy woolen overcoats. By the time the bugler announced the dressing hour at 6 p.m., the mercury plunged toward thirty-nine degrees and promised to plummet below freezing as the evening evolved. The water would be colder yet.

Lucy's stomach turned on her again but she refused to give in and miss this dinner, too. In London, she bought an opulent Lucille gown for this very banquet and was determined to use it. The satin frock was a two-toned purple creation with a darker colored floor-length lining and a shorter one dropping from shoulders to knees in a lighter hue. The bodice had a deep V-neck cut nearly to the waist and an embroidered inset. Shiny purple satin ribbon edged the sleeves, hem lines, and accented the V neck. A wide tassel-trimmed sash surrounded her waist and flowed to the bottom of the overdress. Fiona volunteered to keep Helen so they could enjoy being alone.

The chef outdid himself and diners feasted on oyster Hors

D'Oeuvres, Consommé Olga, poached salmon in mousseline sauce, filet mignon, and peaches in chartreuse jelly. Lucy ate little but vowed to taste each delectable morsel.

Sharing the table were Mr. John Cumings, a stockbroker from New York City and partner in the firm of Cumings & Marckwald, and his wife Florence. Harry mentioned the brief layover in the city and Mr. Cumings extolled its many virtues and listed sites they simply must see before returning to Texas. Florence, who developed an instant fondness for the couple, graciously extended an invitation to stay at their home for a while after docking. A blushing Lucy quietly told her about the pregnancy and sickness. She thanked her for the kind offer and, if possible, agreed to accept.

Following the dinner in his honor, Captain Smith surveyed the endless stretch of water around him. The mercury rested below freezing and the wind died down. Neither brought a smile to his bearded face. Waves lapping the base of the icebergs made the monsters easier to pick out in a moonless night. The fact the clouds gave way to a clear sky enhanced visibility but a slight haze hovered on the horizon.

All day cautionary messages continually interrupted wireless operator Jack Phelps as he tried desperately to finish sending passenger requested wires to friends or family in New York. At 10:30, when the *Californian* broke in once more to say she'd stopped due to dangerous ice, Phelps cried enough. He shot back demanding the operator shut up and quit bothering him because he was busy. The other operator continued listening to the transmissions for an hour then turned off his radio and went to bed. No regulation required the receiver be monitored constantly.

Quartermaster Robert Hichens ordered Sixth Officer Moody to extinguish the lights in the wheelhouse in an effort to improve the view. At 11:40, Frederick Fleet spotted a gigantic iceberg dead ahead and instantly alerted the bridge but the warning came too late. A mere thirty-seven seconds later the starboard bow collided with the floating frozen mountain and sent chunks of ice crashing to the deck. In their stateroom, the Fawcett's slept soundly. The vast ship muffled the scraping and shuddering to the point it was barely noticeable in most parts of the vessel. In the Fawcett's suite Helen, who woke to pull up the blanket, noticed the jar and she quickly drifted back to sleep as the *Titanic* continued on course.

CHAPTER 16

Below decks, the crew was acutely aware of the impact. Contact with the berg ripped a long, narrow gash in the hull and the raw sea poured in. They scrambled as water rose higher and higher, each man trying to escape its deadly rampage but tragically few made it. The liquid death topped the bulkhead in the forward section and rushed into the next since it didn't go to the ceiling. In rapid succession, the supposedly water tight compartments filled and proved the walls were not going to halt the charging onslaught.

Word swiftly reached the captain and he turned cold as the murky, foreboding sea. Succeeding damage reports got worse and worse. He knew the craft could sustain the loss of four compartments. If the fifth went, she'd be doomed. By midnight, the water progressed far enough he anticipated the worst and ordered stewards to wake passengers, instruct them to dress warmly, put on life vests, and go to the decks. Scarcely half would fit into lifeboats but, in case he had to abandon her, the lucky few should be ready to go on a moment's notice.

Violet dashed from cabin to cabin pounding on doors and giving instructions. Harry answered the strident banging and knew something terrible happened. The desperate expression on the girl's face and the listing floor convinced him the stewardess meant business.

"Mr. Fawcett, sir, we've hit an iceberg and the captain wants you on deck. Bring coats, blankets, hats, gloves, and move to 'A' deck right away." Then she added what she'd been ordered to say. "It's a precaution, please come quickly."

He woke the family and they hastily put on warm clothes, thick socks, gloves, hats, heavy coats, and took all the blankets in the suite. Harry carried Helen while Lucy and Fiona struggled with the covers. Topside others already gathered and watched anxiously as crewmen worked to lower lifeboats into position. In the Marconi Room, chief radio operator Jack Phillips repeatedly tapped out QED, the emergency signal, in Morse Code and the *Titanic's* position. Junior radio operator Harold Bride suggested he try SOS, the newer distress call, and he did, alternating between the two.

At twelve-thirty, as the first boat left, Second Officer Lightoller brought portside Boat 4 in position on 'A' deck. Chief Officer Wilde twice denied him permission to launch so the man went over his head to the Captain and received approval to load and lower the craft. At 1:40 a.m. Colonel Gracie assisted his wife and Mrs. Astor into the small vessel. Mr. Astor asked to accompany his pregnant wife and was told no. Instead, he tossed Madeleine his gloves and said he'd see her soon. Mrs. Ryerson and her two daughters entered right behind her. When her son tried to board, Lightoller refused until Mr. Ryerson explained the boy recently turned thirteen. He could, Lightoller said, but no more boys. Lucille Carter heard the exchange and shoved her large hat on her eleven-year-old son's head and they climbed in arm in arm.

Harry urged Lucy, Helen, and Fiona onward. Wives hated parting from their husbands and balked at leaving. Everyone believed the liner unsinkable and assumed this merely an unnecessary precaution. It'd turned too cold to sit in the open air for a drill. Harry insisted and convinced her by saying Helen and the baby needed to go. He reassured her he'd get another ride if necessary, which he doubted. Harry feared he lied to Lucy for the first time ever but it didn't matter. All he cared about now was making sure his wife and children were safe. Most of the ladies eventually acquiesced and got in the lifeboat. Mrs. Straus, however, flatly refused and remained with her husband. She stood by him through forty-one years of marriage and had no intention of stopping now.

As Lifeboat 4 maneuvered slowly away, Lucy saw those still abroad throwing deck chairs, barrels, and doors into the water in case they jumped. It gave her a frightening flashback to scenes during the Galveston hurricane when people grabbed onto anything floating. A number of people already took the drastic measure of plunging in and Lucy guessed no one lived long in the below-freezing brine. She noticed the ship listed more sharply with each passing second, bow down and stern rising ever higher until the three enormous propellers rose from the sea. Mrs. Astor, buried deep in fur, looked to see John standing calmly at the rail, his faithful dog Kitty at his heels.

Lucy vainly scanned the deck trying to catch a glimpse of Oliver. She never spotted him once her raft hit the water. He worked his way to the opposite side to minimize the chance she'd see him die or find his dead body floating in the frigid water. That image is one he did not want seared into her brain forever.

Quartermaster Perkis, the sole crewmember and adult male on the boat, operated the tiller. Marion Thayer, Madeleine Astor, Emily Ryerson, Lucy, and Fiona grabbed oars and rowed away from the mortally wounded vessel. Mr. Perkis believed the suction, should the monster sink, would pull the craft under if it was too near. On the way, the women dragged seven crewmembers from the water, unfortunately two died shortly thereafter.

Aboard the ill-fated liner, the sole remaining flare shattered the gloom. A lookout on the *Californian* saw the lights yet her captain hadn't bothered to find out why they'd been deployed. On the next closet ship, the *Carpathia*, radio operator Harold Cottam removed the headpiece, laid it on the table, and bent to untie his shoes. Since he'd yet to turn off the set, he faintly heard the rapid tapping through the earphones. He put them on and hardly believed the message. The mighty *Titanic* was sinking. He immediately responded, assured Jack Phillips he'd hurry, and alerted the captain. It'd take four hours even though the vessel managed to exceed her maximum estimated speed.

The last lifeboat left at 2:05 a.m., all had empty seats. Jack Phillips and Harold Bride continued sending the Morse Code signals for help to the very end. Ultimately, the deck's slant became too steep and the transmissions couldn't continue. At 2:17 Phillips sent the final message, "Come quick. Engine room full." At the same time, the captain announced 'every man for himself' and crewmembers still at their stations scrambled to survive. Captain Smith returned to the bridge to await his fate.

Sobbing uncontrollably yet digging the oars deep into the Atlantic, Lucy felt Harry slip away. She knew the exact instant she lost him forever. She sensed it deep in her heart as his soul was wrenched out of his body and his life extinguished. Her grief and the horrible screams of those in the water ceased for a few seconds, overshadowed by the horrendous, dreadful death throes of the unsinkable *Titanic*. The practically vertical liner erupted in a terrifying explosion and spewed scolding hot steam into the air. The furnaces filled with water and tore loose from the bolts. The upturned stern snapped free with a tremendous groan, rending the vessel in two. The separated parts rose briefly, unencumbered by the other's weight, and then dove 12,500 feet to the bottom where it wouldn't be seen until 1985.

Suddenly, the world stood still. No one spoke, or sobbed, or called out. The silence didn't last and the noises of desperation resumed. The cries for help ultimately ceased as those in the water froze to death. The tears of loss and moans of despair continued for another hour when suddenly shouts of hope rang forth. Far in the distance, flares from the *Carpathia* sparked a renewed optimism they'd be saved. The *Californian*, a mere eight or ten miles away, responded much, much later. If she answered immediately, it could have arrived before the ship sank and many more would be alive.

At 4:10 on the morning of April 15th, the *Carpathia* flanked Lifeboat 2 and dropped a rope ladder to the beleaguered, shocked victims. Her crew fashioned lifts from chairs and large canvas bags to hoist the ladies, children, and men too weak to climb. Quartermaster Perkis urged Lucy and the exhausted women to row toward the rescuers. It was Lucy's turn to go and her tears were a mixture of sorrow and relief as she, Helen, and Fiona were pulled to the deck.

As dawn broke, bodies floated all around and they realized the rafts sat in a field of ice. Questions formed in their minds—why didn't the captain stop? Or at least slow down? Did Smith post additional watches? Who deserved the blame? Somebody had to be blamed.

Those bobbing on the choppy water or standing on deck weren't the only people asking these questions as word of the cataclysm was telegraphed back to shore and across the Earth. President Taft, who learned of the sinking while attending a play, demanded answers and vowed to hold an inquest. Likewise, the British Board of Trade wanted an explanation and the White Star Line had none to give.

From above on the *Carpathia's* deck, William Carter gazed intently into Boat 4. He was one of the few lucky males who managed to find a ride after his wife departed. The frantic man's heart jumped for joy on seeing his wife and two daughters, then it fell when he couldn't locate his son. Desperately he yelled the boy's name. Thrilled at hearing the voice, Billy threw off the hat he wore and gazed excitedly into his father's face.

Once onboard, survivors followed the crew to the dining halls where hot coffee, brandy, water, and sandwiches waited. Doctors examined the injured and, especially, the pregnant ladies. Madelaine Astor and Lucy were fine and the physician expected both to deliver normally. It thrilled Lucy to know her baby survived but wrenched out her heart to remember it'd grow up missing such a wonderful father.

Most of the women Lucy befriended during the voyage survived, most of the gentlemen did not. Mrs. Cumings reiterated her invitation for Lucy, Helen, and Fiona to stay at her house prior to returning to Dallas. Molly Brown organized groups to make children's clothing out of blankets and gather garments for those who escaped in pajamas. She insisted the second and third-class travelers get the same care as those in first-class. The woman also spearheaded a drive to raise money to aide those from steerage who lost everything and reward *Carpathia's* captain and crew. Eva Dean, Bertram, and wee Millvina made it through with just cold feet and a few scrapes. Millvina went on to be the last living survivor of the unprecedented disaster, dying peacefully in 2009 at the age of 97. Bruce and Julia Ismay survived. Three small dogs, sneaked into lifeboats by determined owners, came safely onto the deck.

Misters Aster, Cumings, Dean, and Lucy's beloved Harry all

perished as did Benjamin Guggenheim, Isidor and Ida Straus, Thomas Andrews and his employees, and Captain Edward Smith. Frank Millet died without seeing the Lincoln Memorial he labored so hard to design. Seven hundred twelve out of 2209 were rescued. Sixty-one percent of those in first-class survived and twenty-four percent from steerage lived. About 75% of the ladies got off but 20% of the men. A mere twenty-four percent of the crew survived, the vast majority being female.

Efforts to aid those plucked from the Atlantic continued. The purser assigned women and children empty cabins to sleep in, requiring several share the space. Following the example of Captain Rostern, some relinquished their beds or took in survivors. A kindly elderly woman, who had a large stateroom to herself, took in Lucy, Helen, Fiona and three ladies now traveling alone. For the second time, Lucy wore clothes donated to her due to a horrendous catastrophe. Others slept on tables in the dining hall or sofas in the lounges. Men claimed places under the stairs, in the smoking lounge, or wherever possible.

For twenty-four hours straight, wireless operator Harold Cottam tapped out lists of those pulled from the sea and as many of the other messages as he could. All wanted to reassure loved ones or break bad news. He became so tired and frustrated at being pressured to work faster that he broke down and demanded they ease up. He'd do it as quickly as he was able. Word of the situation in the Marconi Room reached Harold Bride, radio operator from the *Titanic*. Disregarding his sprained ankle and frost-bitten feet, the man volunteered to help. He knew his partner, Jack Phillips, would, too, but he died when the ship sank. Harold took charge of the messages and organized all for processing. Lucy sent wires to the Sayers', Dorothy, the Beaumont's, and Madge, who'd spread the word. The short note read: Helen, Fiona, and I safe. Harry lost.

At nine o'clock in the morning, the *Carpathia* sailed for New York. Several other vessels converged at the site of the collision including the delinquent *Californian*. Sailors searched the area for weeks but discovered no living souls. The taskforce recovered 334 bodies, however. Of these, forty percent were buried at sea due to the condition of the remains where they'd sleep beside the ones never found. A short service in memory of those who perished preceded the watery funerals.

Three and a half days later the *Carpathia* docked at Pier 54 in New York amid a media frenzy and dark, rainy weather perfectly matching the mood on the ship. Reporters barged in on mourning families, badgered injured passengers, and further traumatized people with no regard whatsoever for their privacy or grief. Intrusive, vulture-like journalists tried to disturb those laying on stretchers while orderlies carried them to ambulances. As the highest-ranking company executive to survive, the press flayed Bruce Ismay for being part of the doomed craft's construction and for managing to escape when so many died.

Perhaps the single positive thing these correspondents did was publish a picture of the so-called *Titanic* Orphans whose father, Louis Hoffman, died. White Star tried unsuccessfully to locate relatives of the youngsters and hoped the articles brought a reply. In Nice, France, Mrs. Marcelle Navratil stared in disbelief at the photo. There stood her two sons, Michael, age three, and two-year-old Edmond. She had no idea her boys sailed on the ill-fated liner. Her estranged husband disappeared with them weeks before. He bought tickets in an assumed name in order to sneak the toddlers out of the country which is why it proved impossible to find family members named Hoffman. She further learned her sons were being cared for by Mrs. Margaret Hayes in New York. White Star happily suppled complimentary tickets so the three could be reunited.

President Taft heard rumors Mr. Ismay planned to rush himself and the surviving crew off the *Carpathia* and onto another ship headed to England as soon as he docked. Accordingly, he ordered subpoenas served prior to disembarking. The document compelled them to testify at a Senate investigation set to start the next day. He'd have to answer to the British inquiry as well.

Editorials dubbed the verdicts a cover up as nobody received blame for the tragedy. The speed Captain Smith ordered was common practice, no regulation demanded radio operators be always on duty, or enough lifeboats be provided for all passengers and crew. The two inquests did lambast the captain of the *Californian* who failed to question the reason for the flares. As a result of the commissions, regulations changed to mandate lifeboat seats for everyone and radios be monitored around the clock. They now stocked spare batteries to ensure any distress call would be intercepted. Additionally, an International Ice Patrol, part of the U.S. Coast Guard, was established. These vessels sail the North Atlantic tracking and reporting positions of any icebergs that might be dangerous to nautical traffic.

Wilber and Barbara Gettings met Lucy at the pier and begged her to come to their house. She expressed her deepest gratitude but Mrs. Cumings already offered her refuge until she and Helen felt like returning home. Once at the Cumings' brownstone, the survivors slept and slept. All were exhausted from the ordeal and grief they experienced. Would Helen remember the horror or her father? Lucy hoped the answer to the first would be no and to the second yes. As for her, this, the hurricane, and Harry's love would fill her heart, mind, and soul forever more.

CHAPTER 17

The trip home took forever. As she'd done since Violet knocked on the door and ordered them on deck, Lucy kept Helen constantly in arm's reach. She held her close at night, ate all her meals with the girl, and rocked her for hours. Deep inside Helen understood and tolerated her insecurity with compliance instead of her usual rebellion. Fiona stayed close, too. The three suffered through hell together and none wanted to let the others out of sight.

Back in Dallas, Lucy locked herself away and instructed Fiona to give callers her regrets and keep out the press. Dorothy came from Austin and she was allowed in. She and Fiona coaxed Lucy to eat, for the baby's sake if not her own, and to dress each morning. Helen recovered quickly and easily got restless and bored. Lucy allowed the women to take her to the park or into town in order to give the tot a release for her boundless energy. Eventually she permitted neighbors to come in and accepted their condolences and the food they brought to the grieving household.

Months passed in a fog of despair and depression. The child grew yet the bulging belly went largely unnoticed. Lucy forced herself to tend to Helen, playing with and reading to her for a few hours daily. She'd rather curl up within herself but her precious daughter needed a mother's comfort and care.

Mr. Gettings wrote her a letter in August again conveying his sympathy and urging her to write about the ghastly calamity. Unbeknownst to Lucy, Dorothy contacted the editor explaining her condition and asked he try and help. Perhaps expressing her torment on paper would allow her to come to terms with what she experienced and Harry's loss. Initially, sharing her anguish horrified her. No one else had a right to intrude. Ultimately, she decided it couldn't hurt. A few weeks before her due date, Lucy outlined her second nonfiction book.

In the wee hours of October 3, 1912, Arthur Mitchell Harry Fawcett popped in with a gusty wail. He was a big boy, healthy, robust, and unharmed from being shipwrecked. She and Harry picked names when the doctor confirmed the pregnancy so she knew exactly what to call her precious son. She honored the decision but added the second middle name to pay tribute to the father forever lost, just as she added Mary to Helen's name to commemorate those killed at the orphanage. The baby lifted the fog further and she happily nursed and cared for the infant. She gained a renewed joy in her daughter, gave her the attention and affection she deserved, and no longer had to force herself to do so.

In 1913, she took an interest in current events for the first time since the accident. Lucy mustered the courage to open and answer the tall piles of cards and letters Fiona neatly stacked on her desk. The note from Mrs. Sayers announced they relocated to Austin in October and built a house at 809 Rio Grande Street. She mentioned the large, two-story contained plenty of room for guests if she felt like visiting. Lucy noted automobile giant Henry Ford introduced an innovative system for building cars. His moving assembly line so revolutionized the industry that completing a Model T decreased from twelve hours to two and a half hours. His improvements slowly lowered the price of the car from $850 to an unbelievable $300 when it was discontinued in 1925. Different companies adapted the technology to their product causing an increase in production and decrease in price. In a very short period, the assembly line became the standard method of manufacturing most products.

The same year, Fred Wolf introduced the DOMELRE, DOMestic ELectric REfrigerator, a separate unit mounted on an icebox. It kept food cool, negated the necessity of ice deliveries and the mess it caused, and made the lives of homemakers easier. They no longer needed to go to the market as frequently for fresh dairy and meat. A lot of people, Lucy among them, had mixed felling when the

16th Amendment passed allowing Congress to impose a federal income tax. The country required money to run, but how far would it go? She bore no such qualms in applauding the 17th and thought it high time Senators were elected by the constituents instead of being appointed by state legislatures. Her dream turned to reality when Woodrow Wilson signed a proclamation declaring the second Sunday in May as Mother's Day and declared it a national holiday.

In June, Lucy recovered enough to complete her summary and begin writing *The Ship of Tears*. It was a tortuous, tearful, heart-wrenching process she vowed to endure. To her surprise, remembering the excitement of being among those to travel on the world's largest liner, the joy of taking pleasant strolls around the decks and dining by romantic candlelight, and the terror of the sinking helped heal the painful wounds. Sooner or later she'd be able to make peace with the memories and move on. Such a time loomed far in the future but would come.

Her memoir hit the shelves in April, exactly two years after the catastrophe and was an instant sensation. It sold twice as many copies as any two of her books put together. Friends urged her to buy a mansion, hire a staff, and travel. She did none of these things. Her house provided plenty of space, Harry's memories were there, she dreaded appearing in public, and Fiona took good care of her. The girl became dear and had a job for life. The success of *The Ship of Tears* invigorated her creative juices and she immediately began a fourth novel, *Second Chance Romance*. The sentimental tale chronicled a widow who got a second chance at love. Lucy didn't see it as a premonition since she couldn't imagine loving another man. It simply let her tender-heartedness and gentle nature shine.

Madge, Lillian, and Gertrude managed to drag Lucy away from work on a warm, sunny day in early June for a lady's adventure out. They ate lunch at a posh restaurant, saw *Texas Bill's Last Ride* at the movies, and went on a shopping spree. Lucy indulged in a creation from the Fashion First Boutique. She adored the above-ankle hem and white, sailor collar design. Gertrude, who owned a car, bought a big motoring hat with a gauzy scarf to wrap around it as she and Carl drove through town. Madge chose a soft, pale peach ensemble with embroidered roses scattered across the fabric, a low squared neckline topped by a lace insert, a high cummerbund waistband, and elbow-length lace trimmed sleeves. Lillian shocked them all by coming from the fitting room in a powder blue maternity dress to announce her fifth pregnancy. Lucy rejoiced at the proclamation, but silently mourned the fact she'd bear no more.

Summer brought terrible news from Europe. On June 28, 1914, a Serbian, Gavrilo Princip, assassinated the heir to the Austro-Hungarian Empire Archduke Franz Ferdinand and his wife Sophia in Sarajevo, Bosnia. The act was the final straw to an ever-growing stack of tensions between powerful nations. It propelled the continent into war yet again. Dubbed the Great War because so many countries were involved, it proved the deadliest conflict ever seen. Over and over, President Wilson proclaimed the United States intended to maintain its neutrality.

Lucy found it impossible to believe she walked Helen to school that morning. It seemed just yesterday she cuddled her babe after giving birth. Miss Gordon, the teacher, greeted each child and parent warmly and showed her students where to sit. Helen, not the least bit shy, instantly fancied the sweet young woman and flitted around meeting her classmates. She and Harry talked of this and planned to do it together. His loss weighed on her mind always, especially at Helen's milestones and when Arthur rolled over, sat up, walked, and uttered his first barely comprehensible word—mama. He'd learn about his father in the future, for now all the toddler knew was mama loved him with all her heart.

With Arthur weaned and Helen gone to school, Lucy agreed to go on a tour but stipulated it be in the U.S. She had no desire to board a boat again. The trip sent her westward and she marveled at the sights of the Grand Canyon, desert landscape, Pueblo dwellings, and the majestic Rocky Mountains. The pictures she saw didn't begin to convey their size and beauty. For the first time, she appreciated what hardships and struggles the settlers faced in moving toward the Pacific. She liked greeting fans and the marvelous sights; she missed the kids terribly. She wished they could be with her, but Helen had class and the endless hours on the train and in a hotel would be torture for Arthur.

Incredibly, a tiny bit of good resulted from the tempest in Europe, at least for women. In February of 1915, Lucy skeptically scrutinized advertisements for a revolutionary type of foundation garment, the brassiere. Corsets were constructed largely of metal and shortages propelled the cooler, briefer, more comfortable alternative into popularity. Lucy and her pals went to try on the liberating clothing and fell in love. It took getting used to though, since she felt naked sans the large, tight, hot, stifling corset she'd worn since the age of sixteen. The ladies quickly adjusted to the freedom and ease of dressing, no help required. The next day Lucy treated Fiona to a shopping trip so she, too, could enjoy the wonderful alternative. In eight years, the corset nearly disappeared from the fashion scene in favor of the bra.

Two weeks prior to Helen finishing the first grade, the German navy torpedoed and sank the *RMS Lusitania* causing an international uproar. The Kaiser claimed it a legitimate target since the liner carried munitions in the cargo hold. The rest of the world reeled at the idea 1,200 civilians drowned, including women and children. It was, in reality, primarily a passenger vessel. Since 128 Americans perished, people back home railed in tumult as well. Some said we should join in the fight against a country willing to slaughter innocents. The majority sought neutrality and Wilson assured citizens he intended to keep them out of war.

In August, a gigantic hurricane hit Galveston head on with 120 mph winds, making it a Category 3. Not as bad as what she lived through, but still a powerful force of nature. It sent chills of fear down Lucy's spine as she held her breath to see if the city survived the assault. It not only survived but came through with flying colors. The Herculean measures taken after the last storm limited the physical damage and kept the human toll at eleven souls lost. While tragic, it paled in comparison to fifteen years earlier. Lucy received a letter at the end of the month from Lena Sayers proudly announcing Joseph was selected to serve on the University of Texas Board of Regents.

Dorothy mailed a special invitation in November. She planned a surprise party for Willie's fortieth birthday on December 12th and wanted Lucy and the children to come. It'd be at the Chelsea Grand Hotel and she was doing it right. She ordered elaborate decorations to fill the space, hired a local band to play, ordered his favorite foods for the buffet supper, and invited fifty guests. And please, Dorothy begged, please stay with them. Their house provided enough space for all three Fawcett's.

Helen and Arthur, ages seven and three, had more fun at the party than anybody else. They ate way too much cake, danced through the ballroom, and hid beneath tables popping up unexpectedly and startling the guests. Hers weren't alone, either. Twelve additional youngsters, plus Dorothy's three, joined in the antics. Lucy lost sight of Arthur for a moment and scanned the room for her son. When she failed to see him, she panicked and rose from the table to hunt for the toddler. Just then, the door opened ushering in a burst of cold air and the most distinguished looking gentleman she'd ever seen, smiling from ear to ear, carried her son.

Lucy rushed over wondering why he held Arthur in his arms. "Does he belong to you, madam?" he asked in a deep, heavy, refined southern drawl.

"Yes, he does. Why, what?"

The stranger chuckled and said, "I scooped him up as he ran down the porch. I spotted him slip out the door when that couple walked in a few seconds ahead of me. They didn't see him."

"Thank you, thank you so much." Lucy hugged her precious boy trying to control the tears. "There's no telling where he'd be by now."

Dorothy joined in and asked if everything was alright. She saw Lucy and Oliver talking and had a sudden brainstorm. Lucy explained what happened and ended with, "and this kind gentlemen rescued him and brought him to me."

"Thank goodness. Mrs. Lucy Fawcett, may I formally introduce you to Dr. Oliver Segar."

Lucy noticed his height and his large, warm, kind brown eyes. He wore his hair fashionably short and a few silver strands glistened in his sideburns. "A pleasure to meet you, Mrs. Fawcett."

"Likewise, Dr. Segar. Do you have a practice here in town?"

"What? Oh, no, I'm not a medical doctor. I'm a professor of mathematics at the University of Texas in Austin."

"Very interesting. I always did well in math and was a bookkeeper for a while, although I'm sure it doesn't hold a candle compared to what you do. Where did you meet the Hightowers?"

"I grew up here in San Antonio but moved to Austin for college and never left. I knew a Harry Fawcett, any relation?"

Dorothy, who'd taken Arthur for a drink of punch, came back. "Lucy is Harry's widow. Oliver was the fifth member of the Harry, Willie, Charles, and Heath gang."

"I can't begin tell you how it devastated me to hear he died on the *Titanic*. He was a great guy. Your name rings a bell from somewhere else, too."

"Lucy's a well-known writer. You likely aren't familiar with her fiction, but I bet you've read...."

Suddenly it clicked. "Of course, *The Ship of Tears* and *The Mighty Blast*. I've read both and thought they were masterful."

"Thank you, again," she said, turning a bright red. It always made her blush when people praised her.

"Oliver is an author, too," Dorothy added.

"Oh, would I have read any?"

The question brought a hearty laugh and wide smile to the man's face. "I doubt it Mrs. Fawcett, unless you're a glutton for punishment. I wrote a few calculus and trigonometry textbooks and several on codebreaking. Are you interested in that?"

Lucy, too, smiled and laughed, "No, sir, however the codebreaking sounds fascinating. I'd like to hear about it. Don't get too technical or I'll be lost."

Dorothy drifted away, Arthur in her arms, to let them talk. These two had a lot in common, writing, a good sense of humor, Harry, losing a spouse, so maybe it'd work out. Both deserved happiness.

CHAPTER 18

The pair talked a little longer after Dorothy left. Oliver told her of losing his wife Bessie to tuberculosis two years after the marriage when he was barely twenty-two. He talked about his daughter, April, and his eyes shown bright as the stars. He explained she studied physics at the University and Lucy declared she'd follow in his footsteps. He asked her to dance and she accepted. A minute later, she turned deathly pale, stopped in the middle of the floor, and looked into his concerned face.

"Dr. Segar, I'm sorry, I can't. Please excuse me."

She turned, retrieved Helen and Arthur, made her apologies to Dorothy, and left. She couldn't do this. What had she been thinking? A wave of guilt assailed her once more. Grief and loss filled her as water filled the *Titanic*, cold and dark and overwhelming. Late that night, she pretended to be asleep so she wouldn't have to discuss it when her friend came home. She walked downstairs the next morning and Dorothy asked what happened.

"I'm so sorry I left early; I hope you and Willie forgive me. You arranged a fabulous party, you did a great job, and he certainly acted surprised. I don't know how you pulled it off and prevented him from finding out."

"Don't think of it. Tell me what happened. I thought you were having a wonderful time."

"I was, until … Dr. Segar and I danced and … well … I suddenly … well … I. It seemed disloyal to Harry." Tears brimmed in her eyes and Dorothy hugged her tightly.

"I can't imagine your suffering. Though three years has passed, I'm sure Harry's loss is raw, but Oliver simply asked for a dance. If

Harry were alive, you'd dance with him. You waltzed with Willie and Heath."

"It's different. They're old friends of mine and married. Dr. Segar, well, it's not the same."

"I doubt he sees it that way. He loved Harry and naturally felt close to you, too."

"Maybe, I guess." The realization helped her feel better and embarrassed for being so rude.

A colorful bouquet of tulips arrived at nine and at two o'clock Oliver knocked on the door. Lucy answered it and invited him in. Before sitting, he apologized.

"I'm so sorry I upset you at the party, Mrs. Fawcett. I certainly meant no disrespect."

"It was entirely my fault, Dr. Segar. I, well, it's the first social soiree I've attended since my husband died and it overwhelmed me I'm afraid. I apologize for being so rude."

Oliver gazed across at the beautiful woman, unconsciously tilted his head to the right a bit, and his strong mouth gently lifted in a small smile as he listened to her soft voice. He'd like to take her in his arms and comfort her, but realized it'd be inappropriate and probably scare her off for good. Twenty years passed since his wife died and he'd never been so attracted to anyone. He dated a number of ladies, briefly contemplated proposing to two, and none drew him in or moved him the way Lucy Fawcett did in a single, brief meeting.

"Don't apologize. It took ages for me to feel comfortable in a room full of strangers."

Lucy and Oliver talked for another hour, Dorothy served tea and cookies, and all five youngsters trooped in to sample the treats. It turned into a pleasant interlude that made her regret overreacting. Dr. Seager proved to be charming and she enjoyed reliving her memories of Harry and listening to him recount youthful adventures they shared.

Lucy returned to Dallas on January 3rd. Helen needed to get to school and her back to writing. Out of the blue, she received a letter from Oliver Segar. He kept it light and casual, told her what classes he taught, of April making the dean's list again, and announced his next work on deciphering would be released in February. The note delighted her and she responded by recounting tales of the children's antics, plans for redecorating the living room, and the progress of *Second Chance Romance*. He said he couldn't wait to read it to which she replied he'd probably be the only male to do so.

Lucy and Oliver enjoyed a lively correspondence throughout the winter and in early March a surprising note from him brought a smile to her lips. He wrote to say the University of Dallas invited him to give a lecture on the role of mathematics in codebreaking. His scholarly books and numerous articles singled him out as a leader in the field and universities countrywide invited him to speak. He'd be there for a few days the first week in May and invited her, plus Helen and Arthur, to lunch on Thursday.

It took Lucy totally by surprise. She enjoyed his letters but didn't expect to see him in person again, at least not so soon. She discussed it with Madge, Gertrude, and Lillian, and none saw it as a problem. She called Dorothy and she thought it a fine idea and urged her to accept. Dorothy knew it'd take a while, Lucy pined for Harry, but hoped ultimately the two got together. She'd become very fond of Oliver, considered him a fine gentleman, and Lucy was her dearest friend in the world. They deserved each other.

In the end, Lucy accepted and Oliver rejoiced. Like Dorothy, he understood she still needed to heal and wanted to be near when she felt ready. He regularly invented excuses to go to Dallas and Dorothy promised to let him know if she came to San Antonio. He'd have no problem creating a reason to come home since his parents lived there.

As the lunch approached, Lucy's anticipation and excitement grew. She told herself it was due to her latest story being published, because of Helen's upcoming eight birthday party, and spring warming the air. Anything except the truth. She half convinced herself the new dress had nothing to do with Oliver's visit. The crisp, white outfit looked fresh and cool and made her feel more youthful than her thirty-five years. Layers of organza topped taffeta for a crisp, clean sheen. Blocks of intricate smocking accented the front of the bodice and were spaced evenly around the skirt forming flattering folds below. A gold taffeta cummerbund encircled the waist, gold buttons adorned the placket, and shiny gold ribbon bordered the pointed collar and wide hat.

Lunch was a huge success. Oliver picked a casual cafe offering a large variety of choices to please everyone and put Lucy at ease. Going with him, or anyone, to a posh establishment might make her uncomfortable. He guessed as much so kept it simple. As the four walked toward her home, he stopped and bought ice cream cones. Lucy and the kids had a wonderful day and Oliver was happier than he'd been in years. The longer he knew the enchanting woman the more he respected and admired her. He always wanted more children and her charming, mischievous brood stole his heart as well.

Oliver came again to give another lecture and convinced Lucy to go to dinner and the opera with him. He chose an elegant restaurant this time. The next afternoon, he took the entire family to see *20,000 Leagues Under the Sea*, a Disney movie based on the Jules Verne novel of the same name. On the walk back, they discussed the unseasonably hot weather, baseball, Woodrow Wilson's campaign for reelection, the war in Europe, and Helen's eighth birthday party in June. She invited him, but he sadly declined. He already accepted an engagement to speak at Harvard and it was too late to cancel.

Down the street, Arthur spotted a Dodge showroom and begged to go in. At three and a half the boy possessed a keen passion for automobiles and jumped excitedly when one clattered past on the street. He climbed on the display models and begged for a ride. The salesman, assuming them to be married, recited the full sales pitch. He adamantly recommended a touring car to fit all four comfortably. He suggested three models, extolled their virtues, and insisted on a test drive. He handed Oliver, who drove a sporty yellow Oakland Model 38 speedster in Austin, the keys and practically forced him to go.

Lucy smiled as the wind caressed her face and she liked the feel of the machine as it rumbled jauntily down the road. She finally realized why Americans had such an affinity for automobiles. It was more comfortable than a wagon or buggy, had a retractable roof and windows that could be closed in cold or rainy weather, and didn't smell of horse or attract flies. Back at the dealership she admitted to Oliver she'd probably get one someday and he said why not today? She protested, for a moment, and then gave in to the urge. The salesman's jaw dropped when she, instead of he, wrote a check for the entire $1,100.

Oliver drove it home for her and extended his stay to begin teaching her to drive. Gertrude's husband volunteered to finished the process. In a couple of months, she and the kids were seen all over town in the sleek, black sedan. Lucy splurged on a motoring hat, driving gloves, and in August hired a crew to erect a garage adjacent to the house. It bore no resemblance to the elaborate tower constructed by Carl Benz, the German who invented the automobile, to house his machines. Benz's building rose two stories tall. The cars sat on the bottom floor and an opulent study occupied the second level. She commissioned a simple frame structure but it made stepping in and out easier on rainy days and she needn't bother with the top.

The Sayers' invited her to Austin in November to attend an election party they were hosting. She'd mentioned Oliver in her letters and Lena suggested she ask him to come as well. He called her as usual on Sunday and she relayed the invitation. He joyfully accepted and said he'd pick her up. Leaving the youngsters with Fiona, she rented a room at the plush Driskill Hotel since the Sayers' home was filled to capacity. Oliver came to get her in his yellow sportscar and she marveled at its style and speed. She chucked to herself and assumed he scrimped and saved to afford it on a professor's salary. Or, maybe he got enough on what he published to pay the cost. She had no idea how much he received for the textbooks and articles.

Lucy caught up with old chums and met many new people including Mr. Sayers' nephews Ralph, Thomas, Albert, Phillip, and Joseph. It'd take weeks to certify all the races, but a boy the Sayers' paid to go back and forth to the Western Union station for the latest results relayed the word at midnight the Democratic incumbent

Woodrow Wilson was projected to win. The announcement brought a rousing cheer from those in the house.

Lucy hooted when Jeannette Rankin, a pacifist, won election to the House of Representatives, the first female to hold national office. Montana, one of roughly a dozen states all west of the Mississippi, legalized full suffrage for women. Voters sent her to Washington for the purpose of keeping the country out of war. Lucy speculated on why some western states allowed females to vote while most still didn't and concluded it was because women played such an integral part in settling the land. They crossed the Rockies in wagon trains, fought hostile natives, plowed fields, and faced the dangers of frontier life alongside husbands, fathers, and sons. It likely gave these men a different opinion than those in the east who forgot three centuries ago women faced the same hardships when Pilgrims sailed to North America.

Three weeks later, Lucy read a disturbing article in the *Dallas Morning News*. On November 21, 1916, the *RMS Britannic*, one of *Titanic's* sisters, hit a mine deployed by a German U-boat and quickly sank killing thirty passengers. The ship, originally intended to join the others as a luxurious transatlantic liner, was diverted to military use on completion. The reporter noted that Violet Jessup, a nurse on the *Britannic*, formerly served as a stewardess on both the *Titanic* and *Olympic*. She survived the collision with the *Hawke* and the sinking, as well as this disaster. Of the triplets, only the *Olympic* survived long once launched and it continued in service until being scrapped in 1935.

Lucy wrote Violet a letter in care of White Star Line reminding her they were on two of the vessels at the same time. She gave thanks the girl survived especially after sustaining a serious head injury from jumping into the water. The woman, who earned the nickname Miss Unsinkable, answered the note and expressed her appreciation for the kindness and said she recalled her, her husband, and baby Helen. She read *The Ship of Tears* and thought Lucy did a marvelous job relating the horror of the awful night. She stopped reading several times, she said, it painted such a vivid picture. Eventually she finished and recommended it to everyone she met. The women continued to correspond sporadically and Miss Jessop, who never married, enjoyed hearing about the children. Lucy sent her a copy of all her books hot off the presses and they spent a few minutes talking when Violet arrived in port while Lucy conferred in New York with Mr. Gettings.

January 1917 took Lucy to Austin again. The University of Texas Board of Regents held a reception for Oliver celebrating his latest article on decryption. His work wasn't a commercial success like hers but it distinguished him as one of the preeminent authorities in the field and earned him the respect and admiration of his peers. Lucy proudly accompanied him to the occasion.

The two visited regularly with no pretense of giving a lecture, attending a function, or anything besides being together. Willie told her Oliver was born on May 17, 1875, the same day Aristides won the premier Kentucky Derby race, and she decided to throw a party for his forty-second birthday. It wouldn't be a surprise, she had to be sure he'd be in town, but it'd be a big to-do and she started planning early. Dorothy's family promised to help and the children couldn't wait to see each other again, regardless of the reason.

Preparations abruptly ended on March 1st when papers splashed the contents of a message intercepted by British intelligence, dubbed the Zimmermann Telegram, on front pages across the United States. It exposed an offer by Germany of substantial financial aid to Mexico if she agreed to ally with the Nazis should the U.S. declare war. Having a collaborator on the southern border gave her a perfect platform from which to launch an invasion. The Kaiser indicated, once victorious, he'd return lost territories, namely Texas, Arizona, and New Mexico. The revelation so outraged the country that on April 6, 1917, Congress passed a declaration of war and America joined the English, French, and Russians in fighting the Hun. Yet, not everybody found it enough reason to enter the fray. Jeanette Rankin and fifty-five other members of Congress voted no in a futile attempt to keep the country neutral.

Oliver already knew his fate. After the Zimmermann Telegram came to light, the War Department contacted him and strongly requested his presence in Washington, D.C. where he'd serve in the intelligence group being formed to decode intercepts from the Central Powers. Before leaving, he had an important question to ask Lucy and prayed five years was enough for her to say yes.

CHAPTER 19

"Washington, D.C. sounds exciting." Lucy beamed at him for an instant and suddenly her face fell as the meaning of the words sunk in. He'd be far away for an extended period with no definite end in sight. A lot of people flippantly declared now the U.S. was in the fight, it'd take just weeks to end the war. She doubted it'd be true. The sides battled to a stalemate and were bogged down in trench warfare from the North Sea, through Belgium, to France. It'd take time to wrench out the foe and end the bloodshed.

"I can't talk about it, dear ..."

"What do you mean? Oliver, what will you do there."

"Sweetheart, I really CAN'T discuss it."

"Oh, I see, I guess. Sorry for pressing you. Do you know how long you'll be gone?"

"For the duration, I suppose. Lucy, dear, I love you. I think I fell in love at Willie's surprise party. Will you marry me; are you ready? I'd like you and the youngsters to come to Washington. If it's too soon, or you'd rather stay here, we'll wait. I'm in no hurry but had to tell you before I left."

Lucy stood dumbfounded for a moment and then hugged him around the neck. "I love you, too. It evolved more slowly for me, although I've known for a while now. I wasn't sure you shared my feelings."

"You must be blind, girl, if you didn't see it. Will you come to D.C.?"

The pair deliberated the pros and cons. In the end she decided no. She preferred not to uproot her brood. Helen, almost nine, adored her school and Lucy hated to make her leave. Arthur would enter first grade next year and she enrolled him in the same fine institute. Lucy couldn't see disrupting their education for a temporary relocation, so they'd postpone the nuptials until the war ended. Hopefully it'd be short as many predicted. In his absence, she'd settle on a wedding, mull where to live following the war, and pray he returned soon.

He reluctantly agreed it seemed best, even if leaving alone depressed him. Oliver anticipated being very busy and often out of town, perhaps for days or weeks on end. It'd leave him little opportunity to bond with his new family and help the children adjust to having a father and Lucy a husband. Neither was an ideal situation but he thought postponing the better option. He did elicit a promise to reconsider if hostilities dragged on.

The head of his department at the recently formed Military Intelligence Division needed him to report in the middle of May. Prior to that, he wanted Lucy, Helen, and Arthur to meet his parents in San Antonio. The Fawcett's packed their suitcases and boarded the train on April 23rd. Oliver met them at the depot in a bright red Auburn Model 6-39 touring car spacious enough for everyone and the luggage. Again, she wondered how a professor afforded such an expensive automobile. Maybe he borrowed or rented it.

He pulled in front of his childhood home and the mystery solved itself. The Segar's owned a huge, eighteen-room Queen Anne style mansion surrounded by a lush, expansive lawn, gorgeous flower beds, pink-blossomed crape myrtles, brilliant redbuds, as well as white and red oaks. The house itself wore cypress siding that weathered the humidity well. It was painted a light tan with darker accents on the trim, railings, and eaves. Lucy ogled at the octagonal turrets, ornate balustrades, steeply sloping roofline, second level balconies, and wide porches.

Oliver walked right in to the large wood-paneled foyer crowned by a stained glass dome. An intricately carved staircase soared elegantly to the second floor. In the center of the entry, a marble-topped mahogany table held a magnificent arrangement of flowers freshly cut from the gardens she'd seen from the driveway. Rosie, the housekeeper, rushed to greet him and Richard and Millicent Segar hurried close behind.

"Mr. Ollie, I'm so glad to see you." He blushed at the nickname used exclusively by his parents and this dear woman and glanced sheepishly toward Lucy who grinned from ear to ear.

"Welcome, my boy. Glad you're back." His father grasped his hand in both of his and his mother hugged him tightly. Lucy remembered he'd been there a few weeks ago, but the joyous reception spoke volumes of the close relationship the three shared. Such scenes caused her to envy those who grew up in the embrace of loving parents.

"Mom, Dad, Rosie, may I present Mrs. Lucy Fawcett, my fiance, and Helen and Arthur."

The raucousness started again with best wishes and warm greetings for the newest members of the clan. Mrs. Segar ushered the guests into the library and Rosie brought coffee and cake. The couple asked a million qestions since Oliver hadn't mentioned anyone in his letters or phone calls. In private, he admitted to his father he questioned whether Lucy was ready to remarry, so he kept the association private in case she said no.

"My dear, are you Lucy Fawcett the writer? Marvelous. Richard and I enjoyed your histories immensely and I wait anxiously for your new novels. Please," she said taking Lucy's hands in hers, "accept our deepest sympathy for all you went through."

Roy, the houseboy, carried the luggage and Rosie showed the visitors to their rooms. The home was so large each got a separate one, with several to spare. Lucy marveled at the large oak four poster bed, tall finials, and curved headboard dominating her room. An upholstered bence with graceful legs sat at the foot, a chest and mirror filled the opposite side, and several deep comfortale chairs were scattered throughout. Pale blue botanical print paper covered the walls, elaborately carved moldings accented the high ceiling, and a sparkling crystal chandelier glowed overhead. It exuded warmth and peace, like the Segars.

At Mrs. Segar's suggestion, Lucy rested prior to dressing for dinner. The children, under the protective eye of Rosie, played in

Oliver's old nursery and then romped among the breathtaking landscape. At four o'clock, she gathered both in to take a bath and change for dinner. Over a delectible meal of roast beef, cabbage salad, mashed potatoes, fresh baked rolls, and cream-topped apples, Lucy learned about her hosts and their son. The stimulating conversation, delicous food, and congenial company enchanted her. Helen and Arthur behaved admirably and participated politely in the table-talk. They relished having grandparents and would pick these two instead of anyone else.

Lucy told of growing up in the orphanage, working for Governor Sayers, and President McKinley setting her on the road to writing. Mr. Segar related the tale of his ancestors immigrating to the U. S. from England in the 1800's as farmers and eventually getting into cotton, lumber, mining, and oil. Oliver actively participated in the corporation although he put most of his effort into instructing students and research. The history fascinated her and all she didn't know about her future husband worried Lucy a bit.

He took her for a stroll through the moonlight to savor the cool breeze and explain why he never mentioned his financial situation previously. "My father gained his fortune through honest hard work and who'd be ashamed of that? I didn't intend to hide it from you, it's just not who I am. I'm a teacher, writer, and researcher. It's what I do best. It's the way I want to be seen instead of all this." He waved his hands around the estate. "My home is modest compared to yours and my single extravegance is the sportscar. It's the life I built for myself and April. I'm on the board of directors mainly to appease Dad. When he retires, we'll sell the business. I've neither the expertise nor patience to takeover permanantly."

She accepted his explanation and, based on what he said regarding his house, asked if it's where he planned to live following the wedding. Laughing, he answered, "No, darling, the cottage was perfect for April and me, but it's way too small for all of us. I, well, how'd you like to remain in Dallas? The University offered me a professorship on several different occasions since I've lectured so often recently." He kissed her softly on the cheek. "The department's building a fine applied mathmatics program and it'd be exciting to be part of it. You and the kids are happy, stability's important, and I've come to appreciate the city, too. We can stay in your house or buy a new one, as you wish. Because I chose a little house before doesn't mean I'm against a grander place now. Income from my shares in the company can give us whatever lifestyle you desire, my precious. Besides, I've saved a good portion of it."

She laughed aloud at his statement and explained. "I followed much the same path, darling. Harry and I bought my house together. After my books sold so well, friends encouraged me to move to a mansion, hire a cook and dedicated nanny, and so forth. I've no need for such extravagance. For now, if you take the job, let's keep my house unless it bothers you Harry and I lived there." He had no problem with the plan so it settled the issue.

The thought of staying put thrilled Lucy. She assumed they'd go to Austin, and being near the Sayer's was a plus, however living in Dallas suited her better. The realization it might be a lenthy separation brought a tear to her eye. When Harry died, she doubted she'd ever care for anyone again. Now she did, and finally admitted it, so being alone left her heartbroken.

He led her down a narrow path through banks of azaleas, lush oleander, and tall Cypress trees until he reached a small nook by a secluded pond. The bright moon filled the natural arbor with soft light and stars blinked festively in the ebony sky. Oliver guided her to a stone bench beside a fragrent rosemary bush and plucked a small box from his pocket.

"I think this is the perfect spot, my darling, to make it official. Will you marry me?" Oliver opened the tiny box, removed a ring, and slipped it on her finger.

"Oh, Oliver, it's the most beautiful thing I've ever seen. Yes, darling, yes." The platinum setting had a square face with a two carat round diamond in the center. An intricate handcrafted filigree design adorned the edge of the setting and graceful shoulders held sixteen smaller diamonds on the stunning gift. He also showed her the matching diamond wedding band.

April came in from Austin and instantly adored Lucy and, especially, Helen and Arthur. As an only child she always wished for siblings and now gained two. She played Hide-and-Seek in the garden, escorted the pair on a walk around the lake, and treated them to a movie and ice cream. She felt she couldn't possibly find a better mother than Lucy. As tragic as it was losing a parent, doing so at such a young age made accepting new ones easier.

The delightful week ended way too soon. Oliver rode the same train as the others to Austin. The sad party of travelers parted at the depot, not sure how long they'd be separated. He returned home to pack, prepare for the man who took a year's lease on his house, and April went back to class. Lucy and the kids continued north to pick up their lives, but it seemed emptier now. The Segar's encouraged them to visit again and she foresaw being there often. Likewise, April hoped they'd come to Austin. She looked forward to having a mother, brother, and sister.

Oliver left for Washington on May second so he'd have time to find a place to live. He settled on an efficiency apartment within walking distance of his office. The job proved grueling and he spent endless hours trying to break the Central Powers' codes to give the Allies an advantage. Though it wasn't easy, he eagerly rose to the challenge. He admitted to himself, and Lucy, it'd be no way to begin a marriarge, much as he missed them. Before accepting the position, he considered enlisting in the infantry. He mentioned it in his interview to which his prospective boss said he'd be more useful in the cramped cubicle in D.C. Discovering the enemy's movements could save thousands and end the war faster.

In June 1917, wealthy publisher Joseph Pulizer established and awarded the Pulitzer Prize to honor American authors. The winner's list embraced several women as well as a number of men. It turned into a month of sadness and excitement in Dallas. As so few men volunteered to fight, Congress passed the Selective Service Act to augment the pathetically small 120,000 man military. This saddened those called into service or who still opposed the war. The excitement came from the openining of Love Field, built to train Army Air Corps pilots. In November, the viciousness at Virginia's Occoquan Workhouse outraged the nation. Suffragette inmates were, on the order of the superintendent, brutalized by guards solely because they dared advocate voting rights for women.

Lucy wrote Oliver almost everyday and filled him in on the children's activities, the lives of mutual acquaintences, word of neighbors fighting in Europe, and the progress of her latest story. *Patriot's Promise* told of a woman's adventures during the Spanish-American War where she served as a nurse trying to heal injured soldiers. She asked Oliver if an intimate wedding, perhaps held at his parents' home, for twenty to twenty-five family members and guests suited him. He wrote as often as his rigorous assignment allowed, never mentioning his job except to say he found it challenging and fullfilling. Anything else constituted a breach of security and would land him in prison. Oliver told her of life in Washington, complimented her idea for the book, and heartily agreed with her proposal for an informal wedding. To be doubly sure he again asked if she'd prefer an elaborate ceremony since she and Harry eloped. Bessie planned a large affair and he enjoyed it immensily. No, she responded, unless he really wanted a big fuss, a small one filled the bill.

The first Americans landed in France in June, 1917 and entered the fray at the front in October. Regardless of the delay, the arrival gave a tremendous morale boost to the weary Allied troops. The Europeans christened the forces Sammies, Uncle Sam sent them. The calvary, forever at odds with the infantry, dubbed the foot soldiers Doughboys. The big brass buttons on the uniforms resembled the cakes of the same name. The U.S. Army deteriorated to such a depleted state, in basic training the raw recruits practiced with wooden rifles and fake armaments. The service still utilized more horses and mules than motorized vehicles. It wasn't until arriving overseas the men trained on real weapons and learned from experienced British and French combat vetrens who'd fought the Huns for the past three years. As the bloody conflict progressed, Lucy often speculated if the armed forces hadn't been so neglicted it might be shorter and fewer killed or wounded.

She went to San Antonio often to see Dorothy. Willie was fighting in France and her friend stayed in a constant state of fear. While there, she called on Oliver's parents to exchange information and compare letters, at least some anyway. Others were exclusively for her. Lucy took it upon herself to visit April frequently and invited her to Dallas. She knew the girl, now studying for a Ph.D., missed her father terribly. She tried to distract her whenever her studies allowed. They attended plays and concerts together and, at Lucy's request, the Sayers' graciously invited the young woman to their parties. At times, April became dispondent and Lucy gently reminded her to be thankful her father was safe and sound unlike so many.

U.S. troops poured into beleagured France, ultimately topping the two million mark, and received a heroes welcome. In certain regions, the Sammies outnumbered local residents 2 to 1. The arrival brought another import, too. Military bands, often comprised of Negros, introduced the French to Ragtime, Jazz's precursor, and the Europeans immediately embraced the exciting rhythm. To make things worse, in December of 1917 following the revolution, Russia signed a separate peace treaty with Germany and the Boshevics left the war. It freed all the German soldiers fighting in the east to throw weight onto the western front.

Lucy jumped in to help the war effort and bring Oliver home. Three shifts a week she assembled rifles in a munitions factory and gave Fiona the chance to do the same on three different days. Both sold Liberty Bonds that financed 60% of the military budget. Around the country women filled slots once reserved for men, not only in producing military equipment but as bank tellers, ticket takers, conductors on trains and busses, clerks, postal workers, police, and firefighters. And, in January of 1918, rationing began. No longer could Fiona buy as much sugar, meat, flour, butter, or milk as she wanted. What everyone, including the soldiers, expected to be a grand adventure turned into hell as they fought, froze, and died in the muddy, miserable trenches of Europe.

CHAPTER 20

In December, Lucy briefly saw Oliver. She piggybacked it on a trip to New York to consummate the deal for *Patriot's Promise* with Mr. Gettings. Oliver managed to wrangle Saturday off, a rarity he informed her, and took her to see the sights: the Washington Monument, White House, Supreme Court, Smithsonian Museum, and whatever else fit into the short visit. She saw the beginnings of the Lincoln Memorial, still under construction. At dinner, the couple dined at the Old Ebbit, the oldest restaurant in the Capital City. Founded in 1856 as a bar, it earned its reputation serving excellent seafood and local delicacies. Oliver returned her to the hotel at ten o'clock. The Willard, on Pennsylvania Avenue a few blocks from the White House, was famous for its luxury and service. The two sat in the richly appointed lobby and talked past midnight before parting. He needed to go in early the next morning, he usually worked seven days a week, to catch up on what he missed.

Lucy, too, wanted to greet the sun and catch the earliest train north. She'd be there two days and hoped to see Oliver on the trip south, too. Unfortunately, he left town so she went straight home to spend the holidays with her children. Although he kept what he did strictly secret, nobody called her stupid. The government didn't hire codebreaking mathematicians to order cleaning supplies. Undoubtedly, he plied his expertise toward the war effort. Lucy prayed constantly it bore fruit quickly.

On January 8, 1918, Woodrow Wilson gave a speech to Congress entitled the *Fourteen Points*. It outlined the principals for peace he envisioned when hostilities ceased and addressed issues such as diplomacy, territorial concerns, and proposed a League of Nations to prevent future global conflicts. It sounded like a good idea to her, however, European leaders were skeptical. It delighted Lucy to read the Postal Service hired Marjorie Stinson as the first federal female airmail pilot. A few years earlier Stinson flew for a local airmail service from Seguin to San Antonio. Marjorie, and her sister Katherine, were among the earliest to earn a license.

The American troops finally joined with other Allied forces, but initially garnered little respect. The Sammies entered the scene late and had yet to exhibit their worth. It all changed in May of 1918. The soldiers unveiled remarkable prowess at the Battle of Cantigny. They withstood the onslaught of German might and pushed them back from Paris before the city fell into enemy hands, greatly surprising the other Allies by demonstrating a ferocious will. The U.S. astounded the world with its staggering manufacturing capability producing an unbelievable quantity of weapons, equipment, and ammunition.

Likewise, her logistical genius in transporting troops and goods to Europe dazzled, as did the number of wounded saved by the hospitals erected near the front lines. The units were self-contained offering doctors, nurses, tents, medical and surgical apparatus, transportation, and independent water and electrical supplies. Considering the military completely lacked a medical corps at the beginning of the war, it caught up swiftly and spared countless lives.

The hospitals were desperately needed, too. The calamity ushered in the most destructive technology ever seen. Airplanes, once Raymond Saulnier invented the Interrupter Gear allowing pilots to shoot between propeller blades, turned into formidable weapons. Arial dogfights pitting aces such as Eddie Rickenbacker and Manfred von Richthofen, the Red Baron, made the men legends. Tanks, depth charges, aircraft carriers, and flame throwers added to the carnage. The U.S. developed a pilotless drone, but it proved too unreliable to use in combat.

The French employed gas in the field first. Neither belligerent deemed the non-lethal tear gas they used a violation of The Hague Treaty of 1899. That changed in April of 1915 when the Germans successfully unleashed a large-scale chlorine gas attack on unsuspecting Allied forces. The fumes burned their eyes, nose, mouth, and lungs causing severe pain, and even blindness or death. Before it ended, both sides used the insidious weapon and worsened an already horrendous clash.

Lucy's latest novel made a big splash and she started on another, going in an entirely different direction. She read an article on Voodoo and decided to shape a story around a shack in a Louisiana swamp, the occult, and how it affected the life of her heroine. Entitled *Voodoo Lair*, it had nothing to do with history. Like *Freida's Fright*, it was a lot of fun.

As the separation dragged on, Lucy missed Oliver more and more. He tried valiantly to write at least twice a week and call on Sundays, but often fell short. He worked harder than ever, frequently traveling across country to confer with colleagues also trying to hasten the war's end. In March, a trip brought him to Tulsa and Lucy, April, Helen, Arthur, and Fiona rode to meet him. They spent a wonderful day having a picnic, going to a fair, and seeing a movie. All five anxiously looked forward to the permanent reunion. In late August, Lucy visited him in Washington during her tour for *Patriot's Promise*. At dinner, she suddenly burst into tears.

"What's wrong, sweetheart. Here, take this." He handed her a handkerchief to dry her eyes.

Sniffling, she replied, "I'm alright, and terribly lonely. We've been separated over a year now and I regret not marrying you then. Do you still want us to move here? Can we marry right away?"

Although Oliver desired it with all his heart, he slowly shook his head and said, "no, my precious. I, well, let's wait until it's over."

Was he having second thoughts, she wondered? Did he regret the engagement? She looked deeply unto his intense eyes and furrowed brow and knew something happened. Oliver lacked the psychic connection she and Harry shared, yet his powerful expression sent a clear message. The winds were about to change.

In September, the Meuse-Argonne Offensive, or the Battle of the Argonne Forest, began and when it ended after forty-seven harrowing days, would be the biggest military action by U.S. forces ever. In excess of two million American's, plus the French, British, and enemy participants, slugged it out the width and breath of the entire Western Front. In the endless bloody conflict, Alvin York became a household name by leading an attack on a machine gun emplacement. He silenced thirty-five of the weapons, killed twenty-five adversaries, and captured one hundred thirty-two prisoners. Sergeant York received the Congressional Medal of Honor and was the most highly decorated soldier of the war. Willie got shot in the leg and riddled with shrapnel from a grenade in the fracas. Fortunately, he'd recover fully and be whole. Tragically, Charles Morgan's luck failed and he died during a mustard gas barrage.

For weeks, the belligerents were locked in bloody combat and each side suffered in excess of 25,000 losses. Then on November 1st, the Allies broke through the adversary's lines and the bloodiest battle in American history ended. The Great War claimed thirty-eight million souls, military and civilian. Of that unimaginable number, the United States lost fifty-three thousand in combat and two hundred thousand suffered wounds. The parties signed an armistice in a railroad car at Compiègne, France at 11 a.m. on November 11, 1918-- the 11th hour of the 11th day of the 11th month. A formal treaty, to be negotiated later, would define the terms of surrender but the shooting stopped, soldiers no longer died, and it's what mattered right now. Although emerging as a military and industrial giant, America shifted to peace mode very quickly and resumed her isolationist stance, determined to stay out of Europe's tangled web of political intrigue.

Word of triumph spread at the speed of light and jubilant hordes poured into the streets to celebrate and praise God for bringing the boys home. The Fawcett's joined the throng reveling in victory, but Lucy cheered for another reason, too. In Washington, Oliver immediately resigned, packed his bags, and hopped on the first train to Texas. He left his associates to wrap up the work and shut the office. He had a wedding to attend, his own.

Richard and Millicent extatically agreed to host the marriage of Oliver to Lucy Fawcett. Mrs. Segar suggested waiting for spring and holding it in the garden, but the pair simultaneously said NO. It'd been a year and a half and neither wanted to postpone it for one more minute. Mrs. Sager arranged to have the large foyer decked with flowers and candles. Twenty-two chairs filled the entry hall. The minister stood by the front door next to Oliver and Willie. Helen, the flower girl, and Arthur, the ring bearer, entered giggling all the way. Dorothy walked down the stairs in a rosey pink dress with Lucy right behind on the arm of Joseph Sayers. She wore an ankle-length pale pink satin gown and the slightly darker pink lace topper had a deep V neck, flowing sleeves, and ended at her knees. A band of lace cinched in the waist and another encirled her head where it secured a large, white feather.

The reception spread across the lower level of the mansion. A string quartet crowded into the corner and guests danced or listened to popular tunes. Large tables laden with delectible meats, salads, fruit, and sweets were artfully displayed in the parlor, sitting room, dining room, and solarium. Cateres, hired so Rosie and Fiona could join the festivities, darted around passing trays of tempting hors d'oeuvres and wine. Officially not on duty, Rosie nonetheless made sure everyone performed perfectly. Lucy, always at Oliver's side, greeted her friends and new family. In addition to the Sayers and Hightowers, the Beaumont's made the ceremony as did Gertrude, Lillian, and Madge. Oliver's old buddies were there and several associates from the University and the Segar's business, too. The whole affair went as she envisioned--small, low keyed, and fast. Lucy and Mrs. Segar put it together in three weeks.

They cut the cake, Lucy tossed the bouquet, and Willie took them to the train station. The couple planned a two week excursion to Miami as a honeymoon. Oliver suggested a number of exotic spots, Cuba, South America, and Spain. Since it remained neutral, Spain wasn't ravaged by the fighting. Lucy begged off of an overseas trip. The thought of sailing frightened her to death and she always wanted to go to Florida. Her tours sent her west, north, and to the east coast, but not that far south. It should be warmer and she looked forward to the sun.

The newlyweds arrived home in plenty of time for Christmas and it was the best since Harry died. Oliver, whose contract at the University of Dallas didn't take effect until mid-January, accompanied Lucy to buy presents for the kids and had a ball. He realized he missed having youngsters in the house at the holiday season. Lucy hosted a big Christmas Eve party so all those who weren't at the wedding could meet her husband. Fiona, Gertrude, Lillian, and Madge organized most of it while they vacationed in Florida, so Lucy had little to do when she returned. What a spectacular way to launch their married life.

On New Year's Helen bounded into their bed announcing the world transformed to an icy wonderland. The temperature dropped to twenty-two degress overnight and the drizzling rain froze to branches, light posts, eaves, cars, lanes, and tracks. Fallen limbs littered yards, broken trees and toppled power lines blocked the streets. Pipes froze and then flooded as the temperature rose. Regardless, inside the Fawcett-Segar's home fires glowed toasty and warm. The family enjoyed a pancake breakfast, proudly fixed by Oliver, and the children squeeled in delight when he gave piggyback rides up and down the hall and braved the weather to take the kids out for a soda. Both thought it wonderful having a father and Lucy got a tear in her eye seeing the three together. At almost forty, she secretly wondered if she might conceive again. It'd be wonderful, if somewhat scandalous, and time would tell.

During the first month of the marriage, Theodore Roosevelt died from a blood clot to his lung and the 18th Amendment became law. Set to take effect a year later, it prohibited the sale, manufacture, distribution, and consumption of alcoholic beverages in the United States. Oliver, Helen, and Arthur went back to school and she and Fiona were left alone. The house felt hollow and quiet following all the bustle of the wedding, party, and Christmas holiday. Oliver's belongings arrived in February. He stored the items at his parent's for the duration and now they were dropped at the door. He told her to expect manuals, academic material, scientific equipment, a desk and chair, momentos, and select pieces of furniture he wanted to keep. What he forgot to tell her was a mountain of crates, stacks of boxes, and a virtual housefull of furniture would be unloaded into her foyer.

The bulk of the items landed in the storage area above the garage, but he used the books and tools for his work so these needed to be inside. Lucy accommodated his desk and shelves next to hers. Since she used the smallest bedroom, his pieces made it cramped and crowded. Plus, both found the other's presence a distraction. Oliver hosted a faculty party to introduce Lucy to his colleges in March. The next day he told her the staff held such receptions frequently, taking turns sponsoring the fête. They'd be entertaining the professors often and members of the Board of Segar Incorporated, that had offices in town, from time to time. April came to town in May and slept in Helen's bed so the girl used the sofa. What once seemed like a reasonably large abode suddenly appeared too small.

They lived with the inconvenience for a while, but Oliver kept having to dig through barrels in the garage to find a particular report. It turned in to a tremendous bother and Lucy suggested a move. She contacted the agent who helped before and began the hunt. It took four tries to find the perfect place. It was three blocks from the University, on Chemsearch Blvd., and significantly larger, too. Oliver saw it on Saturday and heartily agreed to the choice. It sat on a beautiful, shady boulevard with lovely residences down both sides of the paved road. It was a scant two years old, completely modern, and had a garage for two cars and storage. The red brick Georgian style residence featured two full stories, a front door in the center, and an equal number of windows to the sides and across the second level. White shutters flanked all the windows, arches topped those below, and a row of dormers broke up the roof line.

Inside, a large entry held an ornate staircase reminiscent of the steps in the Segar home, minus the dome top. The previous owners left behind a dining table to seat fourteen and the salon accommodated many more guests than hers. Behind the living room, a huge library offered bookcases on three of the walls. It'd make an ideal work space for Oliver and he admitted even his collection wouldn't begin to fill it. At the rear, a big kitchen with a monstrous walk-in butler's pantry, casual eating and sitting areas, comfortable quarters for Fiona, and a service porch rounded out the features. Upstairs were five generously sized bed chambers: the master, one for each child, a guest room, and an office for Lucy. It also boasted two bathrooms. It was considerably bigger than the current residence and provided the kind of space needed to work, host parties, and be comfortable. Lucy decided to enclose a portion of the rear porch and add a small bathroom on the main level. She never understood why people didn't put toilets downstairs in the first place.

They moved in after Thanksgiving and Lucy wrote a letter to April describing it and her decorating plans. She told the girl she'd wait to furnish the guest suite until she arrived in March. They'd go shopping and she could pick out whatever she fancied, since it'd be hers where guests occasionally stayed. Lucy mentioned how disappointed she was Congress rejected the League of Nations. Like President Wilson, she feared the crippling reparations and economic sanctions demanded by the European Allies in the Treaty of Versailles virtually ensured a second war in the not too distant future.

CHAPTER 21

Lucy recognized the signs but wondered if it was age instead of pregnancy. Once her cloths started getting too tight, she went to the doctor. He confirmed her suspensions and placed her due date earlier than she believed reasonable. Regardless, she rushed to Oliver and broke the exciting news to her husband, unsure of his reaction. She'd be forty when this one arrived and he forty-five. Oliver grabbed his wife and swung her around excitedly. He couldn't wait and assured her having another child thrilled him immensely. The couple opted to delay spreading the word until it became obvious, just in case. Dr. Fillmore warned of the dangers in carrying a baby at her age.

She soon let the world in on her condition. Helen and Arthur took it in stride and looked forward to a new sibling. Lucy worried April might be jealous and then scolded herself for imaging the girl so immature when she whooped for joy at the announcement. At twenty-three, she saw no romantic prospects and doubted she ever would. The men at school scoffed at her aspirations to be a physicist. It largely stemmed from jealously since she ranked number two in the class. Her studies left her no opportunity to socialize in a way likely to lead to an introduction. Females with her ambition often remained single and she resolved herself to it.

The girls, as Lucy, Lillian, Gertrude, and Madge called each other, were shocked but happy for her. Gertrude retrieved Lucy's old maternity dresses from the attic and declared them awfully dated. So, on a clear, warm spring morning, the quartet trooped to Marsha's Motherhood Mart and choose a fashionable wardrobe. Since she was due in October, she'd make do with summer outfits. If it turned chilly before she gave birth, she'd wear a sweater. As usual, the ladies went to lunch and gathered at Lillian's to pass the day in pleasant company and a gossip fest.

The much anticipated 19th Amendment became a reality on August 18, 1920. It guaranteed all women the right to vote and Lucy looked forward to casting her ballot for president in November. Helen entered the seventh grade and Arthur the third. She found it hard to believe they were getting so old or soon she'd have four. Glancing down removed all doubt. She'd grown huge, larger than she'd been at this point with Helen or Arthur. Ultimately, Dr. Fillmore concluded she probably carried twins. That's why he set the date in October and why she grew so big and tired. He put her to bed, sure she'd deliver shortly since twins typically came very early. Oliver insisted on hiring a nurse. Fiona had enough to do even after Lucy hired additional help. Once married, she asked Mrs. Flowers to come twice a week and do all the laundry instead of just the sheets and towels on Mondays. There were now mountains of dirty clothes, more people to feed, a bigger place to clean, and before long, two infants living in the home. Fiona couldn't possibly do it all and wash, too. Because of all the changes, Lucy declared drastic actions should be taken.

She and Oliver decided to expand. A wide staircase led to an attic brightly lit by the dormer windows across the front and back of the house. She consulted a designer during the pregnancy and diagrammed two rooms and a bath. Lucy planned to put the babies in her office so she'd shift to the third level. It'd be larger with storage for her collection of reference material, a spot for a generously sized desk, a chalkboard to plot her storyline, and a comfortable corner to think or enjoy reading somebody else's book. Helen could invite bunches of friends for sleepovers in her new bedroom. Lucy hoped the girl didn't feel she was being banished, but Helen relished the idea of having her own space away from her brother's prying eyes and the noise of crying babies. Plus, she'd have a bath to herself, except while her mother wrote upstairs. Lucy accepted Oliver's standing proposal to hire a nanny. Four little ones and a booming career sending her out of town made her admit she needed help.

They offered the job to Fiona and she cried tears of joy as she said yes. Although the Segar's treated her well and respectfully, she was, in fact, a servant. Nannies weren't servants, but like family members. It represented a big step up for a poor Irish immigrant. Oliver moved her into Helen's former room, adjoining the nursery, and set about hiring another maid. Fiona held the initial interviews, narrowed the search to three candidates, and Lucy and Oliver would break the tie. On October sixth, Miss Addie Mae Winston took over the quarters by the kitchen.

Oliver took his excited daughter to find furniture. Helen already selected a pink and mint striped wallpaper, white lace curtains, and a large, beige rug ringed in a floral design of the same colors as the wallpaper. After scrutinizing everything in the store twice, she picked a suite in a green several shades darker than the mint color. She wanted a slatted headboard, chest of drawers, vanity, bookcase, arm chair, and desk for studying. The girl noticed a ruffled lace bedspread with a pink satin border and embroidered flowers and she asked for it, too. The store delivered the furniture the next day and Lucy admired it as the men hauled it past her door. "It's beautiful, sweetie," she told Helen, "I can't wait to see how you arrange it."

April resolved herself to spinsterhood too soon. At the beginning of the fall semester, a physicist from the University of Tennessee in Knoxville arrived on campus for a series of guest lectures on the relatively recent theory of quantum mechanics. It was her exact area of interest so she elected to attend and Dr. Marmaduke Prentiss immediately enthralled her. He proved a mesmerizing speaker, terribly attractive, and a renowned expert in the field. He gave an overview in simple terms, to orient those who weren't too familiar with the topic, and then delved into the deep end giving detailed information, diagrams, and formulas. She had difficulty following his logic and not because of the material's complexity. His sense of humor made her laugh and turned what could be a dry, boring lecture into an enlightening and enthralling interlude. His chestnut brown hair, large hazel eyes, round spectacles, strong, square chin, and tall, lean frame frequently drew her attention away from what he said. On occasion, she sensed him looking at her, too, but felt sure it must be her imagination or since only one other female sat in the auditorium. The second lady was sixty-three-year-old Professor Donaldson who supervised the chemistry lab.

She didn't imagine the interest and he approached her at the small reception given in his honor. "Excuse me, Miss, would you care for punch? I'm Duke Prentiss." He handed her a small crystal cup. She chuckled at his humility in introducing himself and said, "Nice to meet you, Dr. Prentiss. I'm April Segar."

"Segar. Are you related to Dr. Oliver Segar, the mathematician?"

"Yes, he's my father. Do you know him?"

"From reputation. I've read all his essays and his volumes on codebreaking are fascinating. What do you think of Einstein's opinion of quantum theory?"

He impressed her by not asking if she attended the University, or if she comprehended what he talked about, or why on Earth she came to the lecture at all. He sought her opinion on a very hot topic in the field. The two passed the hour debating the issue, often interrupted by attendees who wanted to speak with him. Nonetheless, the pair managed to engage in a stimulating conversation. Afterwards he offered to take her to dinner and she accepted. They spent an entertaining meal discussing the future of the discipline, Ernest Rutherford's efforts in nuclear physics, splitting the atom, and going to see *The Cabinet of Dr. Caligari* at the movies the next night. He stayed in town three days to complete the lectures and then traveled back to Tennessee. April took him to the station and he promised to write often. She smiled and waved cheerfully as the train pulled away and drove off with tears in her eyes.

September and October drug by and Lucy waited impatiently for the babies to come. The doctor switched the due date to mid-November and reminded her to expect to deliver sooner, yet nothing happened. November third passed and still no twins. To keep busy she worked but found it hard to concentrate. She caught up on a few of the latest publications including Sinclair Lewis' *Main Street*, F. Scott Fitzgerald's *Flappers and Philosophers,* and Sigmund Freud's *Dream Psychology: Psychoanalysis for Beginners.* At bedtime, the kids snuggled in with her and she read to them. All three laughed at *The Story of Doctor Dolittle* by Hugh Lofting. Though Helen was a bit beyond stories, she liked lying close to her mother. She missed having her bustling around and being the center of her life. As much as she adored Fiona, she wanted her mom.

Lucy, too, felt terrible missing part of their lives. She hated being stuck in bed; knowing they yearned for her made it worse. Her biggest pleasure in life at the moment, besides bedtime rituals, was seeing the paper and keeping abreast of world affairs. On November 2, 1920, station KDKA, Pittsburg, sent the nation's first commercial radio broadcast. Short-ranged, sporadic transmissions started in 1906, but this represented the sole regularly scheduled one. The owners intentionally chose then to begin so commentators could announce the winner of the Harding-Cox presidential race hours before people read about it. Lucy wondered if the medium would replace newspapers since it reported important events faster.

Three days later Oliver amazed her by bringing in a set and installing it in the bedroom to ease her boredom. Even if the battery-operated device didn't produce great sound, it provided a diversion. Twenty-four hours earlier, WRR began broadcasting in Dallas as the first commercial station in Texas and one of the earliest in the nation. Later, Lucy went into labor and delivered at 4:30 a.m. Annie Alice and Asher Oliver entered the world with gusty wails. The duo weighed six pounds apiece and the doctor pronounced both very healthy. Their parents gave thanks, brother and sister rejoiced, and neighbors brought food for Oliver and the kids. Addie, an excellent cook, deserved a respite in advance of the onslaught.

Lucy left the hospital and friends dropped by to see her and the babies, so the woman slaved constantly at the stove making cakes, hors d'oeuvres, sandwiches, cookies, and coffee or tea for the visiting hordes. Lucy received banks of flowers, hundreds of cards, letters, and telegrams, and scores of gifts. The girls threw her a party in August and she received plenty of blankets, diapers, rattles, and clothes suitable for either sex. Now people sent tiny outfits specifically for a boy and girl. Because she was famous, reporters between New York and California spread the word. Having brother-sister twins garnered added interest.

The pregnancy hit Lucy hard and she recovered slowly. She baulked at the idea of a dedicated nanny for years and appreciated the help now. Fiona cared for the children with devotion and tenderness and pampered Lucy, too. She requested Addie prepare her favorite dishes, kept fresh flowers on the table, and ensured she rested until all her strength returned. She and Addie got along well and enjoyed socializing, but Fiona left no doubt Mrs. Segar and the youngsters were her domain.

Lucy tried to interest Helen in ballet lessons, piano lessons, art lessons, and voice lessons. None of it appealed to the girl. She loved Girl Scouts and looked forward to camping trips and hikes. She embraced the Jazz era and endlessly listened to the radio. Lucy restrained her from going full flapper and steered her toward trendy but conservatively styled dresses. She zoomed around the block on her bike and often Arthur rode close behind. Most surprising of all, the girl acquired a fascination with airplanes. She ran out when one flew overhead as everyone did since they were pretty rare. Helen sought out local airshows and begged to go. The budding flying enthusiast applauded newly scheduled routes, innovations, and the advancements of women in aviation.

Arthur developed a passion for sports and building. Oliver bought season tickets to the Dallas Submarines, part of the Texas Baseball League, and cheered the home team who faced the Houston Buffaloes, Galveston Pirates, and San Antonio Bears. Father and son often saw the University of Texas Longhorns in Austin or the Texas A&M Aggies in College Station battle an opponent. Arthur watched excitedly as craftsmen toiled to raise houses, businesses, schools, bridges, roads, or barns. His dad tried to interest him in math and codebreaking by devising simple cyphers for him to solve, to no avail. He earned excellent grades in the subject but displayed no great interest or talent in the field. Oliver wished he knew how to use tools so he could teach his son. He slipped the carpenters a few dollars to let Arthur 'help' when they remodeled the attic.

Annie and Asher grew and changed daily, or so it seemed. Right on schedule each slept through the night, lifted their heads, and rolled over. The two would be fine together for years, but Lucy and Oliver decided to go ahead and give them separate spaces. None of the others shared and the twins shouldn't have to, either. Besides, Arthur was big enough Lucy didn't mind letting him go upstairs. So, Oliver called in the contractor, added a second bedroom to the attic, moved Arthur into the new space, and put Asher where his brother formerly slept.

Lucy's writing slowed down. Whereas she once released a novel every twelve to eighteen months, it'd take her at least twenty-four now. Between caring for two infants, the other's activities, managing a large, hectic household, spending alone time with her husband, and keeping track of friends, she no longer had hours on end to write. Instead, Lucy stole opportunities here and there to work on her book. Mr. Gettings urged her on, but as much as she liked writing, she'd always put her family first. They'd forever be her priority.

As 1921 dawned, Lucy reminisced and marveled at how much had changed. The National Negro Baseball League was formed and the inauguration of the League of Nations took place in Paris, the United States being conspicuously absent. Prohibition became effective on January 17th and ushered in thirteen years of violence and lawlessness as gangsters and bootleggers clashed with federal agents trying to enforce the doomed Amendment. In April, a massive eruption of tornadoes killed 219 from Alabama to Mississippi. On May 1st, the Brooklyn Dodgers and Boston Braves slugged it out to a 1-1 tie in twenty-six innings, setting the record for innings played in a single game and possibly becoming the most boring as well. Lucy chuckled when in June the United States Post Office issued a directive stating children couldn't be sent via parcel post. She wondered what in heavens promoted such a regulation. The week prior to Thanksgiving, President Wilson received the Nobel Peace Prize for his efforts in establishing the League of Nations even though the United

States, firmly reverting to isolationism, rejected joining it twice. And, on January 3, 1921 at Kinner Field, an obscure airport near Long Beach, California, with no fanfare whatsoever, Amelia Earhart took a flying lesson. In less than a year she broke the altitude record for women.

CHAPTER 22

"Mom, pleeeease. Why not? You let me drive."

"Helen, it's hardly the same." Lucy signed and told her again. "You're sixteen and I won't allow you to take flying lessons. When you grow up, and pay for it yourself, you can do as you please. Until then, the answer is no."

"Please, …."

"Enough! Stop arguing. Go study."

She huffed out and briefly considered asking her father, but it'd be no use. The first question he'd pose is have you talked to your mother. It's what he always said. Lucy and Oliver agreed on the tactic as the children grew and tried to get their way by going to a different parent if one said no. The couple vowed to support the other's decision rather than giving a contradictory answer and causing turmoil.

The argument caused Lucy to pause and reflect on how fast time flew. April turned twenty-six and earned her Ph.D. The next week she announced her engagement to Duke Prentiss. The scientists corresponded regularly and visited occasionally during the past three years. On his recommendation, her extortionary grades, and a stellar interview, April got an associate professorship at the University of Tennessee where he taught and conducted research.

They held the wedding in the University's chapel in July. The bride chose a light ecru silk gown richly embroidered with gold thread across the sleeveless bodice and down the softly gathered skirt to the end of the short train. She encircled her forehead with a simple band instead of a veil. Long gloves, a gold choker, and bouquet of ivory roses completed the ensemble. Helen served as the youngest of four bridesmaids and Arthur a groomsman. Annie and Asher were the cutest ever ring bearer and flower girl. The reception was held at a local country club and the guests enjoyed the delectable food and delightful orchestra. After cutting the cake and tossing the bouquet, April changed into a calf-length pale blue linen suit accented by beige lace on top of the shoulders, at the end of the jacket sleeves and hem, and around the hipline. The pair then set off for London on a two-week honeymoon and the rest of the relatives returned home hoping grandkids appeared soon.

Helen's interest in airplanes grew to the point she declared she not only wanted to fly but make it a career. Lucy was proud of her daughter's determination and ambition, but the very word scared her to death. Every few weeks stories of fatal aeronautical accidents filled the papers and the airwaves. She prayed the forced delay and the International Commission for Aviation's ban changed her mind. The organization prohibited ladies from serving as a member of a flight crew carrying passengers fearing they'd encounter difficulty controlling the craft while having periods. Lucy realized it was absurd and abhorred the pathetic excuse to exclude women, but she'd use any means available to keep her daughter's feet on the ground.

She grossly underestimated Helen's resolve. The week following the argument she cut school, a first, and drove to the airfield at the edge of town. She accumulated $10 and used it to take a ride in a Jenny. Whatever doubt remained in her mind vanished. Helen saw her destiny lay in the air. She'd never be able to put aside enough money to pay for lessons and felt sure her mother wouldn't change her mind. Right now, she had a bigger problem.

"Helen, where have you been?" Lucy grabbed her daughter's arms when she walked in the door and hugged her tightly. Tears welled in her eyes as she held her precious child. "Mr. Vandenberg said you were truant today. That just isn't like you. You scared me to death, your father called the police, and he and the entire neighborhood are searching for you."

"WHAT??" Helen couldn't believe it. She failed to consider the fact the principal checked on absent students or they'd call the police. Oh boy, I'm in for it now.

Lucy let go and sent Arthur to the police station to end the hunt. She seated Helen in the parlor and demanded an explanation. For a moment, the girl mulled over the options. Skipping class was one thing; lying to her mother's face was another. "What on Earth made me believe I'd get away with it?" she chided herself.

"Mom, I'm really sorry, really. I...went, rode, saw.... well, I went for a ride in an airplane. I saved forever to pay for it and I'm positive I want to be a pilot, like Marjorie Stinson and Amelia Earhart."

"Those are grown women, you're not. Helen, go to your room. Your dad and I'll discuss it and decide on a punishment. You mustn't do this again."

Reluctantly Helen nodded yes and trudged upstairs. Her parents let her know in no uncertain terms the seriousness of her transgression. She'd miss Patricia's birthday party, couldn't leave the house for a month, and assumed responsibility for several of Addie's chores: scrubbing the floors, washing dishes, and beating the rugs. The grueling punishment changed nothing except her tactics. Helen never again skipped classes, instead she got a job in the afternoons. She horded every penny she earned at Lone Star Dry Goods store to take lessons in the summer. It'd cost six hundred dollars, a quarter of the average annual income, and Helen knew part time employment wouldn't provide enough to get her there. So, as soon as school ended in May, she headed back to the airfield.

"Welcome to Asbury Aviation & Academy, I'm John Asbury. What can I do for you, Miss?" he asked the petite, blue eyed, blonde haired beauty who walked tentatively into the hanger.

"Uh, Smith, Helen Smith. I, well, I simply must learn to fly."

"Really? Have you ever been in a plane?"

"Yes, I took a ride in October and loved it. But, well, all I have is fifty dollars. I hoped, wondered, perhaps I could help here to pay for lessons." She stopped to take a breath and then continued. "By the way, are you the instructor?" He nodded yes. "Are you any good?"

Helen enchanted him from the instant she walked in. At fifteen or sixteen, he guessed, she possessed extraordinary courage and determination. Women gained more and more rights, yet most contentedly fulfilled traditional roles as wife and mother. This one wouldn't be satisfied with homemaking, or not merely homemaking, honorable and important as it may be. She had a fire, a rebellious streak that promised to take her far in life and he found it charming.

"How old are you?"

"Seventeen. And you? You haven't answered my question, Mr. Asbury."

"Well, Miss Smith, I'm twenty-four. I joined the Army when I turned eighteen, grabbed the stick, and discovered my passion. The war ended the week I finished flight training and the Army discharged me. I borrowed the money and bought a surplus Douglas DT."

Her eyes popped open and she exclaimed, "You mean the kind the Army used for the trans global flight?"

"Sort of. Those were a modified version and brand new. Mine's older. Anyway, for two years I gave rides, ran charter flights to San Antonio, Austin, and Houston, and picked up a couple of airmail routes. I still do all that, and opened the academy in April of 1924, around the time J. Edgar Hoover was appointed director of the Bureau of Investigation. So, you see, I've taught for a year and flown for six. What else?"

"Will you teach me—and give me a job to pay for it?"

John feared it'd be terribly difficult to refuse her anything. He already fell half in love with this captivating, determined, and, he suspected, head strong girl. "Here's the deal. I'll give you lessons for your $50, five dollars a week, and ten hours labor on Saturday. OK?"

She'd barely bring in the five-dollar fee without a cent left over. It's OK, she thought, I'll be flying. Being absent ten additional hours could be a problem. She didn't resent the effort, but how'd she explain it? "I can worry about it later," she told herself. "I'll think it over."

"Deal. When?"

"Saturdays, six o'clock, provided you finish your duties."

"Great." She clapped her hands together and smiled wider than John believed possible. This will be quite an experience, he warned himself. She already convinced him to practically give away the lessons. What else might he do for her? More importantly, he was in danger of giving away his heart. He needed to be very, very cautious and keep her at arm's length.

Helen came up with a scheme and enlisted her best friend's help. Dolly Madison hated her name because of the anguish inflicted by cruel classmates. She looked forward to getting married and changing it. Dolly got a position on the weekends as a babysitter for a family with five children. She amused them, walked all five to the park or lake, and supervised homework while the parents ran their combination service station, grocery store, and shoe repair shop. Helen lent a hand watching the kids now and then. The two devised a way to convince Lucy Mrs. Winston hired her, too. Since her parents didn't know the Winston's, the rouse had a chance of succeeding.

"Helen, you're tackling a lot. Between the store and babysitting, you won't have a free minute to yourself."

"I don't care, Mom, Dad, and it'll give me a lot of extra money. I'm saving for a car of my own, remember." The old goal changed and she decided to use the income for lessons instead. She unsuccessfully tried to convince herself the means justified the ends.

Both applauded her industriousness. They could easily buy her a car but thought it best she learn the value of a dollar. To receive her allowance, Helen minded the twins on Fiona's day off, run errands, set the table for dinner, and took a turn in the kitchen on Addie's break. On top of it, she wanted more to do.

"OK, for the summer. You can't keep both once school starts again."

"Deal. Thanks." The bargain simultaneously thrilled and devastated Helen. She seldom lied and this was a whopper. She'd taken the initial step to fulfill her dream of being an aviator and the happy thought soothed her aching conscience—a little. She'd sweep the hanger, mop the floor, file, pump gas into airplanes, wash wings, and give prospective customers tours of the facility; it'd be worth it to realize her goal.

Soaring through the sky brought Helen to life as nothing else had, and so did John. For the first time she found herself wildly attracted to a man. She hoped he felt the same, but through the summer he stuck strictly to business. He employed her on the ground and instructed her in the air. She caught him staring at her across the hanger, but he quickly returned to his task. He simply refused to become involved with a student.

He'd been engaged once, until his seventeen-year-old fiancée cancelled the wedding and eloped with a distant cousin. Her parents opposed their union at the beginning. John staked his future on a very uncertain industry and they threw her at the successful banker. It broke his heart and cooled him on dating anyone that age. He admitted to himself Helen seemed more mature and down to Earth than the fickle girl. Still, she was seventeen and a student.

Helen worked hard all summer at her jobs and learning to fly. Shortly after she started her senior year, she soloed and secured a license. John's business grew steadily. As the idea of climbing aloft grew more comfortable, people wanted to give it a try. In October, he hired her again but mopping and cleaning wasn't part of the bargain. He begged her to come in on the weekend and give joy rides to the curious or those considering lessons. Helen Pauline Mary Fawcett claimed the title of professional pilot. She wanted to shout it from the rooftop but told no one except Dolly.

John decided he'd risk another relationship and invited Helen to a buddy's Christmas party. Tearfully she declined, saying she made other plans. Keeping secrets exacted a huge toll on her and she wouldn't compound it by lying to him, too.

"My folks are having a party that night."

"It'd be my honor to take you to both. If you asked a date—"

"No date. There's, well, there's stuff I never told you. I kept my lessons confidential and invented excuses for being away when I'm here. My parents don't know and I must keep it private. If I introduce you, it'd be impossible to hide."

"So, Miss Smith, what other lies did you tell me?"

"Nothing, well, except my name, it's not Smith. My mother is sort of famous so I invented one. If anybody knew about this, it'd be in the paper. John, I'm sorry. I really want to go with you. Can we please wait? I promise I'll introduce you and come clean as soon as I graduate. I can't live without flying, you admit I'm a natural, and I lo—like helping you. Be patient for a few months."

It infuriated him, hated she misled her family and he played an unwitting part in it, and wondered what her real name might be. Helen suggested meeting surreptitiously for lunch or dinner and he said no. He wouldn't go unless she confessed. If he must wait, so did she.

John accepted yet another mail run in February, Dallas to Fort Worth twice a week, and gave it to Helen. On her part, it thrilled her even when it became difficult to hide the absences. The round trip took an hour and a half, including loading and unloading, so she rushed to the airfield right from class. She needed to complete the circuit during daylight. She'd yet to land in the darkness and had no desire to try. Some touched down after dark, using small fires or lanterns to delineate the runway, but it seemed risky. No matter how good or how much she enjoyed it, Helen wasn't a fool. She always exercised good judgement and extreme caution.

The year 1926 turned out to be an exciting one. In March, an experimental transatlantic telephone call was made between New York and London. Commercial service would begin in December. On May 16, Robert Goddard successfully launched a fueled rocket in Auburn, Massachusetts. Shortly before Helen graduated, aviation took two giant leaps forward. On April 17th, Western Air Express inaugurated the U.S.'s first regularly scheduled overland routes, ferrying passengers back and forth to Salt Lake City and Los Angeles. Short coastal hops commenced a few years ago, but this signaled a new frontier in commercial airline service. In May, pilot Floyd Bennet and navigator Richard Evelyn Byrd made a round trip flight to the North Pole. It was an exciting age for the industry as opportunities opened up nationwide.

CHAPTER 23

"WHAT!" her father screamed when she said she invited a date, her boss, to the graduation party. "He's married. Have you lost your mind?"

"What?? No, Dad, NO. Relax, I don't mean at the store. I have two. I'm a pilot at—."

Lucy propelled herself out of the chair and yelled in horror. "A PILOT. You can't possibly be serious."

"Mom, Dad, calm down. Let me explain." She confessed to the lessons, delivering airmail, and John. "And don't blame him. I hid my identity from him until recently I, well, lied, again. I invented a phony name so he wouldn't tell you." Helen's tears were exceeded by her mother's. She wasn't the perfect child, there are none, but she generally behaved very well. Helen's grades were exemplary, she mostly obeyed the rules, always acted respectfully, and seldom lied, the biggest being when she skipped class—and now. Flying induced her to perpetrate the biggest fibs of all.

"Helen," Oliver stated, "your mom and I love you more than anything in the world and we're extremely proud of you. I admit, this disappoints me as I'm sure it does her." Lucy nodded. "We asked you delay this until you graduated. I hardly think it's unreasonable."

"It's not, I just couldn't. I'm terribly sorry I hurt you. It's a passion. I regret lying but I'm glad I learned. Please forgive me."

Oliver saw no reason to continue arguing and put a stop to the discussion. The deed was done, she earned her license, and finished school. Both encouraged her to go to college, but she flatly said no. She had a career she adored and it's all she wanted to do. John promised her additional postal runs and she took him up on it.

Although Helen swore he played no part in the subterfuge, they felt animosity, justified or not, toward the person who endangered their daughter. He got a cold reception when Helen introduced him at the party.

"Mom, Dad, please meet John Asbury. He owns the—well, you know."

John extended his hand and, following a moment's hesitation, Oliver shook it without enthusiasm and with a scowl on his face. Lucy starred at him between narrowed eyes and barely acknowledge the man's presence.

"it's a pleasure to meet you, sir, ma'am. I deeply regret any anxiety we gave you." He offered no excuses nor did he try to shift the blame, he simply apologized. It spoke well of his character and loyalty to Helen. He stood beside her and shouldered the guilt even if he shared none of it. After exchanging a few forced pleasantries, Lucy and Oliver walked away and left the younger two alone.

"I don't blame your folks. I'd be furious."

"Me, too. I feel terrible and swear not to keep secrets from them again. It's a relief to get it into the open. At least now you understand why I used an assumed name."

"I do. When you told me your real name I recognized it."

She introduced him to her friends and here he received a warm, congenial welcome. They were fascinated by his job, and Helen's, and wanted to hear all about flying and where it'd take humankind. He distributed cards because people insisted but had an uneasy feeling soliciting business in a social setting. It was her celebration and he aimed to keep a low profile especially given the circumstances. From across the room, Lucy watched him closely. She admitted he was handsome, polite, supportive, socially adept, and well received by the other guests. Still, she couldn't help harboring resentment against him.

True to his word, John asked Helen on a date the next day and nearly each week from then on. The two worked together, shared lunch, often went to dinner, and to movies, plays, concerts, picnics, or the like on weekends. The pair became an item around town and it surprised no one when John requested her hand in marriage. Oliver, who warmed to him a bit, gave his permission if somewhat tentatively. Over Thanksgiving dinner, the couple reveled plans to marry soon so decided on a small wedding.

April and Duke, who arrived for the holidays, announced she'd been promoted to associate professor and put on a tenure track. Duke remarked he and April teamed up and did a lot of investigation in the area of particle theory. Only Oliver truly comprehended, nonetheless everyone found it interesting. Lucy imagined both to be wonderful teachers since they reduced complex concepts to common terms so it made at least a little sense.

Amidst the frenzy of wedding preparations, the world moved forward. In August 1926, *Don Juan*, the first movie with a musical score imbedded on the film, premiered at the Warner Theater in New York. Although no words were spoken, reporters dubbed it a talkie. A year later, the *Jazz Singer* would become the first film to have music and dialog in a few scenes. Henry Ford flipped industry on its ear when he introduced an eight-hour, five-day work week and NBC began broadcasting as the first radio network in the country. It encompassed twenty-four stations reaching from its New York headquarters to as far away as Kansas City. And, in December, a failed artist named Adolph Hitler published the second part of his manifesto entitled *Mein Kampf*.

As pledged, Helen kept the wedding in January a small affair. She reserved St. Theresa's chapel and Lucy decked it full of boughs of flowers and dozens of candles. The bride chose a white satin dress embellished by embroidery and beads. It fell straight to slightly below her knees and at the bottom a chiffon ruffle with a scalloped hem peeked out underneath. An oriental looking pointed hat secured the veil and a string of pearls, her parents' gift, graced her neck. She carried a huge bouquet of lilies and roses. Dolly, her sole attendant, wore a mint green gown in a similar style. The Segar's hosted the reception and hired the best restaurant in town to cater it, placing delicacies on small tables throughout the downstairs. The foyer and dining room were emptied of large pieces of furniture for dancing. It was a wonderful start to a new life and the New Year.

Lucy and Oliver traveled to Austin to celebrate Joseph Sayer's appointment to the Board of Pardons the same month. She hadn't seen them in quite a while and it felt wonderful to catch up. As the four talked, an attractive man joined them to pay his respects.

"Mr. and Mrs. Segar, may I introduce my nephew Ralph Sayers."

As the men shook hands, Lucy commented, "Mr. Sayers, I'm sure you don't remember, you were very young, but we met at the election party in 1916."

"It's a pleasure to see you again, Mrs. Segar." He knew Lucy by reputation since his aunt and uncle spoke of her often and gave him a copy of *Ship of Tears* on his eightieth birthday.

He walked away to mingle with other guests and Lena Sayers commented, "Ralph's an accountant at Sears, Roebuck and Company. He attended Texas A&M but quit to accept the job. He's such a fine gentleman."

The four chatted a bit until recently elected Governor Dan Moody called Mr. Sayers aside. Mrs. Sayers excused herself to greet guests at the door and Oliver led Lucy to the buffet for punch and refreshments and then to the dance floor. The divine night ended at twelve and the couple enjoyed the interlude before returning home on Sunday.

The nation gained a hero when, at 7:52 a.m. on May 20, 1927, Charles Lindbergh lifted off from Roosevelt Field on Long Island to make the first solo, nonstop flight across the Atlantic. Eight years earlier British aviators Arthur Brown and John Alcock crossed, however two shared the task. Their route, Newfoundland to Ireland, spanned a shorter distance than Lindbergh's 3600-mile trek. Using the stars to navigate, for 33 ½ hours he battled storm clouds, skimmed wave tops, fought icing cold and blinding fog to land at Le Bourget Airport near Paris at 10:22 p.m. on the 21st. A throng of 150,000 met the exhausted American and gave him a hero's reception, inflicting damage to his now famous plane *The Spirit of St. Louis*. A year later, the custom-built, single engine monoplane would go on permanent display at the Smithsonian in Washington, D.C.

The twins started second grade in September and the milestone absolutely astounded Lucy. It seemed just yesterday they were born. It felt like that for all of them. Helen, who survived the *Titanic*, too, was married and worked as a pilot. The memory brought Harry to mind and she wondered what life would be if he survived. She loved Oliver with every fiber of her being but couldn't help speculating. It saddened her Helen's sole memory of him resided in stories and a few pictures. Arthur, who arrived after his father died, turned fifteen and grew to be the splitting image of his dad. His childhood interest in construction grew as he matured and he took a part time job with the contractor who remodeled the house. Here he became a skilled carpenter, electrician, and plumber.

April's accomplishments continued to amaze her. The woman and her husband gained a great deal of notoriety in the realm of physics due to innovative, progressive analysis and research. And, Oliver firmly established himself as a well-respected, in demand speaker on the mathematics of codebreaking, not to mention as a gifted and popular instructor. Students often gathered in their living room in the evenings for impromptu brain storming sessions or to discuss assignments.

Helen's rebellion, lie, and career inspired Lucy to write a novel examining family relationships, changing societal values, and women's progress in gaining equality. Although pure fiction, it contained a touch of her own life as well. The main character, Polly, lived through the tumultuous battle to win universal suffrage and courageously entered a man's realm by becoming a pilot. Polly, like Helen, faced prejudice and doubt of ability on a daily basis. *Journey of Light*, as she entitled it, won both popular and literary acclaim. It garnered her a lot of attention from women's groups and earned her a Pulitzer Prize nod, but she didn't reach the finals.

Arthur thoroughly adored working with tools and seeing something stand where once nothing existed. When his boss added a bulldozer, invented in 1923 by a farmer in Kansas using parts of a Model T, Deere tractor, and a windmill, he found his passion. The massive piece of machinery personified pure beauty on wheels. It magnificently magnified productivity using brain over brawn. He begged his boss to teach him to use it and instantly mastered the beast. He was the operator called in for difficult challenges requiring a unique touch. If it'd been up to him, he'd quit school and operate the cacophonous contraption full time. His parents absolutely required he finish, so he waited.

At the end of the year, Helen and John took a big step in their careers. The city of Dallas purchased decommissioned Love Field and turned it into a commercial airport. National Air Transport Company, the first carrier making cross country flights, intended to schedule passenger service from there as soon as it opened. First, though, they approached John and offered him a position as a senior pilot. He talked to Helen and accepted. She would run the business, Asbury & Asbury Aviation as John renamed it, and he'd work at the airlines. John hired a pilot, Bernie Short, to take his place. It turned out to be perfect timing because in February Helen discovered she was expecting. The doctor suggested she not fly; medical science really didn't know what effect it'd have on the baby. Regardless of what the doctor said, her husband insisted and grounded her for the duration of the pregnancy. Between Bernie, and John pitching in on his days off, they managed to keep the business going for a while. It grew so fast, by her due date John took on yet another pilot, a woman he previously taught to fly.

On September 13, 1928, David William Asbury burst into the world wailing at the top of his lungs. The Segar's finally had a grandchild. Most of their friends married earlier and already boasted several. Both Lucy and Oliver eventually warmed to John and realized what a wonderful, loving, devoted husband he was. He worshipped Helen, and she him, and that's what really mattered. Neither doubted he'd be a great father, too.

Lucy threw a party when Helen recovered. David reveled in his role as guest of honor and relished the part. He charmed everyone who held him and cried only if he needed to nurse. Dorothy drove in and stayed a week to be with the chum she missed terribly. The two hadn't seen each other in a year and Lucy reserved lots of time for her. She and 'the girls' spent a pleasant few days shopping, dining, and going to the movies.

In April 1929, Lucy traveled to Austin to attend a reception at the Sayers' celebrating the anniversary of nephew Philip's wedding to Elizabeth. As always, Lena put on a stunning event that enchanted all the guests.

"Mrs. Segar, it's nice to see you again." Ralph Sayers greeted her warmly. "May I introduce Miss Charlena Dawson, my fiancée. We're getting married in a month."

Lucy greeted the gorgeous blue-eyed lady with light brown hair and a petite frame and congratulated them. They chatted a few minutes about the impending wedding and the couple went to speak to others as Lena Sayers walked in.

"I see you met Miss Dawson. Isn't she beautiful? And so accomplished, too. We're delighted at the match."

Unfortunately, the delight quickly turned to sorrow. On May 15, just prior to the much-anticipated wedding, Joseph Draper Sayers died at the age of eighty-seven. Lucy and Oliver attended the funeral and spoke a few words to Ralph Sayers and his fiancée Charlena.

"I can't tell you how sorry I am," said Lucy through a stream of tears. He'd been a surrogate father to her and the devastating loss hit her hard. "Will you postpone the ceremony?"

"We considered it, but Aunt Lena urged us to go ahead. She's confident Uncle Joseph would want us to. She won't be there, of course."

An additional piece of news came a few months later and it was good. Mr. Segar retired and sold the company. Oliver's stock brought him a tidy sum and it prompted them to think about their financial arrangements. With four children, a grandchild, and a substantial estate, Lucy wanted to reexamine the investments and visit an advisor. The man suggested setting up trusts and reorganizing the portfolio. Mr. Curtis sold their stock in banking institutions and automakers, except Ford, at a tidy profit. He reinvested the funds in public utilities, food canners and bakers, and the electronics industry. These, he stated, promised more stability and safety in the future than the others. He agreed retaining Lucy's publishing shares made sense.

The consultant applauded the fact they were debt free. All of this resulted in a safe, enviable fiscal position.

Shortly, the wisdom of these decisions became painfully obvious as headlines nationwide read: DOW PLUMMETS 25% IN FOUR DAYS. On October 29, 1929, the Great Depression threw the world into the worst financial crisis in history.

CHAPTER 24

As the world spiraled deeper and deeper into the Depression, Lucy and Oliver gave thanks daily for Mr. Curtis. The Segar's took a hit, no doubt, but not as severe as most. The reorganization of the portfolio proved to be the best decision ever. The stocks the consultant recommended weathered the assault fairly well. That, the facts they owed nothing, Oliver had tenue, and Lucy's books sold briskly, allowed them to maintain a high standard of living. Their offspring survived the crash but had a rougher ride.

John, as National Air Transport's ranking pilot in Dallas, kept his job and Asbury Aviation kept its head above water, too. The flight academy shut since few signed up for lessons or joy rides these days. Helen snared four additional mail routes and eked a slight profit without having to fire anyone. Arthur received the worst blow since the building industry screeched to a halt and his boss's company failed. After graduating, Oliver lent him enough to buy the bulldozer and tools from his former employer and open his own company: Ace Construction Services. In addition to dozer work, he handled general contracting services such as carpentry, plumbing, and electrical. Investing in a new business in the midst of a depression posed a risk, he knew.

Arthur got the equipment at bargain basement prices, lived at home, and owed only what he took from his folks. For a bit it looked as though he'd go broke, but he managed to win a big contract with the city to do road repair and forge new ones. Virtually every penny went to repay his loan and in four years he cleared the debt. His reputation as a skilled craftsman and honest business owner spread city-wide and he earned enough to support himself well and employ help as needed. The following year, borrowing $1,200 from Lucy and Oliver, Arthur bought a small place near where he grew up.

Like Oliver, April and Duke were tenured. Grant money evaporated, but the teaching salaries enabled them to survive. Asher lost his drug store job and Annie no longer babysat down the street. It wasn't the end of the world, but both missed the pocket money. Lucy discussed it with her husband and increased the allowances, and the responsibilities, to give them a little more. Compared to the third of the population who lost careers, homes, hope, and sometimes their lives, the Fawcett-Segar-Asbury clan fared well.

Since the Depression, life changed fundamentally. As the standard of living plummeted, shanty towns dubbed Hooverville's to ridicule the president blamed for the disaster popped up on the landscape. Formerly middle-class families now subsisted in shacks and cardboard boxes and depended on soup kitchens to survive. As if that wasn't bad enough, the worst drought in history devastated midwestern growers, sent food prices soaring, and caused countless foreclosures. Farmers who'd tilled the land for generations joined the ranks of the homeless and unemployed. Even weddings felt the impact as people ditched elaborate affairs in favor of no-frills ceremonies.

Aviation continued to progress following the Stock Market crash. Amelia Earhart dominated headlines by flying solo across the Atlantic and then America. Wiley Post cemented his place in history by winging solo around the globe and the Navy commissioned a ship designed exclusively as an aircraft carrier, the *USS Ranger*. In 1934, Central Airlines hired Helen Richey as the first female passenger pilot. Congress officially adopted the *Star-Spangled Banner* as the national anthem and the Empire State Building opened in New York. Al Capone, the notorious gangster, was convicted of tax evasion and sent to prison, a tourist in Scotland made the original sighting of the Lock Ness Monster, and the 21st Amendment put an end to Prohibition. Bank robbers Bonnie and Clyde died in a fierce gun battle in Louisiana and the Hoover Dam began operation.

In reaction to the ever-deteriorating financial crisis, Franklin

Roosevelt won a landslide victory over incumbent Herbert Hoover in the election of 1932. The president set about establishing programs to create jobs and put millions back to work. He abolished questionable deals negotiated during the former administration. Roosevelt approved the Tennessee Valley Authority to construct dams, generate electricity, improve navigation, enact flood control, and stimulate the economy. And, in 1935, he sponsored and signed into law the Social Security Act providing older citizens a safety net for retirement.

Lucy's family grew and changed, too. David turned six and Helen had two more children. James Scott emerged on February 22, 1932 and Irene Christine debuted on May 1, 1935. Arthur met Miss Mina Louise Allgood at church in January and announced their engagement in March. The pair planned to marry in November and, since her family was struggling, the Segar's insisted on paying for the wedding. The ecstatic couple gratefully accepted and stipulated it be a simple, small event.

"Mom, can I talk to you?" Helen asked as she peeled potatoes for the big Sunday dinner her parents hosted. Everybody looked forward to getting together, socializing, and catching up.

"Sure, sweetheart, what's on your mind?"

"Well, you realize the twins will be fifteen soon, right?"

Lucy laughed and replied, "Yes, I remember. Why?"

"They outgrew a nanny ages ago, right? I, well, we'd, John and I, want to use Fiona, if you don't mind. Bernie recently moved away so we're short a pilot. We either hire someone else or I start flying regularly again. That's what I'd opt to do. Since David was born I've pitched in here and there and I miss being in the air routinely. With three under the age of seven it'll be impossible without help. I can bring her aboard, do routes myself, and it'd be less than a pilot. What do you think?"

Lucy thought a few minutes before answering. She loved Fiona and the girl always had a place, but Helen definitely made a good point. "Helen, I say it's up to her. If she agrees, so do I. Addie can take care of us, especially since it's the four of us. Let's talk to Fiona, shall we? She's in the den cuddling Irene."

The arrangement greatly relieved Fiona. The Segar twins could fend for themselves and was equally certain she'd never be fired. She suffered pangs of guilt taking the salary, but domestic posts virtually disappeared since 1929. "Yes, I'd like that, Miss Helen. Your children are wonderful," she babysat occasionally, "and I adore taking care of the tykes." She smiled tearfully at Lucy and continued, "I can't even begin to thank you enough, Mrs. Segar. You gave me a home, a job, and the opportunity to advance farther than I ever believed. Thank you from the bottom of my heart. I realize you don't need me, as a nanny, and this is the perfect solution." All three hugged and cried and helped Fiona pack her belongings.

Lucy threw Oliver a surprise 60th birthday party. The entire family, dozens of friends, and hordes of university associates crowded into the house. Lucy sent him on several errands, ending at the airfield where Helen delayed him until Annie signaled the all clear. He walked in, the guests jumped out, yelled, and bid him well. The raucous group ate cake and ice cream, drank punch and wine, and enjoyed dancing to the radio. Later, the tired couple sat in the parlor reflecting on the evening's festivities.

"I'm glad so many of the professors stopped in, Oliver. It's been ages since we invited people for dinner." Her face clouded a moment and then she continued. "I wish your parents lived to see it."

"Yeah, me, too. Dad appreciated a good party and you threw a great one."

She nestled close to him and asked, "darling, have you given serious thought to retiring? You've avoided discussing the topic, but you can, you know."

"Yes, and I'll say it crossed my mind even though I love what I do. I find it hard to picture myself puttering around here all the time and being a nuisance. It'd drive you crazy in a week. I'll pester you to death if I'm bored. You wouldn't be able to write a word."

Once the dust settled on the party, Lucy, Mina, and Mrs. Allgood dove into wedding preparations. Lucy tried hard to keep the bride and her mother from feeling bad about needing help to finance the festivities. Regardless, the women expressed their gratitude to the point of embarrassment. She was delighted to do it, she assured them, she simply wanted the kids to have a nice ceremony and reception. Mrs. Allgood, a superb seamstress, insisted on taking care of the gown. Mina chose a pattern that draped gracefully across the bust. It featured a wide, domed, inset waistband with a bow around the center. The dropped skirt fell straight to the floor and flared to a short train behind. A narrow band held the trailing tulle veil on her hair. The frock bore no lace, pearls, or embellishments, yet the shimmering antique satin fabric made it rich nonetheless. The bridesmaids wore emerald ones in the same style, excluding the train. Prior to the showers, Mina completed a gift registry at the local department store, a service originated by Macy's in New York in 1924, for china, silver, and crystal. They decided to hold the wedding at St. Theresa's, as did Helen, and the reception at a banquet hall.

The newlyweds refused the Segar's offer of a honeymoon, saying they'd done too much already. Instead, Arthur managed to treat them to a night at the elegant Adolphus Hotel in downtown Dallas. He hated not taking her on a trip but couldn't afford the cost or time. He secured several contracts in October and had to strike while the iron was hot, as he said. It might be months, or years, until he got additional work. Because of his new responsibilities as a husband, he also made the monumental decision to hire an employee, go to college, and get a degree in engineering. It'd be hard being married, running a business, and going to school, but both he and his wife agreed it'd be worth it in the end. Mina now worked at a law firm and made a nice salary. They should just be able to make it.

After seeing the gorgeous dresses Mrs. Allgood created, Lucy, Helen, and April, who stayed several days, paid her a visit and ordered garments. Only Lucy, who treated the other two, really needed the attire. It let her help these family members in a way that didn't involve charity. The clothing was expertly sewn and Lucy took the gray tweed wool suit with an asymmetrical buttoned opening, long belted peplum jacket, and narrow calf length skirt on tour in December. This and the burgundy hounds tooth skirt and matching hip hugging jacket, dropped front yoke, and buttons down the sleeves became her favorite career apparel. Helen, who refused to wear skirts to fly in, settled on wide-legged trousers in black, navy, and deep forest green. April selected a burnt orange print dress for winter and a lavender chiffon sleeveless summer frock. Mrs. Allgood tailored each to perfection and soon her client list mushroomed as Lucy spread the word and friends commissioned the woman to design things as well.

The conversation with Lucy set Oliver to pondering retirement as he hadn't before. Although he joked, sort of, about getting bored, he began to deliberate the possibility. He loved teaching even if it left him too few hours to research, read, and write. He liked the idea of spending extra time with the kids, grandchildren, and Lucy. At fifty-five her career thrived, despite the Depression. The new, cheaper paperbacks sold well and she agreed to more personal appearances. It'd be fun to accompany her instead of missing her from home. He always understood the importance of these tours and never caused a fuss but hated it when she went away.

The next year, 1936. Lucy read Margaret Mitchell's epic saga of the south, *Gone with the Wind*. During August, Jesse Owens, a Negro track and field athlete, bedazzled the audience and humiliated Hitler's fantasy of Arian supremacy by dominating the Berlin Olympics. Stories of an invention called television being demonstrated in London fascinated Asher. Reporters described it as radio with pictures similar to the movies. The very thought sent his imagination into high gear. He loved the movies, hoped to work in the industry, and having it in the living room sounded heavenly. In December, England gasped at the revelation King Edward VIII abdicated the throne of England to marry twice divorced American socialite Wallis Simpson.

In May of 1937, the world witnessed a horror beyond comparison thanks to video technology. Moviemakers combined Herbert Morrison's narration and footage of the German dirigible *Hindenburg* bursting into flames and crashing at Lakehurst, New Jersey to produce a truly terrifying account. Lucy took the grandchildren to see Disney's *Snow White and the Seven Dwarfs*. The horrific newsreel started and she rushed them out. It upset them and she let the theater manager know how inappropriate it'd been to run it with a film designed to attract youngsters. Also in May, Prince Albert, the Duke of York, inherited the crown as King George VI following his brother's abdication. His ten-year-old daughter, Elizabeth, stole the hearts of the Empire and beyond. Helen suffered heartbreak in July when Amelia Earhart disappeared in the Pacific Ocean trying to be the first woman to circumnavigate the globe.

On August 3, Mina shocked and delighted them all by giving birth to twin boys, Jeffry Clay and Oliver Wayne. They called him Wayne to avoid any confusion. The babies were small and the doctor warned their frantic parents it'd be touch and go for weeks, maybe months. Twice the physician summoned the two in to say goodbye but the determined preemies rallied and were released in time for Halloween. Lucy asked Mrs. Allgood to create costumes and the grandkids joined in the fairly recent tradition of trick or treating.

As the end of the decade approached, Lucy reflected back on the 1930's. By then, Houston overtook San Antonio as Texas' largest city and never surrender the title. She remembered David's excitement the day Oliver bought him a copy of a comic book featuring a new hero, Superman. The boy wanted each issue the moment it hit the shelves. As David enjoyed the fictional character flying through the air, Howard Hughes set a record by circling the Earth in three days and nineteen hours. Arthur, who won a big contract from the city to erect a terminal at Love Field, treated everyone to lunch and tickets to see the *Wizard of Oz*.

The deadly grip of despair loosened a little as the economy gradually improved. It was good to see, but the reason why was not. The political situation deteriorated steadily due to Nazi aggression, Hitler's persecution of the Jews, rearmament of Germany in direct violation of the Treaty of Versailles, Japan's continuing invasion of China, and the Spanish Civil War. The events thrust fears of another global conflict to the forefront. England and the rest of Europe appeased and pandered to the Fuehrer for so long, the disarmed nation grew into a powerful foe. Although vowing to remain neutral, the U.S. quietly increased production of essential military supplies and beefed up the woefully inadequate armed forces.

The dawn of 1939 brought wonderful news when Helen announced her fourth pregnancy. Irene would be four then, James seven, and David nearly eleven. Arthur and Mina also shared word another baby was due at exactly the same time. The twins would be barely two if this one came on schedule. It'd be Lucy and Oliver's sixth and seventh grandchild and they couldn't be happier.

On September 1, 1939 India Maureen arrived to Helen and John with no trouble whatsoever. Mina gave birth two hours afterwards and Rebecca Coreen joined the clan. All day the proud fathers, grandparents, and assorted uncles, aunts, and cousins bounced between hospital rooms. By dinner the nurses got tired of the commotion and put the moms in the same place to reduce the traffic. Asher and Annie went to the deli on the corner to buy sandwiches. The glowing faces the pair left with had turned ashen gray when they came back.

"Mom, Dad, everybody," Annie blurted sadly, "the German's invaded Poland."

"Prime Minister Chamberlain is asking for a declaration of war," finished Asher.

CHAPTER 25

"Don't worry, sweetheart, I told him thanks, but no thanks," Oliver assured her.

"I hope you didn't use those exact words," she chuckled.

"No, I couched it in very respectful, appreciative, regretful terms."

Oliver met William Friedman on several occasions. The men shared a common interest, the mathematics of code breaking, and frequently attended the same seminars and lectures, including each other's. Friedman and his associate Frank Rowlett called repeatedly asking him to come to headquarters and work for the Signal Intelligence Service. The men never revealed exactly why, but Oliver easily connected the dots. He'd heard rumors the English feverously labored to unravel the German code Enigma. The machine-generated encryption resulted in millions of possible combinations so it'd be a tough nut to crack. He assumed Freidman and Rowlett targeted the Japanese counterpart.

"Good. I can't stand the idea of being separated like in the Great War."

"We weren't married then. You can go, too."

It hadn't occurred to her, but of course he was right. Circumstances were entirely different. Well, D.C. might not be too bad.

Asher began his senior year of college at the University of Houston in 1938. He majored in business and wanted to get a job in the film industry upon graduation. Annie went to nursing school in Dallas and was hired by Parkland Hospital in the emergency room. Lucy respected her strength and dedication and knew she couldn't handle the trauma her daughter witnessed on a daily basis. All her children where healthy, grown, independent, or nearly so, and Lucy recognized she was fortunate indeed.

The full magnitude of the European conflict hit in May of 1940 when the German Army pinned the British Expeditionary Force to the beaches of Dunkirk. With a colossal effort, every available boat, civilian and military, made perilous trips back and forth across the Channel ultimately rescuing 300,000 troops. France surrendered in June and Prime Minister Winston Churchill warned the populace "The Battle of France is over. The Battle of Britain is about to begin." A few weeks later, the Emperor aligned himself to Germany and Italy, and Japan entered as the third member of the Axis Powers.

Partially due to reports on the miracle and tragedy at Dunkirk, Annie enlisted in the Army Nurse Corp. She believed the U.S. would undoubtable be dragged in. When it happened, nurses would be desperately needed and she wanted to be ready. Although women weren't given full military status until 1944, Annie nevertheless had as much dedication and pride being in the service as the men she cared for at the hospital in San Antonio. It was great to be so close to home and go there on leave. Her parents and siblings visited often and it eased the loneliness. She pitied those whose post kept them far from kith and kin. Unfortunately, she'd know exactly how it felt in an unimaginably horrible way she couldn't have dreamed of in a hundred lifetimes.

As awful as it was, the war in Europe skyrocketed the United States out of the Depression. Roosevelt vowed neutrality, but American manufacturing prowess churned out an unbelievable volume of arms and material to supply the Allies and the U.S. armed forces, just in case. The speed with which guns, tanks, planes, and ships rolled off the assembly lines staggered the imagination. It should have served as a deterrent, too, for those contemplating action against the U.S. Due to the ever increasing Nazi and Japanese aggression, Congress authorized the first ever peacetime draft on September 16, 1940. Men between the ages of twenty-one and forty-five were ordered to register. Papers printed details of the Lend-Lease Agreement with England that transferred fifty old destroyers to the

Royal Navy in exchange for ninety-nine-year leases on bases in the North Atlantic.

Lucy sat in silence weighing the implications of the Selective Service Act. All of her boys were of age and eligible for the draft. As a tear rolled down her cheek, the phone in the hall rang obnoxiously.

"I'll get it," she called as she wiped her eyes and blew her nose. "Hello. Oh, my. Yes, sir, he's here. Hold a moment, please." Lucy set the receiver on the table and walked into the library where Oliver graded tests. "Sweetheart, its…. the president."

"Of what?" he asked.

"The country. It's President Roosevelt."

Surely someone was playing a joke, he reasoned. He got on the line and all doubts vanished. He'd recognize the voice anywhere. "Yes, sir. Of course. Thank you."

The men talked briefly and what he said caused Oliver to turn deathly pale. He hung up slowly, stood stone still a second, and looked at his wife. "I guess we should pack. The President wants me in the Capital by next week. I turned down Friedman, but you don't say no to him." Secretly Oliver rejoiced. He hated uprooting Lucy yet relished contributing at his age.

It took just a few days to get ready to go. Addie was staying there, so Lucy didn't have to pack the house or rent it to strangers. Oliver arranged for his attorney to pay the bills and the bank to send a housekeeping stipend to Addie each month. He grabbed a bag and left immediately to find a place to live while Lucy packed the trunks that'd be forwarded to the new address. First, the entire family gathered for a last dinner before being flung to the four corners of the world. Although officially neutral, a lot more now believed the U.S. must take sides. Lucy placed great importance on the event since a war promised to scatter them far and wide.

Oliver leased a small furnished brownstone in Georgetown, an exclusive area of Washington. A shortage of rental properties, thanks to the influx of people responding to the mounting crisis, pushed the price to an exorbitant amount. He was glad they came now because costs would soar if war was declared. The charming, quaint, narrow home had three stories. A sitting room, dining room, and kitchen filled the ground floor. Three bed chambers and a bath occupied the second level and a small den and attic the third. Oliver took the den for his office and Lucy used the smallest bedroom as hers. He warned her he'd be working endless, hard hours so she'd do a lot of writing to fill the lonely days. She started a journal, or diary, chronicling life in D.C. with the thought it'd be the basis of a novel or maybe a third nonfiction book. She prayed it'd remain empty and they returned to Dallas shortly.

Before Oliver arrived, the team already made a lot of progress toward unlocking Purple, the code name for Japan's diplomatic encryption. Using a pencil, note pad, and adding machine, the cryptanalysts endeavored to read the intercepted wires. Part of the problem was a lack of Japanese speakers and the complexity of the language itself. Friedman gave their efforts a huge boost by linking three IBM tabulating machines in tandem to fashion a crude computer enabling the testing of millions of potential solutions quickly. The mathematician ultimately realized the cypher utilized automatic telephone relay switches. This leap led to further success. Without ever seeing one, the codebreakers fabricated a duplicate of the Purple machine and read a message as soon as it'd been sent. Tragically, William Friedman suffered an emotional collapse and retired. The crippling stress claimed a victim and Lucy worried constantly about Oliver's health.

The British, feverously trying to crack the German code at Bletchley Park, got a windfall in May, 1941. The Royal Navy captured a U-boat, recovered an intact Enigma machine, and managed to convince the crew the vessel sank thus keeping the prize a secret. Eventually, the staff regularly read the Reich's top-secret transmissions enabling the military to locate and destroy submarines, discover combat plans in advance, and pinpoint when bombers would attack during the Blitz.

European war bulletins dominated the headlines, but other stories occasionally came out alongside these. Bob Hope's initial USO show entertained airmen at March Field in California. Also in May, Hitler's super-battleship *Bismarck* is sunk after terrorizing convoys in the North Atlantic for two years. On July 1st, the FCC authorized two television networks. NBC hit the airwaves and CBS followed suit hours later. Jacqueline Cochrane ferried a bomber across the Atlantic to Britain on the same day, the first woman to do so. And, in September, construction began on the military services headquarters in Arlington, Virginia, near Washington. Due to its five-sided shape, the builders named it The Pentagon.

Surprisingly, Lucy adored the Capital city. It bustled with excitement, and dread, and the atmosphere sparked like electricity. She visited all the monuments, historical landmarks, the Smithsonian, and spent hours at the National Gallery of Art. The family's welcomed distractions didn't slow her here and she finished a book in July while volunteering twice a week at the library. She rarely saw her husband, but more than if they lived 1,300 miles apart. At least he came home briefly almost daily. As in the previous war, he said little about his job. He counseled her not to mention anything she questioned or guessed, or who employed him, even here. He assured her a planted listening device was a remote possibility, nonetheless every precaution should be taken.

As she finally settled in, Oliver shared surprising news. They were moving temporarily to the territory of Hawaii. Station HYPO, known as Fleet Radio Unit Pacific, requested assistance deciphering the Japanese naval code that differed drastically from Purple. Located in the basement of the Old Administration Building, the group regularly intercepted and tried to read the Imperial Fleet's transmissions. High ranking bureaucrats in both Hawaii and D.C. guessed at some point the Empire would attempt to expand its Pacific holdings and wanted a heads up. His boss ordered Oliver over to lend a hand. The Army arranged for the couple to live in an 'ohana, or guest house, on the estate of a wealthy planter. The small cottage boasted a breathtaking view of the ocean and was surrounded by lush tropical flowers and tall majestic palm trees.

The lack of preparedness appalled Oliver. Security on base looked lax, the radar prototype operated only a few hours in the morning, and planes clustered together as easy targets in an aerial attack. He never served in the armed forces, but it appeared foolish since he believed war was inevitable. Surely the professionals could foresee the danger. What he found disconcerting, Lucy thought wonderful. The locals went about their daily routine with scant regard for impending danger and seemed happy, light-hearted, and content. She had a ball picking Christmas gifts to send to Texas prior to Thanksgiving so they'd arrive in time. At least once a week she sat on the beach and marveled at the warm, sunny November weather. The temperature often stayed mild into November back home, but not like this. On top of that, it'd been a long time since she enjoyed surf and sand. The Beaumont's passed away years ago so her trips to Galveston stopped. Every few days Lucy bought fresh vegetables and the luscious mouthwatering tropical fruit she loved.

Far across the ocean on November 26th, six aircraft carriers sailed from Hitokapu Bay in northern Japan heading toward Hawaii. Kichisaburō Nomura, ambassador to the United States, made a pretense of conducting diplomatic discussions with Secretary of State Cordell Hull to prevent hostilities as the flotilla steamed eastward. Negotiations didn't produce the results hoped for, so the high command sent a coded message to the task force, "Climb Mount Niitaka". It verified to Vice Admiral Chūichi Nagumo the attack should take place as designed. In the predawn hours of December 7, 1941, the initial wave of planes, armed with bombs and torpedoes, roared into the dark sky.

The Segar's planned on going to mass when Oliver showered and dressed. They had plenty of time yet so Lucy sliced a pineapple to serve with the ham she baked yesterday. The sound of planes on the way to Hickam Field was commonplace, however not usually before eight o'clock on Sunday, or so low, or so many. As the rumble of engines grew louder, she put down her knife, opened the door, and walked onto the lanai. Overhead, hundreds soared past. As she stood open mouthed, Oliver joined her on the porch.

"What're you staring at, sweetheart?" She pointed shakily skyward. Oliver gazed beyond her finger, spotted the big red circles painted on the wings and fuselage, and shouted as he ran to the phone. "Those are Japanese. Go back in and take cover under the table. I'll call it in and then go to the base." As he picked up the receiver, Oliver heard explosions in the distance and knew he witnessed the beginning of war.

Lucy, frozen on the porch, watched in horror as the Zero's swarmed above Pearl Harbor like frenzied hornets and clutched her chest as plumes of smoke and flames filled the horizon. Oliver tried to call the base, and his headquarters, and the police but the lines were jammed. He ran to his car and headed to the naval base and his office. It took forever. Civilians fleeing the area clogged streets and sidewalks. He tried to pass through the gate and discovered it shut tight. The sentries allowed only uniformed military personnel to enter. Even his top security clearance didn't sway the guards to let him in. When his boss cleared him, the second wave already attacked leaving the vessels on Battleship Row decimated, Scofield Barracks in shambles, the aircraft huddled together at Hickam Field destroyed, and 2,400 soldiers, sailors, and airmen dead or dying. Oliver said a prayer for those caught in the attack and of thanksgiving that he'd seen the carriers put to sea.

The second attack wave arrived back at the fleet expecting to find a third preparing to depart. Admiral Nagumo decided not to because the Americans regrouped and now inflicted unacceptable losses in the air, it'd take time to prepare, the task force might be located, and fuel was getting low. So, the armada reversed course and headed home, proud of a job well done and confident the thrashing ended America's ability to halt Japan's march to control the Pacific. Admiral Isoroku Yamamoto, commander and chief of the fleet, wondered if it'd been a mistake. Following the attack, he wrote in his diary "I fear all we have done is to awaken a sleeping giant and fill him with a terrible resolve."

President Roosevelt spoke to a Joint session of Congress and uttered the words destined to be as famous as the attack itself. "Yesterday, Dec. 7, 1941 - a date which will live in infamy - the United States of America was suddenly and deliberately attacked by naval and air forces of the Empire of Japan." He concluded the speech saying, "With confidence in our armed forces - with the unbounding determination of our people - we will gain the inevitable triumph - so help us God. I ask that the Congress declare that since the unprovoked and dastardly attack by Japan on Sunday, Dec. 7, a state of war has existed between the United States and the Japanese Empire."

Congress, in a near unanimous decision, agreed and declared war. Montana's Jeannette Rankin cast the sole opposing vote. She also cast one of the few votes opposed to intervening in 1917. Germany and Italy declared war against the United States on the 11th. In a display of comradery and solidarity, Winston Churchill became the first British Prime Minister to address a joint session of Congress.

Three weeks earlier on November 17th, the United States ambassador to Japan, Joseph Grew, sent an urgent wire to Washington. He anticipated an imminent, sudden, surprise attack to occur. Word reached Hawaii, the codebreakers redoubled their efforts, and couldn't believe the cable had no discernable effect on the state of readiness. In D.C., Oliver's former unit decoded the diplomatic telegrams faster than the Japanese did. On Saturday preceding the attack, the final installment of fourteen transmissions to their embassy was intercepted. It gave strict instructions for terminating relations with the U.S. and dictated the exact time to deliver the message. Nobody acted on it until the next day, however. This, and several additional missed opportunities, led many to speculate Roosevelt and top military personnel intentionally delayed informing Pearl Harbor of the danger, thus allowing the base to be caught off guard and thrusting the country into war.

CHAPTER 26

The Japanese invaded the Philippines the following day and, inside a week, Annie received orders to ship out to Bataan and treat the troops battling to repel the onslaught. She endured miserable conditions, brutal weather, constant attacks, too little sleep, and felt more useful than in her entire life. A momentary lull in the fighting sent her and five other nurses into the open to enjoy the fresh air and forget the horror of war, if only for an instant.

"Oh, hell. Not again," exclaimed Edna as the shrill wail of the air raid siren interrupted the pleasant interlude. Annie, sitting beside her, shoved the unfinished letter to her mother in her pocket and abandoned the idea of putting it in today's mail.

All six women clamped helmets on their heads and ran at top speed into the cave that served as hospital and refuge when bombs rained down. Every explosion rocked the sanctuary, sent clouds of dust into the air, and terrified the already traumatized wounded men and nurses alike. Regardless, these Angles of Bataan, as the soldiers called them, labored calmly and efficiently to give as much comfort and protection as possible.

In reaction to a German scientist's discovery of nuclear fission, Leó Szilárd and Albert Einstein wrote a letter to President Roosevelt in 1939. In it the eminent physicists urged him to begin a research program as well. They feared the Reich might develop weapons of unimaginable destructive power and the United States needed to get there first or face annihilation. In 1942, William Oppenheimer and Enrico Fermi confirmed the plausibility of a nuclear bomb. This convinced Roosevelt and he established the top-secret Manhattan Project to ensure the U.S. beat Hitler to the atomic punch. He put

Major General L.R. Groves in command who then recruited Oppenheimer to head the Los Alamos, New Mexico facility where the actual bomb would be assembled and tested. The Army built a number of facilities across the country and each attempted to unravel one piece of the nuclear puzzle. Disbursing the centers and isolating the various aspects of the endeavor disguised the exact nature of the task since very few were privy to the overall scheme. Each scientist worked on his or her bit independently but had an inkling of what was going on. These represented some of the most brilliant minds in the world, after all.

"Why on Earth does an Army colonel want to see us?" April asked for the fifth time in half an hour.

"Sweetheart," Duke answered with exasperation, "I've no clue. The dean simply told me to meet him and to be sure you came, too. He should be here any minute." It couldn't come fast enough.

"You're 4-F because of your eyesight. Surely you aren't being drafted now. You're too old," she said frantically.

"Baby, relax. The Army doesn't send colonels to fetch recruits. Please calm down. Thank goodness." He got up to open the door.

"Dr. Prentiss, and, uh, Dr. Prentiss, I'm Lt. Colonel Beber, it's a pleasure to meet you."

"Please sit, Colonel. Can we help you?" Duke indicated the chair.

"The government requests your services, both of you. We're inviting top scientists to do research in support of the war effort."

"What kind of research?"

"All I'll say right now is it's in your field, you'd live on-site, and you'd be serving your country. If you agree, you'll be required to sign confidentiality agreements and you must take it seriously. Violating it amounts to treason and is punishable by death. No one, especially your family, is allowed to know what you're doing."

The two looked at each other in astonishment. "Why especially the family?"

"It's harder to keep secrets from people you know than complete strangers," he answered.

"Where'd we be?"

"Sorry, I can't give you specifics; I will say it's nearby. I realize it's a lot to take in all at once. I'll give you the night to think it over. I need an answer in the morning, say 9 a.m. here." His 'invitation' sounded more like an order or ultimatum.

Neither slept a wink. They talked to three a.m. without coming to a conclusion and tossed and turned before getting up at seven. At breakfast, April and Duke finally decided to accept the challenge. Oliver took pride in helping at sixty-seven and they would, too. Neither envisioned what the assignment entailed; both wanted to serve.

A month later, the couple arrived at a development in Oak Ridge, TN, a mere twenty-five miles away from home. Roosevelt put the Manhattan Project under the command of Army Chief of staff George Marshal who delegated this arm of the venture to Major General Kenneth Nichols. Here scientists took responsibility for uranium enrichment, liquid thermal diffusion, and building a plutonium reactor. "Beber had been right," Helen thought, "it's exactly our specialty." A sergeant met them at the gate and escorted the pair to one of the hundreds of prefab structures dotting the area. To reach the rustic hut, the couple sloshed through knee deep mud churned up by the Corps of Engineers that frantically developed the land to facilitate research and accommodate those working on it. The anticipated 13,000 residents swelled to 75,000 prior to the war's end. Oak Ridge grew to the fifth largest city in the state of Tennessee and consumed 1/7th of all the electricity in the country.

"So, this is it for the duration," April commented sarcastically as she glanced around. "It's pretty, uh, basic. I'll go and pick up things to make it less dismal." She had no concept yet how busy she'd be or how utterly unimportant the surroundings would be once she immersed herself in the project.

Accommodations were pretty primitive but the job exhilarating. April and Duke met men and women whose names were household words, in scientific circles at least. The close-knit group spent endless hours stretching themselves to the brink of collapse to end the war. In the lab, speculation on uses for the technology ran rampant. Beyond these walls, no one spoke of it. Not in the privacy of their own cottage, or at parties, or church, or grocery store. It proved frustrating to married couples where one was sworn to secrecy. April couldn't imagine how hard it must be not chatting with your spouse and she made a point of talking to Duke every day, even if it meant staying late at the lab to do so.

In June, Oliver disappeared. He managed to leave Lucy a short note warning her he'd be gone for a few days, to keep quiet, and don't worry, although she would. On the fourth of June, six months following the attack at Pearl Harbor, the U.S. Navy engaged and soundly defeated the pride of Japan in the Battle of Midway. Outgunned four carriers to three, America achieved what some called a turning point in the Pacific war. The *USS Lexington* sank but the Imperial Navy lost all four carriers, all of which sailed with the task force attacking Hawaii. It represented a substantial percentage of the fleet, plus the loss of additional ships, planes, and pilots. Long after his death, declassified documents revealed Oliver's team pinpointed the fleet's location thus allowing Admiral Nimitz to lay a trap and turn the tides of war.

As soon as Congress declared war, as feared, Lucy's clan dispersed around the globe. Helen and Mina remained in Dallas. Helen joined the WASP's, Women's Airforce Service Pilots. Facing a severe shortage of combat pilots, women were trained to ferry planes from place to place, tow targets for shooting practice, and deliver vital cargo, freeing males to go to war. A few exceptionally talented women served as test pilots in prototypes of rocket powered crafts. Fortunately, Helen worked out of Love Field, but frequently left for days at a time. To that end, she rented her house to an elderly couple and moved into Lucy's, as did Mina and Fiona. They watched the children while she flew. Many did their part by taking care of the offspring of those in war related industries when childcare wasn't available. These unsung heroes made Rosie the Riveter possible.

"Oh, Mom, why do you have to leave again?" Irene whined. Her father was a flight instructor at Kelly Field in San Antonio. Even though he came home occasionally, or they visited, she missed him terribly. "Why'd you join the Army, too?"

"I'm not in the Army, not really. It's the Civil Service. I learned to fly—"

"You already knew how."

"I learned the Army way. I trained the same as the men, except for combat maneuvers and formation flying. What I do is important. It's helping win faster so Dad, and Granddad, Granny, Uncle Asher, well, everybody will get back. Besides, Addie, Fiona, and Aunt Mina spoil you shamelessly when I'm gone. Right?" The girl nodded reluctantly. Still, she missed her Mom when she flew extended missions and wished she never went away. At eight, she grasped the importance so didn't complain too often.

At thirteen and ten, David and James understood better. They, too, missed their parents and grandparents but weathered the separation better than the younger ones. Both listened to the radio so knew about the struggle. Three-year-old India hated her mom and dad being gone so much since she had no idea why. The battle front reports were extremely grim at the beginning of the war. The Allies took a beating in the Pacific, particularly when the Japanese conquered the Philippines and General MacArthur and his family evacuated Corregidor Island in March of 1942.

Bataan fell in April, trapping 10,000 troops on the southern peninsula, including eighty Army and Navy nurses, Annie among them. The prisoners marched sixty-five miles through dense jungle, ferocious heat, and inhumane treatment at the hands of the guards. The heroic efforts of the nurses notwithstanding, 1,000 died on the trek and Annie lost her best friends Edna and Dotty. Finally reaching the POW camp, the group joined 12,000 other detainees. Here the squalid conditions and sadism of the captors weren't any better. Throughout the confinement, Annie and all the nurses tried their best to heal and comfort the captives. Regardless, barely 15,000 returned following liberation shortly before the war ended, a death rate of thirty percent.

When he finished college, Arthur enlisted in the Navy's new unit called the Construction Battalion, better known as the Seabees due to the initials of the official designation, C-B. This complement replaced unarmed civilian contractors who weren't allowed to carry weapons. The Seabees instantly dropped the task of building roads, harbors, airfields, or bridges and reverted to a fighting unit as needed. These men, trained in combat by the Marines, worked in all parts of the globe during the war. Because of his engineering degree, Arthur received a commission as a second lieutenant and attended training in Davisville, Rhode Island.

"Hey, Red, what's the latest scuttlebutt on where we're going?" Arthur asked his ginger-haired comrade.

"Protection detail at the Panama Canal, but yesterday Thad felt certain we'd go to the Aleutian Islands. I can't decide if I'd rather cook in the tropics or freeze my ass up north. Guess we won't know until we get there." As usually happened, neither rumor got it right. His unit shoved off for Europe to reinforce the Allies in the struggle to capture, hold, build, and repair bridges across Italy.

Asher enlisted in the Marines and went to boot camp at Parris Island, South Carolina. To meet the demand, the Corps shortened the course from its customary twelve weeks to a mere six weeks in duration. At that, it proved grueling enough. Dawn til dark, he marched, ran, exercised, learned to use pistols, rifles, hand grenades, and bazookas, and attended classes on military protocol and procedure. He slept when he could, ate deplorable food, and missed his family terribly. Asher assumed he'd go to the Pacific and it suited him fine. Although also at odds with Germany and Italy, the Japanese attacked his homeland and he wanted to ensure they came no closer. He arrived on Midway after the battle and found it relatively easy duty. What he didn't find easy was the trip over.

"Ash, you sick again?"

Vomiting became a twenty-four-hour occupation, it seemed. "Yeah, whatever I eat comes right back. The sergeant told me it'd pass, what a joke. I'll be glad to be ashore. I don't get how these swabbies do it. Glad I joined the Marines instead of the Navy. At least I'm generally on solid ground."

His easy duty quickly came to an end. Now that the area surrounding Midway was secure, his company sailed to Guadalcanal on August 7, 1942 for Operation Watchtower. The bloody six-month struggle took the lives of 1600 Americans. Its capture gave the U.S. a strong foothold in the Pacific and provided a base from which to launch future island-hopping missions. Asher stayed on as part of the defense battery to ensure it never reverted to enemy hands. Once fighting ended, he settled into a fairly routine job.

"Oliver, where are you going?" Lucy questioned as he walked downstairs carrying a suitcase. She knew better but asked nonetheless. They were back in the brownstone in D.C. now and he often went on short trips for business.

"Sorry, sweetheart, I can't say. Don't expect me for at least a week, maybe more."

"Love you." She kissed him as he left the apartment. Typically, his trips were overnight or a few days at most. To be gone this long, she assumed he was headed to Hawaii. There'd been no attacks on the island since Pearl Harbor, however the thought of him being so near a war zone scared her to death.

Lucy guessed right. Oliver hopped on a plane for Honolulu in support of Operation Vengeance. Navy radio operators picked up chatter stating Admiral Isoroku Yamamoto, architect of the December 7th attack, planned to fly from one base to another in the area of the Solomon Islands. Oliver and the codebreakers toiled feverishly to determine exactly where and when it would happen. On April 18, 1943, fighters operating out of Kukum Field on Guadalcanal intercepted and shot down his aircraft over Bougainville Island. Yamamoto's death dealt a tremendous blow to Japan. They lost a brilliant strategist and morale plummeted. That, and the victory at Midway, practically evened the score for Pearl Harbor. The news hit the papers and Lucy grinned to herself, realizing exactly where her husband spent the last week and a half. It was one of the few times she'd smiled since learning of Annie's capture, maybe, six months before. Nobody knew if she'd been taken prisoner or died. Japan divulged precious little information and many of the casualties remained unidentified or lost to the jungle.

CHAPTER 27

"Dear Lord, please not again," Annie cried to herself. He was coming. She avoided eye contact and stared at the soldier she tried to help, hoping against hope he'd keep moving. As the most ruthless, sadistic guard grabbed her roughly on the arm, the injured sergeant raised his head to protest and she restrained him. Both shed tears as the brute roughly pulled her away toward his hut.

The first time one of the captors dragged her away, she resisted with all her strength and suffered a concussion as a result. Two Marines rushed to her aid and were shot on the spot. The second time, a brave soul tried to stop him and also died. Afterwards, resistance to the merciless rape of the nurses ceased. She'd endure the attack rather than put up a useless fight with no chance of success. All the female prisoners became victims of the captors' atrocities regardless of age. As much as the assaults nauseated her, Annie deduced the reason the women were spared is because they served this perverse purpose. Given a choice, many would choose death.

Headway in the Pacific progressed at a snail's pace for two years, but progress did come. In April of 1942, sixteen B25's launched from the USS Hornet roared into the sky. Lt. Colonel James Doolittle's mission was to take the war to the Japanese by bombing Tokyo. It inflicted just minor damage but boosted the morale of the Americans who'd rarely heard good news so far.

A year later, the enemy destroyer Amagiri rammed Lt. John Kennedy's boat, PT-109, setting it afire. The survivors managed to swim to a small island. A canoe full of locals paddled by, Kennedy flagged down the natives, carved a message into a coconut, asked it be delivered to the closest Allied base, and subsequently a rescue party arrived. Kennedy received a hero's welcome, yet some questioned how the accident happened at all and why a captain who lost his ship got such positive press. The day following Christmas, 1943, Lucy received word of yet another loss. Lena Sayers, her cherished friend and wife of the late Governor Joseph Sayers, died.

Victory in Africa set the stage for the Italian campaign launched in July of 1943 with the invasion of Sicily. It progressed inch by inch, and at a great cost, until the country surrendered. The dawn of 1944 saw the Allies gaining the advantage in all theaters of operation from Africa, to Europe, to the Pacific. U.S., British, Canadian, and French troops stormed ashore on the beaches of Normandy in June and drove relentlessly toward Nazi soil. Flying Fortresses pummeled Axis strongholds and strategic targets. Rumors of death camps proved true when Soviet troops discovered the remnants of one at Lublin, Poland.

Although the fleeing Germans tried to destroy the evidence, the gas chambers bore witness to the Holocaust. As the liberators thrust further and further into the Reich's domain, more and more camps and mounds of bodies were discovered and skeletal captives located and freed. The brutality of the regime horrified the world and humiliated those who opposed taking action sooner. The outcome in the Pacific was less certain than in Europe. The Japanese were definitely on the run but had a lot of fight left in them. As promised, Douglas MacArthur returned to the Philippines in October of 1944. Bit by bit American and Filipino forces regained control of the occupied area. The effort continued to the day Japan capitulated.

Annie woke early, as usual, hoping to be at the head of the line and get food while it lasted. As she walked out of the tiny hut she and twelve nurses shared, she noticed an eerie silence. Most of the detainees still slept but she saw none of the guards. She foresaw the first, not the second. By now, they generally rousted prisoners, rattled pots and pans for breakfast, and trolled for victims. The calm terrified her. What new torture did these animals have in store? The harder she looked the less she saw.

Rushing inside she called loudly, "Wake up, the beasts are gone."

Her elated cries brought her hut-mates instantly to their feet and woke those still asleep. Very quickly, the entire camp stirred and cautiously explored the unguarded prison. Nobody challenged them, so a group broke into the commissary, hauled out the few remaining scraps of food, and distributed it to the starving inmates. The jubilation quieted a bit, Annie heard distant gun fire, and a sound she couldn't identify sent chills of terror through her. The faraway raucous clanking and booming got noisier by the minute.

"What's that?" asked a sailor sitting beside Annie.

"I don't know," she replied even though he hadn't directed the question at her personally.

"Tanks, a bunch of 'um, too," exclaimed a Marine huddled a few feet away. "They're sending tanks to destroy the camp."

Horror instantly replaced joy. Men frantically searched the supply sheds for tools to pry open the locks or breach the wire fence, but found these empty, too. The fleeing forces took everything that'd help the prisoners. The petrified hostages scattered to the edges of the huge camp hoping to find shelter. Annie took cover with dozens of others in one of the guards' barracks since it offered more protection than the huts internees slept in. The already traumatized victims quivered as the racket grew louder, and louder, and louder. Unexpectedly, shouts of joy replaced the mechanical tumult. Those closest to the gates spotted the vehicles and raised a joyous cry, "it's the Cavalry." The hell she imagined would continue forever at last ended. "Liberty, hush your crying. We're free," Annie said as streams of tears poured down her face.

Fifteen hundred miles away, Asher vomited his way across the sea. His unit left Guadalcanal and now approached Iwo Jima. Once taken, it'd be the jumping off point for the invasion of the home island of Honshu. He hit the sand with the first wave and encountered surprisingly light resistance. The biggest impediment faced by the invaders turned out to be a fifteen-foot high ash embankment the strategists at Pearl Harbor completely missed. It slowed progress and was useless for digging foxholes.

"I guess the Navy's shelling knocked out the big guns," remarked

Asher as he trudged up the unstable terrain.

"Maybe," replied Chester. "I heard General Schmidt asked Admiral Blandy for a ten-day salvo. He said we didn't need so much and it wouldn't give him time to replace the ammo before we headed ashore. He figured three'd do it. Blandy blew his top, I can tell you. Hodges heard the screaming through the bulkhead. I guess it was enough after all. Things seem pretty quiet."

When men and equipment lay clustered at the mound's edge, he realized how wrong it'd been. The Japanese unleashed the big guns, relatively unharmed in the short barrage, on the sitting ducks below. Machine guns, mortars, and heavy artillery, lots of it positioned atop Mount Suribachi, rained death on those trapped on the beach. The Navy fired and thick steel doors were shut to protect the bunker from the volley.

Marines and matériel sat exposed and vulnerable until bulldozers plowed a path through the ash and troops stormed forward. With heroic effort and repelling a charge of a hundred enemy soldiers, they overran and held Airfield No. 1. A second contingent isolated those dug in atop Mt. Suribachi, depriving them of resupply and replacements. Using tanks, flame throwers, grenades, and air support, the Leathernecks methodically and surely eliminated the threat and made a trail across the land.

Seabees swarmed ashore bringing in heavy construction equipment. The mission was to build or repair airstrips, provide the U.S. a platform for future invasions, and allow reconnaissance planes to scout the area and warn of incoming attacks.

"Artie, hey Artie." Arthur spun around in disbelief. Only Asher called him Artie.

The men looked at each other, hugged tightly, and Asher exclaimed. "Isn't this the wildest coincidence ever? There're millions of us here, on dozens of islands, and we land on the same rock. WOW." They talked fast, at any minute one might have to run, and caught up on the news. Asher hadn't heard about his twin sisters' disappearance and paled at the thought she died or fell into the hands of the enemy. He'd seen the barbarians in action.

"Sorry, Artie, I gotta go. My sergeant's coming and he'll rip me apart if I don't hustle. Let's try to meet soon, OK?"

The brothers spent a few minutes together the following day, but the Japanese opened the doors on the mountain and pounded the area with shells. The two scattered and raced to join their unit. A final fierce American assault silenced the big guns permanently. As Asher gazed skywards toward the mountain, he silently prayed Arthur would be alright. Suddenly, he felt a sensation he hadn't in months. He shivered with cold. His body froze, he couldn't move, and he lay flat on his back. As darkness slowly replaced the glaring midday sunlight, he lifted his dimming eyes toward the summit of Mt. Suribachi and saw six Marines struggling to raise Old Glory at the peak. As one stretched above the rest to give it a boost, Asher's eyelids shut and he slipped away.

Lucy and Oliver received word Asher died and Annie lived at the same time. Both went into shock, unable to process the grief and joy simultaneously. Oliver got permission to go to Dallas to comfort, and be consoled by, his family. Helen and John received a week off. The couple met the anguished parents at the airport and took them home. Mina and Addie prepared the rooms and served a delicious dinner nobody touched. Grandkids Jeffry, Wayne, and Rebecca, who barely remembered the grandparents, were old enough to understand a terrible thing happened and clung to their mother. Neighbors dropped in with food and sympathy, and David, sixteen, replaced Asher's blue star hanging in the window with a gold one. If the war kept going, he'd be drafted into the fray, too. April and Duke opted to stay at Oak Ridge and mourned standing in the lab. The project reached a critical stage and neither left even when the general granted permission to do so. Success was too close to walk away now. Dorothy drove in from San Antonio and Lucy cried herself to sleep in the woman's arms.

The next week a telegram told them of Annie's arrival in San Diego on April 9th. Lucy and Oliver booked a flight, checked into the Grande Colonial Hotel, reserved her a room, and waited. Late in the day she, the rest of the nurses, and some of the men held captive with her, walked cautiously down the gangplank. Like Annie, most wore dazed traumatized faces from suffering unspeakable horrors over the preceding three years. As Lucy rushed to her, she wondered why the girl wrapped a blanket tightly around her. The weather was warm, so maybe it represented security. The Navy doctor assigned to brief the families warned recovery would be difficult and painful, physically and emotionally. As she enveloped her daughter, the blanket twitched. A three-month-old with narrow eyes and dark hair squirmed when awakened by the embrace.

Neither said a word. They dodged reporters, whisked the beleaguered pair to the hotel, tucked their daughter into bed, tended the newborn, and let Annie sleep until the infant started crying. She needed to eat and her mother had to remedy the problem. As she nursed, Lucy asked the question she already knew the answer to. "Was it rape?"

Annie nodded and a tear rolled down her cheek. "Some of the girls left them behind, but I refused. She's mine. She isn't to blame, not one bit. Mom, this is Liberty. I named her for the Statue of Liberty and my prayers we'd be freed."

"Of course, you'd never abandon her. I guess I can sympathize to a point, but can't imagine it for myself or you."

Lucy kissed the child, assured Annie how much she loved her, and walked into the adjoining suite where Oliver stood in front of the window gazing at the sea. After closing the door, Lucy broke into gasping, uncontrollable sobs that wracked her small body with grief almost as strong as when she heard Asher died. As the heaves abated, Oliver inquired, "is it what we thought?"

She nodded yes and wept harder. "My poor baby," she wailed. It tore Lucy apart to visualize what agony the girl endured. She sat at the desk beside the window and wrote a letter to Helen explaining the circumstances. She wanted the others to adjust and prepare Liberty's nursery. She was the newest family member and Lucy vowed to make her welcome. She took Annie's measurements and went shopping for her and the infant. Her daughter turned to skin and bones at the hands of her tormenters and although it was difficult finding anything to fit, she managed to bring back two suits and a dress that weren't terribly baggy. She bought her a pair of shoes, underclothing, and a night gown. Liberty proved a lot easier to accommodate. She got six rompers, socks, a blanket, three packages of diapers, sleepers, and a rattle. It'd suffice for a while. Before going to bed, Oliver brought Annie up to date on the war, since she had no idea what happened, the status of her siblings, and broke the tragedy of Asher's death at Iwo Jima. Lucy and Oliver debated whether to tell her here or at home. Both agreed it'd be best to let her digest the loss prior to returning to the pandemonium waiting in Dallas.

On April 12th, one headline dominated papers around the world: PRESIDENT ROOSEVELT DEAD. The man, elected to an unprecedented four terms, died of a cerebral hemorrhage as the victory he fought so valiantly to win approached. Supreme Court Chief Justice Harlan F. Stone swore in Harry Truman as the 33rd president and twelve days later the new chief executive learned of the existence of the Manhattan Project. They guarded the secret so carefully, even the vice president had negligible knowledge of its magnitude. As the Allies closed in on his Berlin bunker, Adolph Hitler committed suicide on the 30th and Germany surrendered a week later. Finally, it ended, half of it at least, and the country rejoiced. Still, fear permeated Lucy's every waking moment. Battles raged in the Pacific and Arthur was in the thick of it.

Oliver knew hostilities were slacking off because when he called to say he'd be coming back soon, the general gave him a wonderful surprise. He'd been invaluable to the extraordinary success of the codebreakers and could stand down. Lucy silently rejoiced. At seventy, the tortuous hours and grueling work took its toll. He lost weight, his shoulders slumped a little, and he didn't sleep well. Oliver contributed significantly to two wars and deserved to take life slower. To her surprise, he agreed to retire instead of returning to teaching. She looked forward to spending more time with him than during the previous part of their marriage.

April hated not joining Annie and the family for the homecoming but was even busier now, as impossible at it seemed given the frenzied pace earlier in the war. Rumors, always ripe, grew to epidemic proportions in the summer. On July 6th, whispers of the phrase 'the gadget worked' spread like wildfire around the Oak Ridge labs. While technically in the dark about what it might be, the scientists put two and two together ages ago. On August 6, 1945, the *Enola Gay*, piloted by Colonel Paul Tibbets, dropped an atomic bomb on Hiroshima. Japan still refused to surrender so a second fell three days later on Nagasaki. Faced with the dreadful task of authorizing the use of the terrible weapon, Truman chose to unleash the nuclear age. If the Allies invaded the main islands, experts estimated as many as 800,000 American deaths and millions of injuries. Additionally, they projected the demise of five to ten million Japanese civilians and servicemen. The loss of 300,000 from the bombs, or even twice that, was small in comparison.

Fearing the United States would drop more of the awful weapons, Japan surrendered on September 2, 1945, exactly six years and a day after the war began, aboard the *USS Missouri*. A simple stroke of the pen ended the deadliest, most destructive conflict ever. Fortunately, the Empire hadn't learned there were no more atomic bombs. The only two in existence blew up as 'Little Boy' and 'Fat Man' exploded.

CHAPTER 28

America survived with her cities intact and fewer casualties than other major participants. Allies and Axis alike suffered far greater devastation in terms of human lives, population displacement, and physical damage. Although not widely known thanks to censorship, she didn't escape entirely unscathed. In addition to the assault on Pearl Harbor and numerous ships sinking in sight of its shores, the enemy attacked, or attempted to attack, the continental U.S. on numerous occasions throughout the course of the conflict.

Following the raid on Hawaii, the Axis powers tried four times to strike the country. In February 1942, a Japanese submarine slipped into a channel near Santa Barbara, California and sent shells hurling toward the Ellwood Oil Field inflicting insignificant losses. In June, an Imperial sub shadowed a fishing boat around a minefield and breached the Columbia River. It surfaced at Fort Stevens and fired seventeen shells at the antiquated garrison. An adjacent baseball field got the worst of the bombardment. Also in June, the Nazis sent eight saboteurs in Operation Pastorius. The mission was to create panic and undermine morale by assailing the infrastructure, disrupting transportation, and destroying industrial centers. One of the men, George Dasch, turned himself in to the FBI, revealed the plot, and identified the co-conspirators before they acted. Six received death sentences while Dasch and an accomplice spent six years in prison and then President Truman deported them. In September, a plane took off from a submarine and dropped fire bombs in an Oregon forest. The sole aircraft-launched attack on the mainland resulted in minimal harm.

Starting in 1944, the Japanese concocted the strangest ever military action. The army released 9,000 Fogos, balloon bombs, into the atmosphere from 5,000 miles away. The jet stream propelled the missiles eastward to the States. On reaching land, these descended and detonated to light cities or woodlands on fire. A mere 350 made it and were spotted as far away as Michigan and Iowa. A pregnant woman and five children chanced on a Fogo in Oregon. They accidentally activated the apparatus and became the sole continental combat deaths of World War II.

Despite being at peace once again, enemy soldiers on isolated Pacific islands remained in hiding decades after hostilities ceased. The Americans and Japanese dropped leaflets urging the warriors to surrender, nevertheless some refused to believe it and fought on. Hirō Onoda held out on a tiny island in the Philippines until 1974, turning himself in when his former commander relieved him of duty.

As she suspected, the diary Lucy kept formed the basis of a book. She couldn't make it a nonfiction volume because her husband and daughter didn't divulge enough information for her to do so. Government records were classified and would be for years to come. Instead, the novel traced the life of a family caught up in the war and tossed to the winds. Like *Journey of Light*, *The Rockets' Red Glare* drew characters and experiences based on her own life and her imagination filled in the blanks. It was intensely personal, often left her in tears, she abandoned the project twice, and finally finished. It sold more than any single one she wrote and spent ten weeks on the *New York Times* Best Seller List that had premiered in 1931.

Annie refused to leave her room on returning to Dallas. She clung tightly to Liberty and rarely let anybody else hold her, even Lucy or Fiona. Both she and the baby gained vital weight and looked healthier, at least physically. Lucy urged her daughter to talk to a therapist and she agreed, provided she hired a woman who came to her. Using Oliver's contacts at the University, she found a psychologist, Mrs. Hamrick, who'd make house calls. Liberty, of course, bore no such emotional scars and her physical problems healed shortly. In a few weeks, she was a happy, healthy, joyful girl who reveled in the love and attention showered on her by the family.

Annie agreed to go shopping when she outgrew the undersized clothing Lucy bought in San Diego. The two women went to the Fashion First Boutique and selected six slightly too large garments. The girl needed to add several pounds and these provided her leeway to grow. She especially liked the navy-blue dress with a button front, pleated skirt, and elbow length sleeves. Her mother insisted she buy open toed heels in the same color to complete the picture. The pair walked down the street to the children's store and picked up several outfits for Liberty. She put on weight more easily than her mom and needed cloths every eight or ten weeks. Although she enjoyed the short excursion, Annie cringed at loud noises and shied away from groups of men she passed on the sidewalk. Lucy knew she often endured anxiety attacks, at home and in public, and prayed she'd recover in short order.

"Boy, it's great to be here," April exclaimed yet again. Duke chuckled and agreed, again. Having lived in such austere surroundings, the bungalow was luxurious in comparison. It was filled with familiar furniture, mementoes, and photographs, and it felt great to be home. They were eager to go back to the university, too. It'd happen in January though. By the time the Army dismissed them from Oak Ridge, the fall term was already underway. That wasn't all bad, either. The couple planned to fly to Dallas to visit the family, take a vacation in the west, and simply relax. That came first. It'd been a grueling endeavor and April relished a rest.

"It felt great driving without worrying about having enough ration stamps for gas," April commented. "Let's go on a nice ride in the country this evening, shall we?" Duke nodded his agreement. "October can't get here fast enough," Annie stated as she removed dust sheets covering the furniture.

"Why?"

"Shoe rationing ends. I haven't had a new pair in ages."

"Right, I remember hearing it on the radio. I heard food rationing will stop in January at the latest, too. I can't wait to sink my teeth into a thick, juicy T-bone whenever I choose. Plus, our tires are threadbare," laughed Duke.

The government imposed rationing following Pearl Harbor, tires being the number one item limited. A lot of articles dropped off the list once the strike on Hiroshima hit the airwaves, even before the surrender. Not so in England. Some rationing continued until 1954, after fourteen years of shortages. France repealed it quickly, however, food remained scarce as production fell far short of demand. One good thing happened during the bleak days of 1945. French women voted for the first time ever in October. And, on October 3rd, ten-year-old Elvis Presley made his public debut at a talent contest at the Mississippi-Alabama Dairy Show where he won second prize.

Helen and John gave their tenants notice and stayed at Lucy and Oliver's waiting for renters to move. They threw a big house re-warming party two weeks later. David brought his girlfriend Priscilla. She was the only person he ever dated and it seemed serious. They liked the girl but prayed he'd go to college instead of marrying soon. The younger children, James, 13, Irene, 10, and India, 6, invited four playmates each. In all, forty attended and celebrated the resumption of normal life.

Arthur returned to a rousing welcome even though Jeffry and Wayne, 8, barely remembered him and Rebecca didn't at all, despite Mina's efforts to keep his memory alive with stories and pictures. They, too, stayed at Lucy's until the renters vacated their home. Arthur sold his business and started looking for a different job that'd utilize his engineering degree. By Christmas, the house was emptier since all left except Annie and Liberty. Annie's assimilation progressed slower than Lucy hoped. After five months, she rarely left home. On one of her outings, she strolled Liberty through the park and passersby stared at the girl and uttered rude, just audible comments. The cruelty set her back and she refused to venture beyond the door.

As spring blossomed, Lucy coaxed her away again. They walked down the lane with Liberty toddling beside her mom and nobody commented, although plenty stared. Lucy and Mrs. Hamrick gently prepared Annie for the inevitability of such reactions. It'd be years before memory of the war faded enough so the resentment lessened. She had to be strong, and make Liberty strong, too. Neither was at fault, still many would blame her regardless. The family did everything possible to protect the child but she'd have to learn to cope with it, as unjust as it may be. Annie, too, suffered prejudice since people assumed the baby to be the product of a voluntary liaison. Few stopped to think how else it happened.

Her therapist left for Biloxi in March of 1946 to be near her brother. Annie agreed to see a man who conducted group sessions on Friday mornings specifically aimed at veterans or civilians directly involved in the war. He'd been in the Marines and wanted to do all he could to repair the shock of the conflict. She went in May and was all excited, especially since there was another female participant.

"Dr. Lightner understands, he really understands," she said jubilantly. "He was a POW, too. Mrs. Hamrick helped me but she never went through it."

"Wonderful! Not because he was a prisoner, of course. It's great you'll relate well."

On June 21st, Annie and Lucy, who'd bring Liberty, agreed to meet at the Baker Hotel after her session. The restaurant served a great lunch buffet and it lay two blocks east of Dr. Lightner's office. The appointment ran late, so Annie didn't get to the hotel where the other two waited until 11:45. As she reached the entrance, a stampede fled the building and stormed past screaming FIRE. Annie grabbed Liberty and the three ran away as fast as possible. The blaze dominated the headlines in Texas. As workers installed refrigeration units in the subbasement, a terrible explosion propelled deadly ammonia gas into the lobby and bedrooms. In all, seven died and forty-one were injured in the blast. Being in the proximity of another trauma triggered a relapse and Annie again isolated herself. She refused to go out, except for the appointments at Dr. Lightner's, but the reaction lessened rapidly with his guidance.

"Sweetheart, you know the Japanese occupied a few small islands in the territory of Alaska in the war, right?" asked Oliver as he sat reading the paper.

"No, I don't think so. Why?"

"There's an article in the travel section on tours to the sites in the

Aleutians. Are you interested in going?"

"Isn't it terribly cold?"

"Usually. We'd go next summer. The problem is, they're very remote and the only way to get there is via boat—." His voice trailed off waiting for an answer. Even thirty-five years after the *Titanic*, she'd yet to board anything larger than a canoe.

"No, I won't go to the islands, sorry. You can if you like. I wouldn't mind going to Alaska if we flew. Let's consider it." Even though fall started the week before, it was hot and sultry in Dallas. Up north the temperature already dropped and it was too late for the trip.

Magistrates at Nuremberg sentenced twelve Nazi war criminals to death. Two weeks later ten were hanged. Hermann Göring, Hitler's designated successor, escaped the noose by swallowing a cyanide capsule smuggled to his cell. The twelfth, Martin Bormann, was convicted in absentia. Unbeknownst to the Allies at that point, he died while trying to flee Berlin as it fell.

Dr. Lightner released Annie following thirteen months of therapy. She made amazing progress and he felt sure she'd cope perfectly well on her own. Nightmares rarely interrupted her sleep, she learned to ignore, if not appreciate, the snide comments regarding Liberty, and didn't duck when a car backfired or an unexpected clap of lightning and thunder boomed across the sky. She avoided close contact with men, except her family, but grew more comfortable in social situations by the week. He had no reservations wishing her the best of luck, signing the work release, and biding his time. Annie was rehired by Parkland Hospital but on the post-op floor instead of the emergency room. It'd be less hectic and less reminiscent of what she experienced in the Philippines. Lucy smiled when she learned about her daughter's assignment. Although Annie seemed perfectly fine, she worried the pressure of emergency medicine might be too much.

"Oliver, listen to this. I remember reading of his rescue. He sure is handsome."

He hurried to the radio to hear the announcer proclaim that John F. Kennedy, son of the former ambassador to Great Britain Joseph Kennedy, beat ten challengers to win election to the House of

Representatives from Massachusetts. The charismatic war hero secured the seat in a special election to replace James Michael Curley who gave it up to be mayor of Boston.

Two weeks prior to Christmas, Annie answered the phone as she and Liberty played on the floor in front of the fire. "Hello." The voice sounded familiar, she just couldn't quite place it.

"Miss Segar, this is Sam Lightner." She hesitated and he added, "Dr. Lightner."

"Oh, yes, of course. What a surprise. How are you?"

"Fine, thank you. Miss Segar, I'm having a reunion of sorts on Friday the twentieth at seven in the VFW Hall. Clients," he didn't want them to think of themselves as patients, "and former clients are invited to a Christmas party I'm giving. I'd appreciate it very much if you came. Please feel free to bring Liberty, too—and an escort if you wish. I'd like to meet your daughter." He sent written invitations to the rest but called Annie personally. He prayed she didn't bring a date.

She contemplated it and then replied, "what a wonderful idea. I'm excited to see my old group. We'll be there, the two of us."

Annie panicked the moment she hung up. She debated with herself for days trying to decide if she should cancel or go. Lucy went mad trying to find out what troubled her. Finally, she told her mother about the invitation.

"It should be fun. Why are you so worried?"

"I, well, I haven't dated since, well, you know."

"I'm not sure I'd call it a date, sweetheart. He invited a lot of guests, right? Liberty's included, too. Why don't you just go and enjoy the fun? Don't think of anything else."

"OK. But, I don't have anything to wear, either."

Lucy laughed and took Annie shopping. She selected a deep plum colored satin dress with a wide-collared princess bodice that bared most of her neck and shoulders. The cocktail gown had a sashed waist and full waltz length skirt. During the war, Regulation L-85 limited the length and fullness of skirts. Now, the ladies craved gathered, longer ones. Liberty got a jumper of red velvet and a white blouse with lace collar and cuffs. The big night quickly arrived and Annie was a nervous wreck. She and her daughter looked wonderful in their party finery and Lucy lent Annie her pearls. Oliver drove them to the hall and walked inside. Sam's heart fell as the three moved toward him.

"Dad, may I present Dr. Lightner?"

"An honor to meet you, doctor. I drove Annie and Liberty, who I see has made herself comfortable in your arms, to the party." Silently Sam heaved a sigh of relief. It was her father rather than an older suitor.

"Please stay, sir. It'd be a pleasure if you joined us."

"I appreciate the invitation, but my wife and I have dinner plans." Turning to his daughter he reminded her, "I'll be back at ten." Annie kissed him on the check and walked across the dance floor beside Sam who carried Liberty on his shoulders.

CHAPTER 29

"Thank you for inviting us, Dr. Lightner."

"You're welcome. Sam, please. You aren't my client, remember?"

"Thank you. I'm Annie." They sat at a small table adjacent to the dance floor watching Liberty whirled around jostling the revelers, and nobody seemed to mind.

"I told you I spent a short while as a POW, but intentionally didn't say where. Annie, I ended up in the same camp as you for four months."

"Really? There were thousands so I guess it's no surprise we never met."

"I mention it now so you realize I understand." He glanced at Liberty.

She smiled in a way that was sad and proud and nodded her head. "A lot stare and point, not as much as at first, though."

"A client, I can't say who, left her son behind in Java. Guilt is eating her alive and she's fighting a terrible battle to make peace with it. I'm not sure she ever will."

Sam and Annie danced several times, twirled Liberty twice, then he gave attention to the other guests, too. Annie enjoyed seeing former groupmates and meeting survivors who shared her experiences. Her family offered lots of support but these people went through the same horrors she did and it felt nice to know they didn't judge. No one pointed and stared at Liberty or whispered nasty comments. Even if not taken prisoner, they heard what happened. She could relax among these friends.

"Helen, take a look." John said on Sunday as they sat sipping coffee.

She read the caption and laughed aloud: KENTUCKY PILOT CRASHES PURSUING FLYING SAUCE.

"Do you believe it? What on Earth was he thinking?" wondered John aloud. "I heard rumors some of the Army pilots saw strange, unidentified craft toward the end of the war and called the objects Foo Fighters. The military assumed the enemy invented a secret weapon. Maybe not," he chuckled.

"Well, if I see a Foo saucer, I'll head the opposite direction, forget nearer," she laughed.

The conversation changed to an upcoming luncheon at the Berry's, James' fifteenth birthday party in February, and David's graduation in May. Helen taught him to fly at sixteen and the boy regularly took short hops to surrounding areas delivering mail. He planned to major in accounting or finance at the University of Texas and earn spending money working at Asbury & Asbury Aviation during breaks. Both took great pride in the boy. He ranked sixth in his class, turned into a responsible pilot, and earned the rank of Eagle Scout. On top of that, he was a kind, caring, and honorable young man.

Only his devotion to Priscilla worried them. The duo was inseparable and Helen fretted over the situation. Since the war started, the traditional values of abstaining until marriage and reluctance to divorce took a beating. Couples conceived more babies out of wedlock than before and divorce didn't hold the stigma it once did. Many married hastily when the Selective Service Act ensured most men would go into the service. Divorce rates skyrocketed as prolonged separations, lack of a firm foundation, and regret at saying "I do" quickly exacted its toll. Oliver and Helen encouraged them to avoid ending up as a statistic. Regardless, the pair continued to get together every day and became even closer as graduation approached.

"I can't believe my baby graduated high school," Helen cooed as she hugged David twice more after the ceremony. "Priscilla, congratulations to you, too. Your parents must be thrilled you're at the top of the heap." She kissed the girl on the cheek and prayed the relationship cooled when David left for Austin. "What do you want to do, dear?" She truly liked the girl and couldn't pick a better wife for David, just hoped they'd postpone any declarations.

"I'm going to study business like Mrs. Segar." Lucy smiled and remembered fondly the years she worked with Governor Sayers and the Reverend Mother.

"It's a good choice. A skilled secretary is in demand. If you're interested, I suggest you learn bookkeeping, too. You'll earn a higher salary."

"Thank you, I'll check into it."

Reveling teenagers filled the house til eleven o'clock. The throng slowly began to disburse and Helen struggled to put the little ones to bed. James, 14, Irene, 12, and India, 8, were hyper-stimulated from all the excitement, noise, and music, not to mention the copious amounts of cake and punch they consumed. The three bounced off the walls all evening and chatted furiously about what kind of party each wanted when the time came.

Lucy briefly encountered her second president in September of 1948. David took a train to Austin to begin his college career and Lucy tagged along to help him settle into the dorm. She then went to San Antonio and stayed two weeks at Dorothy's. On the way back, she spent the night in the capital to take David to dinner yet again. He'd been gone a few days, but the proud grandmother missed him already. While waiting for her luggage, a special train pulled into the station. President Truman chose Austin to give a speech on his whistle-stop campaign across the United States. He spoke briefly, shook hands with those nearby, and left twenty-five minutes later sporting a ten-gallon hat and carrying a pair of silver spurs. Lucy was lucky enough to be in the front row.

If she'd been in Dallas, and owned a television, she could have watched Truman on the set. Station WBAP-TV, an NBC affiliate, made its broadcasting debut ahead of schedule to cover his arrival in Fort Worth. Viewers saw his forty-nine-minute speech and endorsement of a Representative now seeking a Senate seat, Lyndon B. Johnson. In November, on the day following the general election, the station aired a photograph destined to become iconic. It showed a beaming Harry

Truman holding a copy of the *Chicago Daily Tribune* sporting a giant headline: DEWEY DEFEATS TRUMAN. In reality, the paper jumped the gun. Dewey was projected to win, but Truman effected an upset victory and retained the presidency. The early edition hit the streets in advance of the certified results. It wouldn't be the last time the media erroneously predicted the winner of the Oval Office, although they weren't irresponsible enough to publish the results prior to the final tally.

David came back for the summer and said he'd transferred to the University of Dallas where Oliver formerly taught. He told them he missed home, however both suspected Priscilla had a lot to do with it. They were absolutely right. On Christmas Day the young couple announced their engagement and set a date in mid-July.

"Where will you live while you're in school? Please don't tell me you're quitting," she added in a terrified, shrill voice.

"Don't worry, mom, I'm not quitting. The Logan's said we can have Priscilla's room. We'll survive until I graduate. I can take runs for you and Priscilla's a bookkeeper at an accounting firm." The four discussed the arrangements and then told the others. Oliver and Lucy shared the same reservations of marrying so young but tried to be happy for the couple.

"Do you want to use the third floor? Annie, Liberty, and Addie are all on the second so you'd have, um, more privacy," Lucy offered.

"Granny, Paw, thank you. Thank you so much. That'd be perfect. The Logan's are very generous, nonetheless their place is small. Thank you."

Once gone, Oliver looked at Lucy and said, "I have a better idea." He explained his brainstorm and invited Helen and John to dinner. As the adults sat in the parlor and the kids played upstairs, Oliver suggested an alternative.

"How'd it be if your mother and I built a guest cottage at the south edge of your property? It's an enormous lot and there's plenty of room. The kids could use it after the wedding. We'd make it big enough for a child, but I hope that's way off."

Helen and John discussed it with David the next morning. He said thanks too often to count. Helen interrupted him and said, "your grandfather thought of the scheme, why don't you thank him." He and Priscilla rushed to express appreciation for the generosity.

Oliver called an architect and told him what he had in mind. The man designed a small bungalow with a combination living-dining-kitchen area, two bedrooms, and a bath. The corner lot allowed him to install a driveway making it truly a separate home. David and his fiancée approved the design and construction started immediately, nevertheless, it wasn't finished before the wedding. Meanwhile, the newlyweds moved into their grandparents' attic space.

"Dad, do you think you'll buy a jet?" James asked his father.

John replied, "I kind of doubt it. Scientists tinkered with rocket-powered flight in the 20's or 30's and I know the British De Havilland Comet airliner made its debut, however they're pretty experimental. Besides, we don't go far enough for the extra speed to matter. I'd sure like to try my hand at it and give it a test drive."

"Has United Airlines talked about using jets?"

"No, and I bet it's a ways off. Addie, you topped yourself again. This roast is perfect. Thank you." United absorbed National Air Transport Company before the war.

Following his Christmas party, Sam Lightner asked Annie on a date every few weeks, always encouraging her to bring Liberty or making it a group affair. Later, he occasionally proposed gettogethers for just the two of them, a movie, concert, or dinner. She became secure enough to invite him to David's wedding and from then on, they went out alone most often. At least twice a month he brought Liberty to ensure she didn't get jealous.

On January 1, 1950, he asked her to marry him. She wanted to, but tearfully said no and tried to explain. "Darling, I love you, it's, well, I'm unsure, I'm afraid —" she stopped, trying to control the tears, and continued. "I'm not sure I'd, well, sleep with you after what happened on Bataan."

"Baby, I get it. I experienced the brutality, too, and witnessed what trauma the nurses bore. We don't have to rush into it, you know. Let's take it slowly. We've rarely kissed. Let's begin there. When you're comfortable, we'll try more. If all goes well, we'll have a wedding. You can call it quits at any point. I promise our life won't bear the slightest resemblance to the horrors you endured."

She nodded shyly and started the ball rolling by reaching up, touching his face, and giving him the deepest kiss so far. Annie and Sam kept the engagement a secret and cautiously became more and more intimate. In the spring, the couple began touching and, as David dubbed it, making love at the edges. In the meantime, the family commemorated the fifth anniversary of Asher's death, mourned the Korean War, celebrated Oliver's seventy-fifth birthday, and watched the third season of *The Ed Sullivan Show* on the TV Lucy bought him.

In July, Annie proudly proclaimed she and Sam planned to marry in October. His restraint, tenderness, kindness, and patience dispelled her fears and she trusted him completely. She knew the honeymoon would be difficult at first, but she'd be able to handle it now, thanks in large part to him.

They decided on an informal wedding held at home. Annie selected a pale-yellow Chantilly lace dress atop layers of tulle. Its strapless bodice had a scalloped edge and the fitted waist was encircled with a wide satin ribbon. The unbelievably full skirt fell in two tiers to a stylish mid-calf length. The layers of crinoline created a soft rustling sound that made Annie giggle and caused her to unconsciously sway her hips. She selected a pair of satin high heels dyed to match and a small hat holding a nose-tip veil. Sam wore a black suit as did his best man. Annie asked Helen to be her bridesmaid and five-year-old Liberty the flower girl. The joyous couple cut the cake and left for a week in Havana, Cuba. Liberty happily stayed behind and looked forward to playing with her cousins and sleeping over at Aunt Helen's. On arriving home, Sam contacted an attorney and adopted Liberty as his very own daughter. Just before their anniversary, Annie had a boy, Sam, Jr.

David, who finished early by taking classes all summer, graduated college without Priscilla getting pregnant, but she wasted no time once he had a degree in hand. The pair shared the exciting news in August. By then, David landed a good paying job at Sears,

Roebuck, and Company as a store auditor. Before the baby arrived, the company transferred him to Houston, at the store on Main Street south of downtown. They bought a small home north of Hobby Airport and settled in to wait for the delivery. On June 30, 1952, Donna Kathleen pushed her way into the world with a wimper. It was the first great grandchild and Lucy and Oliver jumped on John's plane to see her. Helen beat them to it, however. She'd ferried two business executives down early in the morning and took the opportunity to visit. Priscilla went into labor at lunch so she volunteered to stay and help tend her granddaughter.

A year later, the U.S. executed Julius and Ethel Rosenberg for espionage. They received the death sentence when convicted of giving information to the USSR about the design of nuclear weapons. Ethel's brother, David Greenglass, stole documents from Los Alamos and handed it off to Julius. The government believed this aided the Soviet's in building an atomic bomb. The Rosenberg's two children asserted their innocence for decades. Eventually, the Cold War ended and declassified documents verified the collusion. The sons admitted Julius committed conspiracy but rejected the spying verdict. Michael and Robert then contended he didn't deserve the death penalty and their mother wasn't aware of the activity and had been falsely judged. Well into the next century, the men continued to campaign for her to be posthumously exonerated.

It hurt Lucy to think of David being so far away, although she could always hop a ride with John or Helen. They often flew to Houston. She rejoiced in the fact her family returned home, or at least were reasonably close by, after being dispersed and prayed the rest stayed put. She didn't believe Helen and John would leave the area. His job at United was stable, Asbury & Asbury Aviation prospered under Helen's leadership, and the youngest were at home. James started his senior year at Dallas Baptist University where he studied biology. Irene, who wanted to teach, just enrolled at the Texas State College for Women in Denton, a short distance north. She'd come back later and India was a high school freshman.

Upon returning from the Pacific, Arthur was hired by Humble Oil

Company, eventually part of Exxon. Founded in 1911 in Humble, Texas by Ross, Frank, and Florence Sterling, it quickly opened offices in a number of different locations. He currently worked on a deep-ocean platform scheduled for construction in the Gulf of Mexico in 1955 in a hundred feet of water, the deepest yet. He frequently traveled to Houston and Galveston, but thought he'd remain in Dallas. Mina dreaded the idea of moving Jeffry and Wayne, 16, and Rebecca, 14, out of the school they grew up in and away from the clan.

The country was as busy as the Segar's. On January 20, 1953, Dwight D. Eisenhower, the commander of Allied Forces in Europe in WWII, was sworn in as President of the United States. In May, a tornado packing winds in excess of 200 miles per hour slammed into Waco, Texas killing one hundred fourteen. This would make it an EF-5, the highest rating, when Tetsuya Theodore Fujita invented the Enhanced Fujita scale in 1971. Months later, Lucy found out Ralph Sayers' daughter Helen, her husband Mayo, and newborn daughter Jo Lynn were in Waco at the time. Fortunately, all escaped injury. An armistice halted the Korean War on July 27th and Lucy gave thanks it ended prior to any of her grandsons being drafted. In September, Senator John F. Kennedy married Jacqueline Bouvier in Newport, Rhode Island. And, in England, the coronation of Elizabeth II formalized her title as queen that fell to her due to the death of her father, George VI, the year before.

CHAPTER 30

Lucy knew her writing slowed down and age definitely played a factor but wasn't the sole reason. She wrote just four novels in the eleven years since World War II ended. The second explanation for the sluggish pace lay with her family. It mushroomed and they kept her busy.

Helen and John boasted four children and four grandchildren. David had three: Donna, Sheila, and newborn Jason. Fiona moved with them to Houston since Priscilla managed a large law firm. James and his wife Sallye were the proud parents of a daughter, Scarlett Beth. Irene was twenty-one and India graduated in June. Of all Lucy's descendants, India alone expressed an interest in writing. *Readers Digest* published a poem she wrote, with a little assistance from her grandmother. India said she hoped to write a children's story and Lucy extatically agreed to coach her.

Arthur and Mina finished at three, Jeffry, Wayne, and Rebecca, and none had married yet. The boys appeared to be following in Arthur's footsteps by majoring in engineering and Rebecca put in half days at the local library. Annie and Sam's brood grew, too. Twelve-year-old Liberty adored her siblings, two-year-old Sam junior and infant Marcus Lee.

Regardless of the excuse for the extended period between books, Lucy was proud of each one she wrote. The latest, *Roman Adventure*, represented a new challenge. All the history-based novels she wrote before were set in the fairly recent past. This reached far back into the era of ancient Italy and their trip to the country in '51 supplied the inspiration.

Wilber Gettings retired and she hired an agent. Mr. Pickman

thought the story wonderful and insisted she do a tour to promote the tale. Lucy agreed because Oliver said he'd join her again. He'd accompanied her on most of the trips since he retired. It made the long hours on the road bearable. The editor offered to pay for plane tickets, however both preferred traveling by train.

In October, the duo pulled out of the station and headed south to Houston and then east the day after. On the way to New Orleans, the locomotive stopped briefly in Baton Rouge. A middle-aged couple sat in the seats facing them.

"Mr. and Mrs. Sayers? Is it you?" Lucy asked.

The man stared at her a moment and remembered. "Mrs. Segar, what a coincidence. It's wonderful to see you again."

"Do you remember my husband Oliver?" The men shook hands. "Do you still live in San Antonio? Are you going to New Orleans, or beyond?"

"Beyond. We're in Baton Rouge now and are going to Mobile to visit our daughter Helen, her husband Mayo Adams, and our grandchildren Jo Lynn and Craig. They're expecting a third and are going to call him John, if it's a boy, for his OTHER grandfather," snorted Charlena. "I don't think they picked a girl's name yet. You're in Dallas, right?"

"Yes, we are. Our oldest daughter is named Helen, too, another coincidence. We're fortunate the whole clan is in the area, except our grandson David. He's an accountant at Sears, Roebuck and transferred to Houston when he graduated."

The Sayers' stared in disbelief. Charlena stated, "Ralph's an accountant for Sears, too. He occasionally goes to the Houston store on business."

"What's your grandson's name?"

"David Asbury."

"I met him on my trip in the summer. Unbelievable! Mayo just got a job with the company, too. He's an accountant as well. Sears, Roebuck is a stable firm."

The foursome chatted pleasantly until Oliver and Lucy disembarked at New Orleans. Here the pair attended three events in two days. They put in an appearance at Montgomery, Alabama and then on to Atlanta, Nashville, Little Rock, Tulsa, and innumerable stops in between. It proved a grueling three-week trip and both were exhausted. At 76, it hit Lucy hard and eighty-two-year-old Oliver looked drained and wane. Annie checked him, suggested he see a doctor, and stubbornly he refused. Instead, he took it easy and napped in the afternoon. He soon bounced back to his former, robust self. Nevertheless, Lucy vowed it'd be her, and his, final promotional tour, except perhaps short hops to nearby cities. She'd simply refuse to do any marathons.

Dwight Eisenhower won reelection against Adlai Stevens again. The two opposed each other in the last campaign and it ended in the same result. During Christmas break, Oliver treated the whole bunch to lunch and Elvis Presley's first movie, *Love Me Tender*. Addie announced her engagement to Mr. Zestly, the butcher. The marriage was way off and she wanted to work for Lucy right up to the wedding. Losing Fiona had been hard, but at least she was with family so they saw her frequently. It wouldn't be the same with Addie. Zestly Meats lay across town and it'd take a special trip. Since he had the best selection and quality in the city, it'd be worth it. She'd do the shopping herself.

"Paw, can I have this?"

"What, sweetheart?" Oliver asked Liberty who read a magazine on the sofa while he thumbed through the February 23, 1957 edition of the *Dallas Times Herald*. She pointed to the paper. A huge Woolworth's ad on the back publicized the arrival of a big shipment of Wham-O's new toy, the Frisbee. Although he couldn't quite imagine what it did, he drove her to the store where a clerk showed him how to throw it. He bought half a dozen and distributed them following Sunday dinner. The kids and the adults alike had fun flinging and chasing the discs.

The world rapidly became a more dangerous place. By the time the Segar's happily tossed the toy, three nations possessed nuclear weapons. The USSR joined the club in 1947 and England in in 1952. Rumors abounded France might add its name to the list. The Cold

War was in full swing. As atomic bombs were tested in isolated areas, an even bigger explosion swept the country: Television. In towns large and small, stations erected tall towers and brought current events and entertainment into thousands of additional homes each week. And, Hurricane Audrey stormed ashore in June of 1957 at Cameron, on the far western coast of Louisiana, killing in excess of five hundred people and inflicting untold devastation and misery in Texas and Louisiana. These monsters always revived terrifying memories for Lucy even six decades later.

The best news Lucy heard came in the late summer. Grandson David, his wife, the children, and Fiona moved back to Dallas when Sears transferred him. The fantastic revelation thrilled Lucy and she offered them the second floor for the duration of the house hunt. Months passed and Priscilla didn't find the perfect place. The longer they stayed, the more Granny enjoyed having the youngsters around. Annie married three years ago and the big place seemed empty and entirely too quiet with just the two of them and Addie to fill it.

"Priscilla, that dress is charming on you, dear." She said as the woman walked downstairs carrying baby Jason. She wore a stylish sky-blue shirtwaist outfit with a slim fitting skirt. It had a small collar, short sleeves accented by three buttons, and a thin belt covered in the same fabric. Large white earrings, a matching bead necklace, white gloves, and a wide straw hat ringed in silk flowers completed the getup. Lucy, too, cut a smart figure in her beige linen suit. The gathered waist jacket flattered her slim figure perfectly.

"Here, let me take him, what a good boy you are." The beaming, cooing great-grandmother put Jason into the stoller, Helen grabbed the hands of Donna and Sheila, and the five made their way down the street. The ladies prefered walking to driving and, besides, the kids always enjoyed an outing. "Sallye's meeting us with Scarlett Beth. Annie is ill so I'll choose a few things for Mark. I can't believe you had babies at pratically the same time. I think giving birth at thirty-five was hard on her, but he sure is a cutie, as are they all."

Annie's ill health proved more than post-partum fatigue and it dragged on for quite a while. The doctor eventually discovered a tumor on her ovary and advised she have surgery right away. It scared her to death, and Sam too, so he urged her to take care of it without delay. She defined his existance and didn't want to take any chances. Dr. Quinn operated and learned he underestimated the extent of the problem. Instead of a single tumor, he dicovered several growing on all parts of her reproductive organs. He performed a hysterectomy and fortunately all the growths were benign. The diagnosis came as a shock, but she'd fully recover and had no desire to have more children anyway so it wasn't terribly tramatic.

Irene stunned everybody in September by abandoning her fledgling teaching career and announcing her engagement to Reggie Quaker. He was thirty-two, a decade her elder, and employed as a partner in a major law firm. Mina introduced them when Irene visited her at work. The two dated quietly for the past year and a half and now intended to marry. Mina respected him even if he was pompous, but less so than the other attorneys at her firm. She knew him to be honest, successful, and extremely wealthy, but thought him too old. Helen and John agreed. The fact he divorced his wife and had three children gave them enough cause to question the union. Regardless, she didn't need permission to marry so the wedding went forward for November.

With the Baby Boom in full swing, Dallas experienced a housing shortage as did much of the nation. Tract subdivisions sprouted in the suburbs like mushrooms, it seemed, however this isn't where the couple wanted to be. David and Priscilla hoped to be near the rest of the family who all settled close to downtown. Houses there were expensive and got snapped up fast. Four months later they still lived at the grandparents' and feared wearing out their welcome.

"Of course we don't mind," Oliver assured him. "Your grandmother and I want you here. Don't rush, save for a bigger initial payment, and relax. Don't even metion paying rent. Priscilla is a big help to Lucy and the grandkids keep me on my toes," he laughed. Both Granny and Paw cherished the time spent with the wonderful children.

Irene and Reggie threw an elaborate wedding at his country club.

Her satin gown featured a full skirt and strapless bodice. Delicate lace covered the shoulders and arms, ending in a point on her hands. It topped the satin as well, envoking an ethereal cloud. A Juliet cap anchored a three-tiered tulle veil, the longest of which formed a train. Most of the law firm attended, as did many clients, his offspring, siblings, and parents. Irene, too, invited scores of guests including relatives, friends, and past classmates. The smaller ballroom served as a chaple to hold the hundred seventy-five guests and the larger provided an area to dine and dance once the ceremony ended. The halls were decked in flowers, lighted by candles, and wrapped in music.

India finished her book about a boy who worried Santa wouldn't come since it rarely snowed in Houston. Her niece Donna inspired the idea while living there. Lucy loved the story, gently proposed a few changes, and sent it to Mr. Pickman. She enclosed a note saying she'd appreciate it if he read it. Getting a first manuscript published was extremely difficult and a push from her might ease the path. The agent begrudgingly opened the envelope, he could hardly refuse his biggest client, and read the material. He immediately phoned India and sent her a contract. Lucy indeed passed on her talent and legacy to her granddaughter.

Arthur, a vice president at Humble Oil, kept extremely busy trying to negotiate the details of a merger with Standard Oil. The amalgamation wouldn't happen quickly; such contracts required time and patience. The innumerable hours he devoted to that deal, drilling projects in the Permian Basin, and erecting rigs in the Gulf often made him an absent member of the family. The job took a heavy toll on the marriage. Mina tried to be supportive but felt frustrated, neglected, and resented being a married widow when facing an empty nest. Now that her sons were at school and Rebecca worked all day, she spent too many hours by herself. She issued him an ultimatum. Either spend more time with her or she'd leave.

Mina's accusation mortified Arthur. He never realized she was so lonely, how frequently he ignored her pleas for attention, or that she'd become so desperate. He buried himself so deep in his endeavors, he completely abandoned his wife. "I'm so sorry, Mina. You're the most important person in the world to me. I promise, I'll do better. Let's take the vacation to Hawaii we've dreamed of." On Monday, he rushed in and placed an ad in the *Chronicle*. He 'd hire the managers the company authorized, one to oversee the west Texas fields and the other exploration in the Gulf. Soon he started getting home to dinner and rarely worked on weekends. His mood, not to mention his marriage, improved drastically. He and Mina had a fabulous second honeymoon and the relationship repaired itself rapidly.

Lucy didn't particularly care for westerns, even at the movies. Besides news and a few variety programs, they filled the small screen, too. Shows such as *Colt 45, Tombstone Territory, Hawkeye and the Last of the Mohicans,* and *Man Without a Gun* dominated the airwaves. She liked legal dramas, though, and loved the movies *12 Angry Men* and *Paths of Glory*. When *Perry Mason,* starring Raymond Burr, premiered her heart leapt for joy. Not only was Mr. Burr a consummate actor, he portrayed an interesting character who possessed a brilliant mind and an uncanny knack of making criminals confess on the witness stand. She dreaded Irene and Reggie visiting while she tried to watch it. He took pleasure in pointing out what the writers got wrong.

Duke decided to retire effective January 1st and April cut back to part time. She still planned to do research but gave up teaching duties to be with her husband. They went to Dallas at Thanksgiving and stayed through Christmas. Oliver invited them and Lucy to attend the math department's holiday party at the University. As a retired professor, he received an invitation and enjoyed seeing former colleagues and meeting the new staff members. It was fun and he looked forward to it. Being able to introduce his well-known daughter and son-in-law delighted him all the more. He took his bragging rights as a proud father very seriously. They were rehashing the wonderful evening when anchor Douglas Edwards of CBS announced the Army called Elvis Presley for active duty.

Christmas Eve 1958 was a zoo. The entire family piled into the Segar's to open presents and eat a sumptuous dinner boasting all the trimmings. Everyone, especially the children, wanted to be home in the morning so the clan celebrated together the night before. A huge tree crowded the parlor and the smell of pine intermingled with the mouth-watering aroma of turkey, green beans, and yams. Scores of gifts and ripped wrapping paper littered the floor and created an obstacle course for anyone trying to pass. On top of that, the hordes of familial bodies made it stuffy and too warm. By the time he finished eating, Oliver needed some air.

"I'm going to take a walk, Lucy. Join me?"

"No, dear, it's too cold out for me. Take one of the kids, OK? The streets are icy and I don't think it's a good idea for you to go alone."

"You fuss too much, but I'll grab Jeff to make you happy. He ought to walk off those three servings of potatoes and two of pecan pie," Oliver laughed, corralled his grandson, and walked into the subfreezing gloom.

CHAPTER 31

"Where on Earth are Oliver and Jeff?" asked Lucy for the tenth time. "Surely those two aren't still walking in this weather." The temperature dropped and sleet pelted the ground. "Rebecca, get it, will you?"

"Hello. Oh, good. Jeff, Granny's worried sick. Where are you? Should we—OK." She responded in disbelief when her brother ordered her to shut up. "God, no. GRANNY!"

Lucy ran to the phone in response to the agonized cry, listened a moment, and then slumped to the floor. Arthur took the receiver while John and Helen lifted her to a chair. "OK, we'll be right over." Oliver slipped on a patch of ice and struck his head. A woman passing in a car saw the accident, stopped, and drove him to the hospital. The perilous roads aggravated the already agonizing slow journey. Once in the door, the doctors rushed him to surgery and Jeff had the opportunity to telephone.

The Segar's wheeled their way cautiously to Parkland Hospital. Annie immediately ran to the emergency room head, Dr. Ross, for an update on her father's condition. He'd been her boss before the war and she'd run into him since returning to work.

"I'm sorry to say it isn't good, Annie. He hit the curb and has a large hematoma on the occipital and, I'm afraid, an intracerebral hemorrhage due to the impact. The surgeons will do their best, you know that. We have to wait and see." He softened the prognosis a little, while not giving her false hope.

She relayed the diagnosis and warned it'd be a long haul. Oliver sustained a serious injury and brain surgery posed significant risks. Annie tried to convince her mother to go, she'd ring the instant anything happened, but Lucy refused. They all congregated in the waiting area, pacing, sniffling, worrying, and comforting each other. In the wee hours, Dr. Laningham emerged and walked purposefully toward them.

"He's in ICU. It's worse than we thought, that's why surgery took hours. Plus, his brain is badly swollen. I, um, we did, tried to, there's no way to predict how much damage he incurred at this point. It's too soon to say if he suffered any deficits or if he'll wake at all. He's badly injured and time will tell. Undoubtedly, he'll be out a good while, perhaps weeks, or more. I urge you to go home. We'll take good care of him. I'll instruct a nurse to call if his condition changes. It'll be a marathon so pace yourselves."

Lucy agreed to the suggestion because Annie pledged not to leave his side. As a nurse working in the building, she had unrestricted access to the ICU. John devised a schedule so somebody was always there should he rally. Lucy stayed during the day with one of her children or adult grandchildren at hand. At night, they alternated keeping watch in the lounge so she could sleep. The arrangement satisfied Lucy and she promised to try to relax. Twelve hours following surgery, Oliver slipped into a coma and the doctors didn't know when, or if, he'd come to.

Her husband's condition so consumed her, Lucy completely ignored the rest of the world. She usually kept a keen eye on the news, but paid attention only to Oliver's progress, or lack thereof. As she sat quietly, desperately praying he'd improve, the space race heated up even if the weather turned colder. Two months prior, the USSR successfully put the first artificial satellite, Sputnik I, into space. In November, the Soviets launched Sputnik 2 and sent a living creature into orbit. Laika, a stray dog from the alleys of Moscow, died a few hours later. Before Oliver's accident, the US attempted to fire its own rocket. Just after liftoff, the Vanguard TV3 exploded at Cape Canaveral.

The New Year passed with less of its customary fanfare, but David and Mina did whatever possible to bolster spirits and make the day happy. The family gathered, as usual, for lunch and Addie served a fabulous feast that was merely picked at and she planned how to serve the leftovers. Oliver had been in the ICU six weeks when the United States succeeded in putting a satellite into space. On January 31, 1958, Explorer I roared skyward and disappeared into the heavens. The scientific equipment it carried radioed back information resulting in the discovery of the Van Ryan Radiation Belt.

The dreaded call came at three a.m. Sallye was at the hospital when Oliver succumbed without regaining consciousness. Lucy moved zombie-like through the viewing, funeral, and afterwards. Nothing seemed to console the grieving widow. In January of 1959 when Congress admitted Alaska as the 49th state, she still sat in a daze except on the rare occasions she agreed to receive visitors. Lucy lost weight, cried often, and seldom left her room.

David and Priscilla temporarily abandoned house hunting and decided, instead, to live at Lucy's indefinitely. She relied on their encouragement and support. On April 9th, the day NASA revealed the names of the Mercury Seven who'd be the first US astronauts, the pair made a startling announcement. They were expecting a baby. It surprised everyone, including the prospective parents, who couldn't be happier and the thought of another great grandchild brought Lucy out of mourning a bit. She left home for just the fifth time since the funeral to buy Priscilla maternity dresses, supplement hand-me-down infant clothing, and replenish newborn paraphernalia. The excursion into the warm spring air perked her up and sparked a revitalized concern for world events.

India, who published her third picture book, proposed writing a novel for pre-teens. The murder mystery featured twin sisters whose crime solving ability astounded the police. Dismissed and ridiculed as meddling amateurs by the professionals, the siblings ultimately solved a case so baffling the FBI failed to find the culprit. She shied away from the genre herself, but Lucy had a ball reading it and assisting India tighten the plot if she lost her way. During the process, India met Jeb Rondeau, a detective at DPD, who gave her invaluable technical advice. Reggie introduced her to his partner's son who'd joined the force nine years ago in the hope he'd be a good resource for his niece. The detective's insight and expertise made the tale more realistic and she gladly said yes to his invitation to dinner. In the dedication of *Sister Sleuths*, she'd thank her grandmother and acknowledge him in the author's note.

Lucy's brainstorm grew faster than Priscilla's belly. In August, Hawaii entered the union as the 50th state and she approached David with a solution to the housing dilemma--take hers. At seventy-nine, it'd become too much to handle. Even though Addie took care of the cleaning, Priscilla lent a hand, and Fiona pitched in when the kids didn't need her, it was a lot to manage. And, she hated to admit, the constant commotion of small children rattled her nerves and soon there'd be four. Besides, the stairs got steeper and taller by the week. It wouldn't be long until she had to sleep downstairs in the maid's room and the last thing Lucy wanted was to be in the way or interfere with the growing brood.

David loved the idea of living in the stately residence, particularly since he'd have another son or daughter. In July, the doctor realized Priscilla carried twins; instead of four, it'd be five. Obviously, it ran in the family since this was the third set in as many generations. None of the properties the real estate agent presented last year were big enough and even the small ones in the vicinity cost too much. With twins on the way, the parents reluctantly agreed to search in the suburbs once Lucy recovered. When Granny offered, he sadly declined. "We simply can't afford it. My job pays well, and so does Priscilla's, but not enough for that. To buy a large place we'll look in a less expensive neighborhood," he explained.

Lucy smiled and said he misinterpreted what she meant. She'd give him the house and adjust her will to compensate for the early gift. He'd get most of his inheritance now instead of in cash upon her death. "Let's talk to the others, but I don't imagine anybody minds." She guessed right, they didn't.

David and Priscilla thanked her over and over and Priscilla added, "And you can live here forever, if you like. It'll be your home always." Lucy appreciated the generosity, but she hadn't mentioned the rest of her scheme yet. She went to see Helen and John to reveal the whole plan.

"May I have the cottage in your backyard?" Several people had used it for short periods, but it'd stood empty for five years. "I'll pay rent, of course."

"Nonsense," chimed John and Helen in unison. "We wouldn't charge you under any circumstances, you and Dad built it remember. I guess it's rightfully yours. Please, please take it over."

Once she agreed, Helen sounded an 'all hands on deck' alert and everyone showed up bright and early on Saturday to clean the bungalow. It was scrubbed from top to bottom and all the dusty, musty furniture, window coverings, and rugs were discarded. James and Jeff striped paper and painted the walls a creamy yellow Lucy picked. Arthur and Sam sanded the floors after a carpenter refurbished the cupboards and built shelves in the second bedroom that'd be her office. A plumber removed the cast iron tub, replaced it with a large shower, and installed a more modern toilet. The older grandchildren filled the space by moving a few of her favorite pieces while Irene, Rebecca, and Liberty helped select drapes and bedding. Two months later, Lucy pronounced it ready and prepared to settled in. She stayed put long enough to welcome Brady Sinclair and Brandy Rose on October 1st.

The guest house suited her perfectly. She liked the cozy, comfortable feel and the fact she could easily walk to see Helen on the spur of the moment, nonetheless vowed not to be a pest. Memories of Oliver didn't lurk around each corner of her small nest so she felt slightly less lonely. She missed him constantly, especially when *The Twilight Zone* premiered in 1959. The spooky story sent chills the length of her spine and she wished she'd accepted John's invitation to spend the evening with them.

India picked her up regularly to work on the novel. At the half way point, Lucy suggested a few changes. It'd be easy to amend it to allow for the possibility of future volumes featuring the same characters. If successful, she'd have the basis for more mysteries. India adored the prospect and the two collaborated to make it conducive to a series of books instead of a single one. *Sister Sleuths* was a great success and she immediately started on the sequel.

Lucy noted the opening of a new exhibition hall, the Solomon R. Guggenheim Museum, in Manhattan at Fifth Avenue and East 89th. Architect Frank Lloyd Wright designed the interior in a unique spiral configuration. Instead of walking through interconnected galleries, visitors rode the elevator to the top and strolled slowly down the ramp viewing the collection. The article brought a mist to her eyes as she remembered meeting Guggenheim's brother, Benjamin, who perished on the *Titanic*. She needed to confer with Mr. Pickman and made a mental note to see it when in the city. Lucy flew to New York instead of taking a train and India went, too. The editor applauded her notion of a series of adventures based on sleuths Amaryllis and Amelia Bernard. It'd appeal to young girls and this was one of the publishing industry's biggest markets. After he and India talked, he turned to Lucy.

"Mrs. Segar, I'd like to see you publish your memoirs. You've led an interesting, if tragic, life and your readers would buy it hand over fist. You told parts of it in *The Mighty Blast* and *Ship of Tears*, but an autobiography allows you to share details." The idea never occurred to her and she promised to think about it. In the meanwhile, she said, she'd come up with the beginnings of a third eerie tale inspired by the popularity of *The Twilight Zone*. Mr. Pickman agreed the time was ripe and spent ninety minutes discussing her thoughts.

Being in the miniature house gave her more opportunity to write since before Helen's birth. Although her family dropped in often or invited her over, there were hours to fill. She finished *Terror's Highway* in June of 1960 and gave it to her granddaughter to preview. India and Granny grew closer as they consulted together on the other's work. The girl acted as her sounding board and recently completed reading her final draft. At eleven o'clock India called and asked her grandmother to meet her at the drug store lunch counter in a few minutes.

"It's perfect, Granny. It'll be a best seller, I'm sure. Maybe we'll co-author a book. You already help me a lot and I'd like to see your name on the cover, too." Both ladies ordered a hamburger and fries when the waitress came to take the order.

"That'd be great fun, sweetheart. What's in the bag?"

The girl hemmed and hawed, and then excitedly blurted out the secret. "Jeb and I are eloping next week. Neither of us care for a big, fussy wedding. We're going to tell Mom and Dad tonight so DON'T SAY A WORD, OK." Then she looked at the bag and continued. "These are those birth control pills the FDA just approved. We'd rather delay having children and this makes it easier," she said blushingly.

Lucy nodded, kissed her, and headed back. Even though the Catholic Church condemned it, she thought it terrific couples had a simple, effective means of delaying pregnancy. It provided greater options if they wanted to postpone having a family, or not start one at all. She did wonder what it'd do to the already deteriorating moral values, however.

Her latest manuscript was scheduled for release in mid-February of 1961. Prior to that, she watched the convention nominate Senator John F. Kennedy of Massachusetts and Texas Senator Lyndon B. Johnson for the 1960 Democratic ticket. If victorious, Kennedy would be the only Catholic and youngest person ever elected to the nation's highest office. The Republicans chose Vice President Richard Nixon and Henry Cabot Lodge to oppose them. These candidates' debates were the first broadcast on TV. In November, in a fiercely fought contest, Kennedy won the Oval Office.

"Hey, Dad," called six-year-old Sam, Jr. as he and his father planted flowers in the bed Annie insisted they dig. "Do you really think a person will go to the moon the way the President says?" In a speech to Congress on May 25, 1961, Kennedy ambitiously committed the country to putting a man there before the end of the decade.

"I don't know, perhaps. When I was a boy, airplanes were a novelty. We'd run outside every time we heard them fly over. You don't even notice. I talked to your Uncle John and he sure thinks it's possible. He'd have a better opinion, and that's a fact. Here, put the white geraniums by the sidewalk." The feat came to pass on July 20, 1969 as Apollo 11 astronauts Neil Armstrong and Buzz Aldrin landed at Tranquility Base while Michael Collins orbited above. It happened nine years after Kennedy's challenge and less than six following his assassination.

It amazed Lucy how quickly she wrote her autobiography once she started. She reread her journals from Galveston, the *Titanic*, and WWII to refresh her memory. Her offspring, and theirs, enjoyed adding reminiscences and stories to spice it up. In her life, she loved two remarkable, kind, thoughtful, and supportive men. Without their encouragement, she'd have never achieved her writing dreams. They gave her four wonderful children, ten delightful grandchildren, and six perfect great grandchildren, so far. She shipped the pages to Mr. Pickman and enclosed a letter announcing her retirement as an active writer. Lucy wanted to spend time with her family and promote India's blossoming career. And maybe, just maybe, this summer she'd finally join the others when Reggie treated everyone to the annual Caribbean cruise.

ABOUT THE AUTHOR

Jo Adams McAuley is a native Texan whose family moved frequently throughout the south and southeast during her childhood. She graduated from the University of Arkansas, worked for a Senator in Washington, D.C., and returned to her roots. Her love of history and personal experiences are infused in her work. She lives in the Houston area along with her two sons.

Thank you so much for reading one of our **Women's Fiction** novels.
If you enjoyed the experience, please check out our recommended title for
your next great read!

Wild Raspberries by Connie Chappell

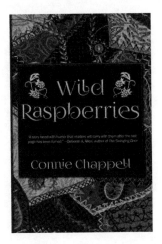

"*Wild Raspberries* artfully captures the struggle to see clearly in the midst of loss, with well-placed comic moments to break the tension." *–Foreword Reviews*

"Chappell unfolds the women's secrets and lies at a good pace, adding interest with minor characters." *–Kirkus Reviews*

CPSIA information can be obtained
at www.ICGtesting.com
Printed in the USA
FSHW02n1716040918
51810FS

9 781684 331345